"Saturday shouldn't have happened," Brad said.

"But the way you responded to me..." Sabrina protested. "The things you whispered while we were making love—that I was magical and beautiful and exciting—you meant them. And you would have called me Sunday morning if it weren't for this misunderstanding."

Brad didn't say a word. Where did she get off telling him how he felt? Whatever she was after—sexual pleasure, his approval, another male notch in her belt—it didn't matter. He didn't want any part of it.

"Brad, please. Can't we talk this out? If I could come to your house, cook you dinner—"

"And rub my feet and take me to bed?" He'd lost his patience. "Exactly what do you want from me? A roll in the hay to remember me by?"

Sabrina flinched at his crude accusation, but his anger was better than his cold indifference. "I just wanted to spend some time with you."

"I'm flattered," he drawled. "Might I ask why?"

Answering him honestly was one of the hardest things she'd ever done. "Because I'm in love with you."

Dear Reader,

Each and every month, to meet your sophisticated standards, to satisfy your taste for substantial, memorable, emotion-packed stories of life and love, of dreams and possibilities, Silhouette brings you six extremely **Special Edition**s.

Now these exclusive editions are wearing a brand-new wrapper, a more sophisticated look—our way of marking Silhouette **Special Edition**'s continually renewed commitment to bring you the very best, the brightest and the most up-to-date in romance writing.

Reach for all six freshly packaged Silhouette **Special Edition**s each month—the insides are every bit as delicious as the outsides—and savor a bounty of meaty, soul-satisfying romantic novels by authors who are already your favorites and those who are about to become so.

And don't forget the two Silhouette *Classics* at your bookseller's every month—the most beloved Silhouette **Special Edition**s and Silhouette *Intimate Moments* of yesteryear, reissued by popular demand.

Today's bestsellers, tomorrow's *Classics*—that's Silhouette **Special Edition**. And now, we're looking more special than ever!

From all the authors and editors of Silhouette **Special Edition**,

Warmest wishes,

Leslie Kazanjian
Senior Editor

BROOKE HASTINGS
Both Sides Now

Silhouette Special Edition

Published by Silhouette Books New York

America's Publisher of Contemporary Romance

For Esther and Maurie Rosen.
Old friends are the most precious.

SILHOUETTE BOOKS
300 East 42nd St., New York, N.Y. 10017

Copyright © 1988 by Deborah Gordon

ISBN: 0-373-09486-8

First Silhouette Books printing October 1988

"Both Sides Now" by Joni Mitchell. © 1967 Siquomb Publishing
Corporation. Used by permission. All rights reserved.

Printed in the U.S.A.

BROOKE HASTINGS

is a transplanted Easterner who now lives in California with her husband and two children. A full-time writer, she won the Romance Writers of America's Golden Medallion Award for her Silhouette Romance, *Winner Take All*. Brooke especially enjoys doing the background research for her books and finds it a real challenge to come up with new plot twists and unique characters for her stories.

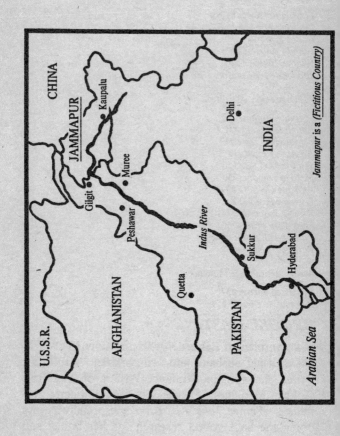

Jammapur is a (Fictitious Country)

Chapter One

Family was important to Brad Fraser. So were prudence and privacy, especially *his* privacy, all of which explained why he was in the Boston Astoria Hotel on a sunny Saturday in June when he would rather have been sailing. It was bad enough that his aunt had taken up with some character out of a Hollywood jungle movie; even worse, her mother wasn't going to give him a moment's peace until he put a stop to it.

Sighing, he knocked on the door in front of him. There was no answer, so he knocked more loudly. After ten seconds he heard someone mutter grumpily, "All right, I'm coming. Whoever said this was a civilized city..." The words trailed off as the door was pulled open.

Brad recognized Howard Lang at once, and not just because he'd done his homework and read a dozen magazine articles about him. The local paper had run a story on Lang the previous week and he turned up on television with tiresome predictability to publicize his incessant adventuring.

A strapping man of fifty, he was a professional tour guide and amateur explorer whom interviewers liked to describe as larger than life. With his dark hair and beard and muscular build, he could have passed for someone ten years younger. Lots of women found his rough-hewn good looks extremely attractive, but Brad was surprised his aunt would be one of them. Kathleen was a quiet, scholarly woman who preferred cultured, intelligent men. As a professor of ancient history, she'd often expressed disdain for Lang's seat-of-the-pants style of archaeology.

Lang looked so fierce that a lesser man than Brad might have been afraid to challenge him. Bradley Royce Fraser IV, however, was the product of over two hundred years of privilege and breeding. It took a lot more than some cheap imitation of Indiana Jones to intimidate him.

"My name is Brad Fraser," he said calmly. "I'd like to speak to Kathleen."

Lang nodded, then smiled. He wasn't being friendly, just showing his amusement at Brad's existence. "Ah, yes. The lawyer." He stepped aside so Brad could enter his suite. "I was wondering how long it would take the family to call in its top gun."

Since Kathleen had been holed up with Howard Lang for nearly a week, Brad didn't consider it unreasonable that her family might be concerned. Lang might style himself a daring adventurer, but others had labeled him an expert hustler. He seemed to have a talent for separating wealthy females from their bank accounts, and Kathleen Fraser Carlisle was very wealthy indeed. Given how unworldly she also was, there was no telling what a charismatic character like Lang might have talked her into.

Brad glanced around the parlor. It was furnished with the kind of understated elegance that cost a thousand a night—silk-upholstered furniture, porcelain lamps, original artwork. He was relieved to see a rumpled blanket and pillow on the couch, indicating that Lang had slept there. Maybe Kathleen hadn't taken leave of her senses, after all.

The suite seemed to contain two bedrooms, prompting Brad to wonder who was staying in the second one. According to the newspaper, Lang had come to Boston alone.

He opened the door on Brad's right and poked his head into the bedroom beyond. "It's your nephew, sweetheart. He has the look of a man who wants to run me out of town."

Brad was pondering the implications of that easy, intimate "sweetheart" when he heard a girlish giggle. He was thirty-two; Kathleen, his father's half sister, was thirty-nine. In all the years he'd known her, she'd never once laughed that way. Flirtatiousness was foreign to her nature, or had been until Lang had gotten hold of her. What had he done to her?

"Is he wearing a suit?" she asked.

"Dark blue pinstripes, complete with vest. Blue shirt. Conservative tie. Very lawyerlike."

"Sounds ominous." She paused. "Is he carrying a briefcase?"

"No."

"Then it could be worse. He's only dressed for a minor crisis." She breezed through the door wearing a besotted smile and a flaming red negligee she couldn't possibly have bought for herself. Even more unnerving, her light brown hair, once prematurely streaked with gray, was now a warm ash blond. Although she looked sensational, she wasn't the staid, serious woman Brad was used to.

She pecked him on the cheek. "It's Saturday. You should be sailing. How's Grace? I'm sorry I had to cancel out of her mother's dinner party last night, but let's face it, Abby Fitzsimmons and her friends are hopeless snobs." She smiled slyly. "Howard is far more interesting."

"Thank you for the endorsement." Lang picked up his blanket and pillow. "I'll have breakfast sent up. Sit down, Brad. You need to learn how to relax."

Brad told Kathleen that Grace was fine and seated himself on the couch. He and his aunt were close, but the only advice she generally asked for was on legal matters. Given how smitten she obviously was, any criticism he made was bound to backfire. She would only defend Lang staunchly and refuse to leave him.

Still, a week of exposure to the man couldn't have changed her in any fundamental way. Brad was far too skillful a lawyer to doubt his ability to maneuver people into doing what he wanted. He considered his task a simple matter of guiding her back to reality.

She joined him on the couch as Lang called room service. "I thought you liked Grace's parents," Brad said, putting more hurt into his voice than he actually felt. Grace Fitzsimmons, his girlfriend, had a master's in art history and worked at a local museum. Her parents, Boston Brahmins to the core, had known Brad for years and treated him like a favorite nephew. "You once told me you enjoyed going to their parties," he added.

Kathleen bit her lip. "I'm sorry—I didn't mean to hurt your feelings. Abby and Charles are okay, but some of their friends are so...so..." She shook her head helplessly.

"Well educated? Well connected? Well-informed?" In Brad's opinion, Congressman and Mrs. Fitzsimmons were all those things; it was hardly something to criticize. Even more to the point, putting Kathleen on the defensive might help him penetrate the spell Lang had cast.

She hesitated, then checked Lang's reaction. "How about stuffy and self-important?" he asked. "We ran into a group of them in a restaurant the other night and they treated me like something the cat had dragged in."

Given Lang's reputation, it was little wonder, but Brad knew better than to arouse Kathleen's protective instincts by saying so. "It's easy to mistake New Englanders' natural reserve for unfriendliness," he remarked instead. Before Lang could argue, he continued, "Your department chairman's been trying to contact you, Kathleen. He finally gave up leaving messages on your machine and called your mother—"

"Who'd figured out where I was by then and decided I needed rescuing. What urgent problem does Ted have now?"

"He wants you to deliver a paper for him in Chicago next week. He was in the hospital Tuesday night and he doesn't think he can make it."

She rolled her eyes. "Believe me, Ted will survive."

"But he was having chest pains—"

"He has chest pains every other week. He runs to a hospital every time he sneezes. Nobody's ever found a thing wrong with him."

It was no secret that Dr. Ted Solomon was one of the worst hypochondriacs in Boston, but Kathleen had never taken such a cavalier attitude toward him before. Although Brad disliked shading the truth, the situation called for drastic measures. "They did this time," he said. "There were some anomalies in his EKG." He didn't find it necessary to add that the doctors had attributed the problem to the medication Ted was taking.

His statement had the intended effect—Kathleen went from indifferent to alarmed in no time flat. "Something's wrong with his EKG?" She jumped to her feet. "I should have kept in touch with him. There could have been questions about my grades or my editor could have called about my book—ten different problems could have come up and I didn't even check my machine. I don't know what I was thinking."

Brad could smell victory now, so he eased the pressure. Putting a comforting arm around her shoulders, he said, "You had a hectic semester and you needed a few days off, but it's time to get back to work. Get dressed and I'll drive you home. You can call Ted, then stop by your office."

She looked distractedly at Lang. Brad was sure she meant to leave, but Lang didn't give her the chance. "He's trying to send you on a guilt trip, Kathleen. It isn't a crime to take a vacation. People can survive not hearing from you for a couple of weeks."

"But it was so irresponsible—"

"Is it your fault that Ted Solomon saw a blip on his EKG and flew into a panic? One of his graduate assistants can deliver the paper—there's no reason for you to do it."

He walked to her side, then removed Brad's arm from her shoulders. Brad had no choice but to step aside; it was either that or get into a physical fight. "You have a tendency to think of everyone and everything but yourself, but you're entitled to be a little selfish now and then. Call Ted if you want to, but don't go back to your house." He cupped her face in his hands. "Stay with me until I talk at the Adventurers' Club, sweetheart. Then, if you really need to go to Chicago, I'll come along."

Brad could see his victory dissolving before his eyes. Kathleen looked mesmerized, a helpless victim of Lang's seductive stare and husky voice. "You will?" she breathed.

"Try and stop me. I'm not going to let anything come between us." She gave a spellbound nod and allowed him to take her into his arms.

It was more than Brad could stomach. This, after all, was his beloved Aunt Kathleen, who'd been more of a mother to him than anyone he could name. He couldn't let her succumb to the charms of a smooth-talking opportunist whose chief interest was probably in her fat bank account.

The cool detachment he prided himself on flew straight out the window. "For God's sake, Kathleen, the man has been married three times. He finds rich women, talks them into financing his expeditions and then ignores them for months at a time. I can see you're infatuated with him—I suppose he's good in bed—but that's no reason to—"

"Just a damn minute!" Lang glared at him in an admirably menacing way. "I've never taken your aunt to bed, not that it's any of your business, and I've never married a woman I didn't love. I resent—"

"Just as easy to love a rich woman as a poor one," Brad said.

Lang ignored him. "I resent the way you barged in here and I resent your crude accusations even more. I want you out of here. Now!"

"Darling, please," Kathleen murmured. "He didn't mean to accuse you of anything. He's just concerned about me."

Brad barely heard a word she said; a stunning revelation had just dawned. Kathleen's husband, Jim, had died in Vietnam when she was only twenty-two, and she'd never gotten over losing him. Howard Lang bore an uncanny resemblance to him, or would have if Jim had lived to the age of fifty.

"Good Lord, Kathleen, wake up and look at the man!" Brad said. "He could be Jim's twin brother—that's what you're responding to. If you're not careful, you'll be married, divorced and broke before you know what's hit you."

"Damn it, Fraser, I ought to knock you clear to Cambridge for that. You have no right—"

"That's what happens when the truth isn't on someone's side," Brad drawled. "They have to resort to violence."

Totally enraged now, Lang charged forward, grabbed Brad by the lapels and began to curse him in language so colorful that even *he* was impressed. Kathleen begged Lang to calm down while Brad waited indifferently, ignoring the way Lang was manhandling his suit. Both Lang and Kathleen were talking so loudly that anything he might have said would have gotten lost in all the commotion.

It was like a scene out of a French farce, so it was only fitting that the other bedroom door should suddenly open and someone should walk out. Kathleen and Lang couldn't see her, but Brad certainly could. A tall brunette with long, wavy hair, she was dressed in an oversize Oakland Athletics sweatshirt that ended at her knees but didn't quite conceal her assets. Of course, it was hard to hide the kind of body that men's magazines feature in their centerfolds.

The photographs Brad had seen of her didn't do her justice. Her mouth was full, her green eyes were large and widely spaced, her skin was alabaster fair and her cheekbones were high and exotically hollowed. He recognized her at once, but then she wasn't the sort of woman a man forgot. Her name was Sabrina, she was Lang's only child, and, like her father, she'd led a less than conventional life.

Brad knew what everyone knew and a little more. Sabrina Lang had married the heir to the throne of a small kingdom in Asia when she was twenty-two and left him four years later, a few months before he'd become king. Their parting was shrouded in mystery, but Sabrina had once admitted to a reporter that *he'd* wanted the divorce, not she. It was the only public comment she'd ever made about the matter.

The rest of Brad's information came from his father, who'd told him the story over drinks one night in Delhi. Bradley Royce Fraser III, called Royce by his friends, had given up his law practice for diplomacy when Brad was still a child. At the time of Sabrina's divorce, he'd been the American ambassador to India. Diplomatic scuttlebutt had it that the prince had caught Sabrina and his sister's husband in bed one morning and started divorce proceedings the next day, blaming the split on irreconcilable differences in order to protect the image of the royal family. Brad wasn't surprised Sabrina had gone along; having the truth come out would have won her precious little sympathy.

She'd been running around the world ever since, going on the trips her father conducted for rich, bored tourists and helping him raise money for his adventures. Gossip columnists occasionally ran items about her romances, which were always with wealthy, successful men, but she'd obstinately refused to comment. A couple of her boyfriends had been less closemouthed, however, describing her in terms only lovesick idiots would use. In the end she'd dumped every one of them, exactly the sort of fickleness Brad would have expected from the daughter of Howard Lang.

She rubbed her eyes and yawned, her gaze coming to rest on Brad's face. Obviously she'd overheard what he'd said; her expression was tense and hostile. Kathleen, meanwhile, had persuaded Lang to release Brad's lapels. He straightened his jacket and tie and awaited further developments.

Sabrina turned to her father and smiled. "Good morning. Is this the Kathleen you've been telling me about?"

Her voice was husky and sleepy, like Debra Winger's, and she radiated sensuality. Brad wasn't surprised that she'd managed to go through men like a scythe slices through wheat, because she was every male's fantasy of the perfect one-night stand. There would be no talk or involvement with someone like Sabrina, just pure animal pleasure with a woman who was built for a man to enjoy.

Lang rushed to hug her, then returned to Kathleen's side and drew her forward. "You would have heard even more if I'd been able to tear myself away from her. Kathleen, this is Sabrina. I hope you'll become good friends."

Sabrina threw out her arms and embraced Kathleen exuberantly. "I'm so glad to meet you. Dad's been waiting a long time for someone like you to come into his life."

A typical Bostonian, Kathleen wasn't used to such gushing familiarity and stiffened. Brad figured Lang and Sabrina used this routine all the time to impress wealthy, susceptible females with their warmth, but personally he thought it was the phoniest display of emotion he'd ever seen. Sabrina seemed to sense her mistake, because she added quickly, "I guess I'm rushing things, but I've never heard Dad sound so much in love."

Not since Mrs. Lang number three, anyway, Brad thought in disgust. Looking flustered, Kathleen answered, "It's nice to meet you, too." She suddenly seemed to remember Brad's existence. "This is my nephew, Brad Fraser. He was a little worried because... That is, I haven't been back to my house since—since your father and I..." She shook her head and blushed, embarrassed for reasons that had gone out of style years ago. Brad felt such a strong surge of protectiveness that he wanted to drag her off to safety.

Sabrina regarded him coolly, as if she longed to kick him but was afraid of offending her next meal ticket. "How do you do, Mr. Fraser?'' she asked politely. "I'm afraid my father didn't say a word about *you*."

It was such a deft put-down that Brad felt a stab of admiration. "I'm not surprised, seeing how wildly in love he is. Obviously my Aunt Kathleen is the only one on his mind these days."

"Obviously," she said, mimicking his dry tone. "I'm sure you have a great deal of experience in that area—in the effects of love on the human psyche, that is."

She was needling him, of course. To the Sabrina Langs of the world, a man who would put on a three-piece suit on a Saturday and speak of things like common sense and responsibility had to be hopelessly stuffy. "Enough to know the difference between love and infatuation," he said, "and enough to spot slick opportunists when I see them."

Her eyes narrowed. "In that case, you must realize that my father is very much in love with your aunt."

"On the contrary, I'd say he's an expert at manipulating women who are too innocent and trusting to recognize what he's really after."

"Marla Moore? Joan March Whitson?" She sounded incredulous.

She had a point. The women she'd named, an actress and socialite respectively, had been her father's second and third wives. Both had been as worldly as it was possible to be, so Brad assumed Lang had given them their money's worth for as long as they'd cared to pay his bills.

"The really great hustlers have an instinct for knowing what people want and giving it to them." Brad pretended he was talking about con men in general rather than her father specifically. "Let's use Kathleen as an example. I'm speaking theoretically, of course."

"Oh, of course," she said.

"Bradley, really!" Kathleen scolded, but nobody paid any attention to her.

"As I understand it, she and her mother, Diana, attended your father's lecture at Boston University last

Wednesday night." B.U. was where Kathleen taught history. "He took questions afterward, and she raised a number of objections to his presentation." In fact, she'd told him with exquisite politeness that he was full of baloney. "Some rather heated exchanges followed." They'd wound up screaming at each other, surely the first time Kathleen had ever lost her temper in public. "Let's assume for the sake of argument that your father is an accomplished hustler. Since Kathleen is well-known in her field, let's also assume he placed her as soon as she mentioned her name. He knew she was rich and he sensed she was interested in the trip he was planning, so he challenged her to meet with him privately and examine his evidence. Once they were alone, he turned on the charm, persuaded her that her expertise was crucial to his success and convinced her he'd fallen for her like a ton of bricks."

Lang had issued the challenge, all right, but the rest was pure conjecture on Brad's part. In reality, Kathleen had told him that a private meeting would be a waste of her time and had stalked out of the hall. The last time Diana had seen her, she'd still been sputtering with indignation about amateurs who couldn't bother to get their facts straight.

Sabrina was taken aback for a moment, but then raised her chin and looked him in the eye. "Only a cynical, suspicious person would put that interpretation on it, Mr. Fraser, and I'm *not* speaking theoretically now." She paused. "You couldn't possibly be anything but a lawyer."

Kathleen giggled in the same unnerving way as before. "How did you know? Did your father tell you?"

She shook her head. "I can recognize them by the way they talk. There's also the way they dress, in very proper and serious three-piece suits. Tell me, Mr. Fraser, aren't you warm in all that clothing?"

If he was, it was emotionally rather than physically. He wasn't some sleazy mouthpiece who sold his services to the highest bidder, but an ethical, honorable man. Still, his quarrel wasn't with Sabrina, so he turned back to Kathleen. Her arm was around Lang's waist now and she was smiling at Brad the way a mother smiles at a fractious child.

Since everything else had failed, he tried a full frontal attack. "Since you're apparently the great love of Mr. Lang's life, I'm sure he'll still be around when you've finished fulfilling your professional responsibilities. I'll wait in the lobby while you dress and pack."

"You told me a lot about your nephew, but you forgot to mention what a pompous ass he was," Lang observed.

"Howard, please—try to behave yourself." She looked at him entreatingly. "I want you and Brad to get along, and if you're going to call him names—"

"What about the names he called Dad?" Sabrina demanded.

"Calm down, darling," Lang said. "It's not your problem."

"But if *you're* not going to set him straight—"

"And how am I supposed to do that? His mind was made up before he even met me."

"Then throw him out."

He grinned at her. "I can't. Kathleen is unaccountably fond of him."

As the two of them argued back and forth, a shirtless, blond-haired boy with the build of a tank strolled out of Sabrina's room. Not only had she slept with her lover right under her father's nose, but the kid couldn't have been more than twenty. It didn't occur to Brad that the same age difference existed between himself and Grace.

The boy had pulled on his jeans so hastily that he'd forgotten to button his fly. "If you're going to yell at each other," he said, "could you do it someplace else? I want to go back to sleep."

"No, Josh, and your underwear is showing," Sabrina replied.

He looked down, then shrugged. "You're right. You want to fix it for me?"

"Very funny. Look, Dad, maybe I overreacted. Maybe you and Mr. Fraser could sit down over dinner tonight and work out your differences—assuming he's capable of acting that civilized, that is."

"I'm willing if he is," Lang said.

There wasn't a chance in hell of the Frasers accepting Lang into Kathleen's life, but Brad didn't say so. Kathleen was a grown woman, and she could do as she pleased. Since she could also be mulishly independent, it was a wonder she hadn't announced she didn't need a pair of men to decide her future for her and thrown *both* of them out.

As for Brad, between Lang, his daughter and his daughter's half-naked boyfriend, he felt as if he'd landed in the middle of the Boston Zoo. "You're staying?" he asked Kathleen, not hiding his displeasure.

She nodded. "I'll call Ted from here."

"Then I'll see you at dinner," he said to Lang. "I suggest we eat up here and avoid the possibility of public bloodshed."

Lang smiled faintly. "Seven o'clock?"

Brad was in no mood for polite goodbyes. He nodded, walked to the door and let himself out, already wondering how he could persuade Lang to find himself another patsy. He was willing to do whatever it took—lie to him, threaten him or even buy him off—but he didn't want to see Kathleen hurt.

Chapter Two

Sabrina dropped onto the couch, thinking that her brother Josh had a positive genius for timely entrances. Brad Fraser had gotten her so riled there was no telling what she might have said if Josh hadn't wandered in when he had. She prided herself on being quick to see the other fellow's point of view, but Fraser's accusations had been outrageous. Her father might be a bit of a scoundrel, but he was certainly no calculating opportunist. Why, he'd never panted after a woman's bank account in his life!

Oblivious to his daughter's agitated mood, he whispered something in Kathleen's ear and grinned. She blushed and laughed, then glanced up in embarrassment. Kathleen Carlisle, Sabrina told herself, was sweet and shy. It was funny how some traits *didn't* run in families.

Josh was buttoning his jeans now, watching the two adults in fascination. Sabrina suddenly realized Kathleen probably had no idea who he was. She'd been visiting her mother and stepfather for the past few weeks and had planned to come to Boston alone, but Josh had tagged along at the last minute. They'd flown all night, arrived at the hotel gruesomely early and gone straight to sleep. Although there were two beds in the room, Sabrina still hadn't slept well. She hadn't shared a bedroom with Josh since they were kids and hoped to heaven she wouldn't have to again. He snored.

"This disreputable-looking person is my little brother," she said to Kathleen. "Josh Rogers, Dr. Kathleen Carlisle."

"Josh is my first wife's son by her second husband," Howard added. "You remember, darling—Sam Rogers, the pharmacist."

Her smiling nod indicated he'd told her about his past. "I'm sorry we woke you up," she said. "We'll try to be quieter from now on."

"It's okay. I'm not tired. I was just trying to get everyone to stop yelling." He looked around the room. "Is there anything to eat?"

"Breakfast should be up any time now," Howard said.

The room service waiter arrived a minute later, leaving a cart set with orange juice, coffee and sweet rolls. "So what brings you to Boston?" Howard asked Josh once everyone had sat down. "Aren't things exciting enough at home?"

"In Redding? Are you kidding?" Josh picked up a croissant and took a huge bite. "Nothing against Dad's pharmacy, but every day I worked there felt like a month. When Sabrina told me you were going to Australia, I decided to come along." He took a long swallow of juice. "Mom and Dad send their regards. They really liked the fertility goddess you sent them from Africa last winter, at least until their Siamese got out and mixed it up with the neighbors' tomcat. She had seven kittens last month. Mom says you have to adopt them if she can't find homes for them."

Kathleen pricked up her ears, probably because she was curious about Sabrina's mother. Howard's lady friends never believed he got along with his ex-wives as well as he

claimed, but he did. None of them had been able to live with
him for long, but all were genuinely fond of him. He had an
exuberance for life that few people could resist.

He laughed at Josh's remark and suggested that Jane and
Sam should mail the goddess back to him. "Kathleen is one
of those stubborn Yankees you always hear about. She'd
like a child but she's not sure I'm the right man to father it.
I'm beginning to think that the only way I'll get her to marry
me is by convincing her of my genetic superiority and guar-
anteeing I'll be able to impregnate her."

Sabrina could hardly believe what she was hearing. Except with her mother, her father had never rushed into
marriage in his life. He claimed marriages had a better
chance of succeeding when the parties involved knew each
other well, not that it had ever made a difference in his particular case.

Josh popped the rest of his croissant into his mouth.
"Then you're in luck." He strode into his bedroom, returning with a small bronze statue of an enormously pregnant female. "After what happened to the cat, Mom was
afraid to have this around. She said to bring it with me."

"But your father had a vasectomy years ago."

"There's always the mailman." Josh placed the statue on
the coffee table. Sabrina studied it for a moment, then
tearfully looked away. Her father and brother wouldn't have
joked about having children if they'd known what she'd
gone through in Jammapur, but she hadn't seen the point in
telling them. Pregnancy after pregnancy, miscarriage after
miscarriage. She took a sip of orange juice and forced herself not to think about it.

Kathleen, meanwhile, had picked up the statue and was
examining it with a professional eye. "Howard, this is real.
It's not just some cheap copy made for the tourist trade."

"Of course it's real," he said indignantly. "Do you think
I'd send the mother of my only child a piece of junk?"

"But if it's a genuine antique..." She frowned. "How did
you get hold of it?"

"I had some information the dealer wanted. He had a statue *I* wanted. We traded. Then I bribed the customs officials to look the other way when they inspected my bags."

"But antiquities belong in their countries of origin. It's unethical to smuggle them out, not to mention illegal."

He sighed. "I never should have gotten mixed up with a professor. Do you want me to return it?"

"Well, maybe not right away. After all, look what it did for Josh's cat." Smiling coyly, Kathleen stroked the statue's belly. "I think I'll keep it around for a while, just in case I do decide to marry you."

"Of course you're going to marry me. Who could resist these genes? Look at what an exceptional daughter they produced."

"True enough, but there's more to marriage than children."

"Umm. There's also making love, an activity at which, with all due modesty, I must say I excel." He grinned at her. "You're depriving yourself of ecstasy, sweetheart."

She set the goddess down and firmly changed the subject. "Tell me, Josh, have you been on many trips with Howard?"

Howard burst out laughing. "You can run but you can't hide. Sooner or later you'll have to give me an answer."

"Then it will be later, because I'm talking to Josh right now." She paused. "Are you really that bored at home, or is it just that Howard's tours are exciting compared to practically anything?"

Josh probably heard the warm interest in her voice because he opened up unusually quickly. "To be honest, I was jealous of Sabrina when we were kids. She'd go off on exotic trips every summer and I'd be stuck at home. The nearest real city is San Francisco and that's two hundred fifty miles away. In other words, Redding's in the middle of nowhere."

"Don't listen to him," Sabrina said. "Redding is a very nice town, and the area around it is beautiful. There are rivers, lakes, forests..."

"Like I said, it's in the middle of nowhere. There's nothing to do there unless you get your kicks from nature. I talked my parents into letting me take my first tour when I was sixteen and I haven't missed a summer since, but I was planning to stick around this year because I'll be going to business school in New York next fall and I won't be able to get home very often. In the end I couldn't take it, though."

"Then you just graduated from college?" Kathleen looked surprised, probably because, like most people, she'd taken Josh for a little younger.

"Berkeley," he said. "My one small act of rebellion."

"Mom and Sam were convinced he'd turn into a wild-eyed radical if he went there," Sabrina explained, "but I told them not to worry—that protest had gone out of style when *they* were kids. They're both real homebodies. Once Josh was born, they had everything they wanted out of life. Sam is so different from my dad that I can't figure out how Mom and Dad got together in the first place."

"Just shows you what hormones can do," Howard remarked. "Besides, I was an idealist back then. I was going to become a teacher and inspire my students to save the world."

"You would have had an interesting life no matter what you'd done," Josh said. "It's the type of person you are."

Kathleen studied him for a moment. "You really mean that. You like Howard a lot."

"He's a great guy, Dr. Carlisle. Don't get me wrong—I love my father—but Howard... He's really *lived*, you know? He's never buried himself in a nine-to-five job and let all the excitement pass him by. Sometimes when I was stuck in Redding and Sabrina was off in some jungle some-where—" He cut himself off, a flush rising on his neck. Then he shrugged and finished the sentence. "If you want the truth, I used to lie in bed at night and tell myself that

Howard was my real father—that *I* belonged in the jungle, too." He stood up. "I should get cleaned up. I'll see you later."

He strode into the bedroom, leaving Sabrina almost speechless. She'd never realized he felt that way, especially since he'd always maintained that Howard was unforgivably irresponsible to go running off all the time when he had a daughter in California to consider. She'd defended Howard staunchly, but despite his letters and gifts she'd felt a little rejected, a little abandoned.

"I thought Josh and I were close, but he's never admitted that to me," she finally said. "He always seemed to feel sorry for me because his father lived with us and mine didn't." She looked at Howard. "If he feels you've led such a terrific life, maybe business school is the wrong choice for him. Maybe he's only going to Columbia to please Mom and Sam. Now that I think about it, I can't picture him trussed up in a suit all day, working in some crowded office. He's not the straitlaced executive type."

"How about the entrepreneurial type? Can you picture him starting his own business?"

"I suppose so, but business school at a yuppie place like Columbia—"

"Is the perfect preparation for going out on his own. He's twenty-two, Sabrina. He can make his own decisions."

Sabrina knew it was pointless to argue, but that didn't mean she would stop worrying. On some level Josh would always be the kid brother who'd come to her for a Band-Aid when he cut himself or sympathy when older, bigger boys bullied him. The role of big sister came naturally to her, so much so that it had gotten her into a great deal of trouble at times.

She poured herself a fresh cup of coffee, her thoughts jumping to Brad Fraser. While she didn't care for his remarks about her father, maybe he was as protective of Kathleen as she was of Josh. The media made Howard out to be far more of a womanizer than he really was, so it was possible he was worried about Kathleen getting hurt.

Of course, the situations weren't parallel. Kathleen was a mature woman, not a girl just out of college, and she was Fraser's aunt rather than his kid sister. She looked about the same age, though, which made Sabrina wonder how they were related. Now that she thought about it, Fraser had called Kathleen's mother "Diana." It was hardly the way most people would refer to their own grandmother.

"I guess I go a little overboard when it comes to worrying about my family, especially about Josh," she said. "Maybe you can understand that, since you and Brad seem to be so close."

"We're more like brother and sister than nephew and aunt. There were just the two of us when we were kids. I practically raised him."

"He lived with you?" Sabrina asked.

"From the time he was seven. That's when Royce—his father—decided he was tired of practicing law and wanted to try diplomacy. The State Department was so thrilled to get somebody with his talents that they posted him to Southeast Asia. They needed people with good negotiating skills, but things were heating up there, so Royce and Emily left Brad in Boston with his grandparents."

"Then Brad's grandparents are your parents." Something about the name Royce Fraser rang a bell, but Sabrina couldn't place it.

"His grandfather is my father," Kathleen corrected. "Dad was widowed when he was in his forties and married my mother two years later. Royce was twenty-three by the time I came along so he's more like an uncle than a brother."

"Then your mother is the only grandmother Brad's ever known." Sabrina still didn't understand why he called her by her first name. It seemed so cold. Was it a lawyer's instinctive precision or a symptom of something deeper?

Kathleen smiled. "True enough, but it irritated her no end to be taken for the real thing. Even being the mother of a teenager made her feel old, but it turned out to be a blessing in disguise. I was exactly the right age for babysitting when Brad moved in—fourteen—with loads of experience in bringing up a child."

"Which child?" Kathleen didn't have any siblings, so what was she talking about?

The smile gave way to a chuckle. "Neither of my parents was very nurturing, I'm afraid. Dad was always at his office or in court and Mother is an unapologetic social butterfly. We had a live-in housekeeper, but she was addicted to soap operas and game shows and never left the TV. In the end I more or less raised myself, so I knew how it felt to be ignored. Brad spent most of his childhood with us, but I never minded taking care of him. It was less lonely with him around."

"His parents never sent for him?" Sabrina felt a pang of sympathy for the abandoned little boy he'd once been.

"Only once, when they were posted to Turkey. Then Royce was sent to the Middle East and entrusted with some very dangerous assignments, so he shipped Brad back to Boston. By the time Royce returned to the States for a tour at the State Department, Brad was seventeen and didn't want to change high schools."

College and law school had obviously followed, and then what Sabrina supposed was a brilliant career as an attorney. "Are his parents still in Washington?" she asked.

"Yes, but Royce spent six years as our ambassador to India in between assignments at State. It's odd, but that's when Brad got to know him. He visited there a couple of times and found that Emily and Royce were fascinating people. Horrible parents, unfortunately, but fascinating people."

Sabrina finally put two and two together and almost blanched. Dear God, the "Royce" Kathleen kept mentioning was Bradley R. Fraser—Bradley *Royce* Fraser, who'd been the American ambassador to India during her marriage to the Crown Prince of Jammapur and a continual thorn in her side.

Jammapur was a small kingdom that bordered Pakistan, India and China. International relations in that part of the world were incredibly complex, but Sabrina had understood that Jammapur would only continue to exist as long as none of her powerful neighbors was willing to provoke the others by trying to take it over. All the same, she'd felt a little lost in the constant political turmoil.

Ambassador Fraser hadn't helped, encouraging her to be more supportive of America one moment and criticizing her for antagonizing India the next. She'd put most of her energies into what had quickly become a difficult marriage, leaving herself little time to worry about the fact that everything she said or did seemed to have political consequences. Since there was no pleasing everyone, she'd done what she thought was best for the Jammapuri people.

It was all she could do to weakly remark that she and Royce had met. "When I was married to the Crown Prince of Jammapur," she added, assuming that Kathleen knew about her past. Everyone did.

"I should have realized that," Kathleen replied. "He's the assistant secretary for Near Eastern and South Asian affairs now. Perhaps you'd like to look him up."

Sabrina never wanted to see Royce Fraser again, but was spared the necessity of lying by Josh, who'd reappeared in the parlor with his usual splendid timing. Showered and neatly dressed, he announced he was going sightseeing and would be back around four.

The telephone rang just as he walked out. Sabrina answered it, then handed it to Kathleen. "It's for you—Dr. Ted Solomon."

After a five-minute conversation that consisted mostly of "Yes, Teds" and "I'll do that, Teds," she hung up the phone looking as if she wanted to kill it. "As soon as I get dressed I'm going to call my mother and give her hell," she grumbled to Howard, who nodded distractedly. "Brad told her where I was and she turned around and told Ted. I was planning to call him later and give him a story about being sick, but *she* had to inform him that I'm at the Astoria, lolling around doing nothing, as she put it. He's having fits because some of my grades got lost in the computer and the original records are locked in my desk. He wants me to come get them out."

"Nobody else has a key?"

"Nobody but one of my friends, and she's in Mexico."

"And it can't wait?"

She sighed in exasperation. "Of course it can. Nobody will even be in the registrar's office to reenter the grades until Monday, but we're talking about Ted. He thinks I could get hit by a car in the meantime. If I don't go into the office, he'll call me again and again until I give in and do what he wants." She got up and marched into her room.

As soon as she was out of earshot, Sabrina smiled and said, "I like her, Dad. She's different from the other women you've married—gentler and more giving."

Instead of the teasing wink she'd expected, he reddened and looked away. Puzzled, she murmured, "Dad? Is something wrong?"

He answered in a low, hoarse voice. "Maybe it's just as well she has to leave. It was bad enough about her nephew's girlfriend, but a brother in the State Department—I had no idea." He picked up the coffeepot, realized it was empty and grimaced. "We have to talk. Later, when we're alone."

She leaned forward, alarmed now. "But, Dad—"

"Later," he repeated firmly. "I don't want her to overhear us."

Sabrina nodded and stood up. She'd never known her father to be anything but self-assured, but he seemed badly shaken now. Something terrible must have happened.

When she reached her doorway, she glanced at him again to make sure she hadn't overreacted. He was still on the couch, staring blankly across the room. The dashing raconteur and larger-than-life adventurer looked like an ordinary human being now. Maybe he always had been. Maybe she just hadn't noticed it before.

Chapter Three

The more Sabrina thought about her father's behavior, the less sense it made. He'd been his usual commanding self that morning, disposing of Brad Fraser quite easily and joking with Kathleen and Josh as if he hadn't a care in the world, so when had things changed? And why?

Frowning, she stepped into the shower. What had Howard said a few minutes ago? Something about "her nephew's girlfriend"—obviously Brad Fraser's girlfriend—and "a brother in the State Department?" Why should he care whom Brad dated or what Royce did for a living?

Piecing things together, she decided that Royce must be the main issue. Whoever Brad's girlfriend was, nobody had mentioned her in the past hour. Howard couldn't have been overly concerned about her or he wouldn't have been so cheerful all morning.

Royce Fraser, though... She frowned again. His name had first come up when she was talking to Kathleen, but Howard had been eating rather than listening. At the very end, though, there had been a period when he'd paid closer attention. Had it been when she'd mentioned meeting Royce in India? Had Howard finally placed him at that point? And if he had, why had he been so interested? Although the man had caused her a lot of heartache, she hadn't whined about him to Howard. Her father barely knew he existed.

As much as she liked Kathleen Carlisle, she was disappointed to find her sitting on the couch when she returned to the parlor. Kathleen was talking to Howard in low tones but fell silent when she noticed Sabrina approaching. Sabrina thought she looked guilty, or at least uncomfortable. What was going on?

Kathleen was wearing a jacket and holding her purse in her lap, so obviously she was about to go out. She glanced uncertainly at Howard, then said, "Are you sure that's the best way to handle it? After all, it's my problem, too."

"I'm sure." He patted her hand. "It's the perfect solution, darling. You need to be going now."

"But shouldn't I at least stay and explain?—"

"I'll do it." He got to his feet and pulled her up. "Ted's expecting you. You really should leave."

Smiling apologetically, Kathleen said she would see Sabrina later and followed him out of the suite. He returned a minute later with a red smudge near the corner of his mouth. Sabrina took a tissue out of the box on the table and silently handed it to him.

"What's this for?" he asked.

"Lipstick. I suppose that's one way to end an argument. What was it about?"

He wiped his mouth. "We have a favor to ask you. Kathleen thought she should help ask you, but she'd already called Ted and arranged to meet him at her office. I didn't want her to keep him waiting."

"Your concern for the man is admirable, considering how annoying you find him." Howard seemed so composed that Sabrina wondered if his problem had worked itself out. "I thought you might have wanted to get rid of her so we could talk in private. That's what you said before.''

"Actually, Sabrina, I've been thinking it over and I realize I overreacted. Sit down for a moment. About that favor I mentioned . . ."

He settled into his favorite chair and Sabrina sat down on the couch. No matter how she looked at it, his attitude didn't add up. Nothing had changed; he'd just admitted that. Maybe he was trying to protect her, but if so, she wanted no part of it. They were business partners as well as father and daughter and she expected to pull her weight.

"I'd be interested in hearing what was wrong first," she said. "You seemed terribly upset before."

He waved his hand in dismissal. "It was nothing—a minor problem. Fraser woke me with his banging and I was tired and irritable enough to let it throw me."

"A minor problem," Sabrina repeated skeptically. "I must say, it's the first time I've ever seen you go pale and grimace over a minor problem."

"Obviously I'm getting old."

"Old, my foot." She gave him a calculating look. "Since it's so *minor*, why don't you tell me about it? I love a good story. In fact, I'd be happy to sit here all day if that's how long it will take you to satisfy my curiosity. Patience is one of my greatest virtues."

"Bullheaded tenacity, you mean." He thought about it a moment longer, then conceded defeat. "It's just that when Kathleen mentioned who her brother was, I realized he wouldn't want her to help us with Maya. You know how the State Department is—always afraid of provoking a diplomatic incident."

Maya was Sabrina's former sister-in-law, now fifteen years old. She'd been a lonely child of six when the two had first met, the product of a mother who'd recently died and a father who was off in some Buddhist monastery seeking nirvana. Not surprisingly, she'd turned to the twenty-year-old Sabrina for love and attention. They'd grown so close over the years that the hardest part about leaving Jammapur had been saying goodbye to her. If Sabrina hadn't promised herself they'd be together again someday, she would have gone wild with grief.

Sabrina's ex-husband Prince Ashoka, now the king, had forbidden the two to have any contact, but he allowed Maya to go to Delhi every few months so the order had been impossible to enforce. Sabrina kept track of Maya's movements with the help of a friend in Jammapur who phoned with news when she could and carried out letters when she accompanied her husband on his business trips to Europe and America. Sabrina and Maya had managed a few brief meetings during the past three years, but not a week went by that she didn't worry about the unsheathed dagger that hung over the girl's head.

As a female, Maya occupied a secondary place in Jammapuri society, and as a princess, she was expected to sacrifice herself to whatever political ends her brother felt necessary. Several months before Sabrina left Jammapur, on Maya's twelfth birthday, Ashoka had announced her betrothal to Hassan Muhmar, a powerful local landowner and a member of the country's Muslim minority. The alliance was designed to strengthen the ties between Jammapuri Muslims and the monarchy.

Ashoka didn't care that Muhmar was in his fifties and had consolidated his position by eliminating those who got in his way; he didn't even care that Muhmar already had a wife and was marrying again only because she'd failed to give him sons. His plans for Jammapur came first, even if it meant using Maya as a pawn.

Sabrina had objected vehemently, earning a blistering reprimand from Ashoka in the process. Jammapuri women, even princesses, were supposed to stay out of politics. Even worse, she'd contaminated Maya with her foolish ideas, inciting the girl to raise an unseemly fuss about the marriage.

At twelve, Maya had only known that she didn't want a flabby old man with a dragon of a first wife and breath like a goat's, but an even more important consideration had eventually arisen. Ashoka had promised that she would convert to Islam, but she'd become a devout Buddhist and refused to comply. In the end, though, she would have no choice. Women did as they were told in that part of the world or died refusing.

King Ashoka wasn't totally provincial; he wanted Maya to receive an education befitting her royal position. He'd decreed that the wedding would take place after her sixteenth birthday, on a date to be determined by the royal astrologers. Sabrina had hoped the political situation would change by then or that a more advantageous match, one that was more acceptable to Maya, would come along.

She was still hoping, but if Ashoka persisted with his plans, she had every intention of going to India the next time Maya visited Delhi and trying to smuggle her out. Her greatest fear was that Maya would be so closely watched that Howard and his shadowy friends wouldn't be able to get to her. He kept telling her not to panic—that Maya's birthday wasn't until the spring and that the rescue would be child's play for a man of his talents and connections.

Of all people, then, the cool and daring Howard Lang should have been the last to agonize over Royce's current position. "It's not like you to worry about something until you have to," Sabrina said, "and even then, your usual response to a difficult situation is to analyze it and take action. As far as Kathleen goes, there's no reason for her to become involved. When are you going to stop hemming and hawing and tell me what's really the matter?"

He looked at her soberly. "I wasn't trying to keep anything from you, honey. It's just that things have gotten more complicated in the past few weeks and I was hoping to work them out before I spoke to you. But if you're determined to have the facts..." He reached for his briefcase. "Ranjeeta Singh tracked me down in New York two weeks ago. She asked me to give you a letter. You'd better read it right now."

Ranjeeta was Sabrina's Jammapuri friend, the one who'd acted as a go-between for her and Maya. She'd been educated in England and was unusually independent, but she was also a dutiful wife. Although her husband was modern enough to take her on his business trips, he would have divorced her on the spot if he'd caught her sabotaging Maya's marriage. Because of that, Sabrina hadn't confided in her.

Howard opened his briefcase and handed Sabrina an envelope. It contained a three-page letter from Ranjeeta and a note from Maya. The note was brief and discreet ... and it broke her heart.

Dear Sabrina,
The king has decided that I am to be married this summer. The astrologers say that the first half of September would be an auspicious time. I am not to leave Jammapur until then, because preparations must be made. I miss you.

Love,
Maya

The blood drained from Sabrina's face; she was so shaken she never even looked at Ranjeeta's letter. "Why would he change the date? Oh, God, he must have found out."

Howard sat down beside her and put his arm around her. "Calm down, honey. Jumping to wild conclusions isn't going to help any."

She was shivering, stricken that things could have reached this state virtually overnight. A fifteen-year-old child forced to abandon her religion and marry a cold opportunist almost four times her age... It was obscene. Even if she hadn't loved Maya like a daughter, she would have been sickened. "She's practically under house arrest," she choked out. "Why won't he let her leave?"

Howard answered in a soft, reassuring voice. "She's a princess, Sabrina. Think back to your own wedding. Between the astrologers and royal protocol, the arrangements took months. And you'd been engaged for two years by then."

"But I went to Delhi constantly—"

"Because you were a grown woman who was handling the details of her wedding by herself. The queen was dead, the king was off contemplating his navel and the crown prince had more important things to worry about than whether new drapes should be ordered for the main receiving room. Maya's situation is completely different. Ashoka's second wife is running the royal household, so there's no reason for a young girl to concern herself with wedding arrangements."

Sabrina fought to get a grip on herself. He was right, but that business about keeping Maya in Jammapur... "You'd think she'd at least go to Delhi for her trousseau. She loves new clothes and Ashoka's always indulged her—"

"She's marrying a Muslim. What does she need fancy clothing for?"

"Jammapuri Muslims dress modestly, but they aren't veiled." The more she thought about it, the surer she was that Maya was a virtual prisoner. "If anything, she'd need a whole new wardrobe—less colorful and more suitable for a married woman. And since she loves to shop—"

"Look, Sabrina, I'm not saying Ashoka isn't keeping Maya under wraps. He probably is, because he realizes she'd take off if he gave her half a chance. But there's no way he could have learned that we intend to help her."

Again Sabrina knew he was right. They'd told nobody about their plans, not even Maya. Still, she felt helpless and overwhelmed. It would have been hard enough to sneak the girl out of India, but Jammapur... She and Howard were persona non grata there. They wouldn't even be able to get *into* the country, much less smuggle anyone *out* of it.

She started pleating Ranjeeta's letter, too distressed to notice what she was doing. "This is all my fault. If I'd listened to you when we met her in the National Museum—"

"We'd probably be in jail right now." He hugged her gently. "You were right to stop me. It was an impulse, not a well thought-out plan, and there was no point provoking a diplomatic incident unless we were sure the wedding would actually take place. Having to get her out of Jammapur will complicate things a bit, but nothing is impossible."

Sabrina opened her mouth to argue, then hesitated. Her father was smiling in a way she recognized only too well. "You've been thinking about this," she said. "You've figured out a way to get into Jammapur."

"Dr. Kathleen Carlisle," he stated.

"Kathleen?" Sweet, unworldly Kathleen? The woman he loved to distraction? Sabrina was dumbfounded.

"Sure," he answered. "It's the perfect solution. It came to me during my lecture, when she announced who she was and started yelling at me. If a scholar like Kathleen asks to enter Jammapur to do research, nobody's going to turn her down. Ancient Asian history is her specialty. She has an international reputation. Hell, she even reads Sanskrit."

"But to use her to get to Maya...to pretend you feel something when you don't... It's unforgivable." She stared at Ranjeeta's letter, which looked like an accordion by now. "I thought you loved her, Dad—really loved her."

"For God's sake, Sabrina, of course I do, but I also care about Maya. That's how it all got started." He sighed heavily. "Maybe I should begin at the beginning."

Having idolized her father from the time she was a child, Sabrina desperately wanted him to explain. She couldn't bear to think he would hurt someone as vulnerable as Kathleen, not even for Maya's sake. Still, she couldn't pretend to be shocked by what he proceeded to tell her—she knew he was far from a saint.

His lecture at Boston University, entitled "In Search of the Ancient Harappans," had been designed with two ends in mind: to educate and entertain his audience by telling them about an ancient civilization and to interest them in going on his August tour. An accomplished showman,

Howard had known that the prospect of poking around Asian ruins in the height of summer would hardly attract the sort of wealthy, jaded travelers he catered to. He'd needed something more intriguing, so he'd told them of a persistent legend—that a golden statue representing the earliest known portrayal of the Hindu god Vishnu had been fashioned by a Harappan artist two thousand years before the birth of Christ and stolen from the site of an ancient city a hundred years ago. Not only was it priceless; it had enormous historical significance. And he meant to find and photograph it.

That was when Kathleen had risen to speak. She'd dismissed the rumors of the statue as rubbish, saying there was no evidence that the Harappans had influenced the development of Hinduism in anything but a broad, basic way. Even if they had, the god Vishnu hadn't been mentioned in early Hindu literature, but had only appeared five to ten centuries later—five to ten centuries *after* Harappan civilization had disappeared. Never one to back down, Howard had answered that the oral tradition must have preserved the old Harappan legends, which had then found their way into the Hindu work in question, the *Bhagavad Gita*. A series of sharp exchanges had followed.

Sabrina was groaning softly by this point. It was bad enough that her father had repeated common gossip about a golden statue, but claiming it was a statue of the god Vishnu was totally beyond the pale. Kathleen had been right.

The worst, however, was yet to come. Aware that his audience was on the edge of its collective seat, Howard had thrown in some mumbo jumbo about one of the great mysteries of the Harappan civilization—the meaning of the Harappan seals. The seals, small squares of soapstone engraved with writings and pictures, had been found in all the major Harappan cities. Numerous scholars had attempted to translate them, but none had succeeded.

Howard had informed his audience that he'd come across a brilliant new translation, as yet unaccepted by the academic community, that indicated the seals contained references to Vishnu. He claimed this supported his belief that the golden statue was fact, not legend. Outraged, Kathleen had insisted no such translation existed, saying that he'd taken the fact that the engravings contained religious motifs and twisted it to suit his own ends. He'd blithely answered that she was the perfect example of a closed-minded academic.

"I wasn't worried when she stormed out—I knew she wouldn't be able to resist phoning me and asking to see my proof once she'd finally cooled down. When I got her alone, I admitted the lecture was mostly showmanship and talked her into having dinner with me. We haven't discussed the Harappans since."

"In other words, you charmed her into falling in love with you."

"I certainly tried."

Sabrina didn't need him to spell out why. He had a weasely little friend in London who could manufacture counterfeit documents for any identify one cared to assume. "You plan to talk her into going to Jammapur. You figure she can sneak us in as her research assistants."

"The thought had occurred to me, yes."

"But that's unconscionable!" she wailed. Dear Lord, Brad Fraser had been righter than she'd dreamed possible. The idea that she owed him an apology was mortifying.

Howard grinned at her. "I was only teasing you, honey. I was smitten with Kathleen from the moment she started chewing me out. Would I be talking about marriage if I didn't love her?"

Sabrina didn't want to think so, but the sequence of events was awfully suspicious. "You already knew about Maya by the night of the lecture. You realized Kathleen could be useful the minute you learned who she was."

"I'm not denying it started out that way, but it's grown into a lot more." He looked at her earnestly. "Believe me, Sabrina, I wouldn't get Kathleen involved in this if there were any way she could get hurt. The only problem—the thing that really bothers me—is that I was planning to tell her the truth as soon as I'd gotten your okay, and now I can't. She's too close to her family."

"You're afraid she'll tell her brother?"

He nodded. "Either him or her nephew. The girl he dates is a congressman's daughter—Charles Fitzsimmons, the senior Republican on the House Foreign Affairs Committee. People like Fraser and Fitzsimmons don't care what happens to one little girl. They're too busy playing global politics."

The situation was relatively simple. If the Muslims in Jammapur became disaffected from the monarchy, Pakistan, an Islamic country, might invade the predominantly Muslim areas near its border in the hope that the inhabitants would rise up against King Ashoka, a Buddhist, and support the Pakistani troops. Maya's betrothal to Hassan Muhmar was designed to prevent that. The Muslims hoped for more of a say in how the country was run and saw this as a promising first step.

India and China were satisfied with the status quo. They couldn't take Jammapur for themselves, but Pakistan couldn't, either. The United States was happy, too, because it favored anything that kept China and India content. If the American government caught wind of Howard and Sabrina's plans, they would never be permitted to leave the country. In other words, she thought wearily, deceiving Kathleen was the price they would have to pay for rescuing Maya.

Howard released her and stood up. "When you run out of alternatives, you take the only course open to you. And that brings me to the favor I need to ask."

She didn't say a word, merely waited for him to continue. "Kathleen called Diana before she left and told her she would make her own decisions regardless of what Diana thought or did. At that point, Diana did a complete about-face. She said she wanted to meet us—all of us—and that she would have a few people over tonight and introduce us around. She probably hopes I'll make a complete fool of myself and get dumped on the spot, but I have no intention of obliging her." He paused, running a tired hand through his hair. "Kathleen is determined to stand her ground, but it would take a lot of the pressure off if I could get her family's approval. The major problem is her nephew. I have a feeling he's not especially susceptible to my charm. He'll do his best to rip me to shreds tonight, and he's smart enough and tough enough to succeed."

"But you're supposed to have dinner with him later," Sabrina said.

"Exactly. Brad told Diana he was going sailing and then coming straight to the hotel. Diana wanted us to wait for him and bring him along to her house, but Kathleen and I came up with a better idea."

The sinking feeling in the pit of Sabrina's stomach told her she was intimately involved. "I can imagine," she said.

"Kathleen, Josh and I will go to Diana's. You'll stay here and wait for Brad. All you have to do is keep him occupied for a while—give me time to win Diana over."

"Occupied *how*? And for how long?" She didn't like the sound of this at all.

He winked at her. "There isn't a man alive who can resist you when you go into that subservient Asian female routine and—"

"It's not a routine," she interrupted, offended now. "I enjoy spoiling people—even men. That's not the same as being subservient."

"So spoil Brad Fraser. Distract him. Delay him."

"Seduce him?" she asked acidly.

"Think how much enjoyment it will give you! The guy will be spoiled rotten after a few hours in your bed."

"Very funny," she muttered.

"Seriously, honey, you have nothing to worry about," he assured her. "According to Kathleen, the man's been faithful to his girlfriend for three straight years. He would probably consider it a breach of his personal code of honor to make a pass at you."

"And how am I supposed to feel about breaching *my* personal code of honor?"

"Lousy, but think of Maya." He sobered. "I know you don't like manipulating people, but it's the only way we're going to get her out of Jammapur. We need Kathleen's help and we need to keep her in the dark after we get it. It will be a lot easier to persuade her to go to Asia if Diana gives us her blessing."

And it would be a lot easier to get Diana's blessing if Brad wasn't around to ask questions. "I suppose you're right, but I'm not sure I can handle her nephew. He'll expect to find you here—"

"Tell him we went sightseeing with Josh—that we should be back at any time."

Brad wouldn't like it when "any time" stretched into hours, but as Howard had said, when you ran out of alternatives, you took the only course open to you. She'd simply have to be amusing and fascinating enough to keep him hanging on. It was a daunting prospect.

Chapter Four

There were only a few things Brad enjoyed more than sailing—ripping a tough opponent to shreds on the witness stand, perhaps, or trying an important, complicated case in front of a jury. When it came to sheer relaxation, though, nothing could compare to a day on his boat, the *Cape Poge*. It had once occurred to him that a day with Grace—talking, dining, making love—should have been equally enjoyable, but it wasn't. The realization had been so unsettling that he'd refused to think about it ever since. His life, he'd told himself, was perfect.

His work was challenging, his social life was busy and interesting, and he and Grace had an agreement—he didn't have to go to operas and she didn't have to go to ball games. She could be alone at art exhibits and he could be alone on his boat. All in all, he preferred a smooth, predictable existence and his relationship with her provided it.

He was mellow and pleasantly tired after a day on the water, and in such a good mood that not even the prospect of dinner with Howard Lang could spoil it. He thought about changing into a suit and decided not to. Sailing always made his feet hurt, the result of a congenital condition he'd learned to live with. The idea of cramming them into a pair of oxfords was distinctly unappealing.

Then again, the meeting with Lang was business. He couldn't show up in a sweaty T-shirt and shorts and expect to be taken seriously. Fortunately, he'd brought along something in between—a taupe sweater and slacks, a long-sleeved shirt and Topsiders. The outfit was a little too preppy, but Lang wasn't exactly a candidate for the fashion hall of fame. He'd never know the difference.

Brad stayed in the shower for an extra ten minutes, letting the hot water beat down on the sore muscles in his shoulders and back. Ordinarily it bothered him to run late, but he was too relaxed to care. He played a tape as he drove into Boston, a folk album from the sixties. Kathleen had loved this music, so he'd grown up listening to it. One of the songs was running through his mind as he rode up to Lang's suite—"Blowin' in the Wind," with its lyrics about life, freedom and death. Kathleen's infatuation with Howard Lang seemed unimportant compared to such cosmic concerns.

Unlike that morning, his knock was answered immediately, but by Sabrina this time. While Brad wasn't surprised to see her, he assumed she and the others would be leaving shortly so he and Howard could talk in private. In the meantime, he allowed himself the pleasure of looking at her.

Her outfit—a silky dress over full pants of the same fabric—covered her completely but hugged every curve. The delicate, flowing fabric, a swirl of greens and blues, reminded him of an Impressionist painting. If this was what the women in Jammapur wore, the men there were lucky. It was feminine and enticing, the sort of thing that sent a guy's imagination into overdrive. It was a shame the kid in the jeans didn't have the sophistication to appreciate it.

She smiled warmly, but he forced himself not to smile back. Her friendliness was out of place in a woman who'd been hard-pressed to be civil before. Besides, she was a certified man-eater. She wrapped guys around her finger, took what she wanted and discarded them. Whatever her game was, he didn't want to play.

"Dad called about half an hour ago," she said. "They were sightseeing up the coast and Kathleen's car broke down. They managed to find a place to get it fixed, but it'll be a while before it's ready. They're grabbing a bite to eat in the meantime. He said we might as well have the dinner he ordered because otherwise it will only go to waste."

Brad could see a room service cart sitting by a table near the window. The table was set for two, complete with crystal goblets, silver candlesticks and shrimp cocktails nestled in ice-filled compotes. He walked inside and closed the door. The meal, the privacy, the beautiful woman... It smelled like a setup, but he couldn't imagine what Lang hoped to gain by it. Brad wasn't some raw kid who could be seduced into dropping his objections.

"How come you didn't go with them?" he asked.

She started across the room. "I was a little tired. Besides, I've been here before and I've toured the whole area. Josh hasn't, though, so Dad and Kathleen took him."

"I trust he managed to get dressed, then."

"And without my help, even though it would have served him right if I'd called his bluff." She grinned impishly and Brad responded in a tangibly physical way. Between her beauty, her husky voice and the mischief in her eyes, it was impossible not to. "He doesn't like to be reminded of it, but I changed a lot of his diapers in my time. I was pretty good at it, too, especially since he used to carry on as if I were trying to kill him."

She paused by her chair, waiting for Brad to pull it out. He couldn't imagine what she saw in the kid—he was much too young for her and had less polish than one of the Hardy boys—but there was no accounting for taste. As he seated her, he noticed the scent of her shampoo and the way her thick, silky hair shone brightly even in the room's dim lighting. The thought brought him up short. Dim lighting? God, he was a sucker! There was even a bottle of champagne on the cart, opened and sitting on ice. Some soft music, and the setting would be complete.

On guard again, he walked around the cart and sat down. "This is nice, but it's also a bit of a surprise. You said something this morning about your father and me having a civilized dinner, but this looks as if he was hoping to make love to me. Should I be flattered?"

Sabrina reddened. She knew how it looked, but it wasn't her fault. Her father had ordered the meal and arranged for the romantic table setting. The lighting in the room was dim, but she'd turned the lamps as high as they would go. And while she did have to take the blame for the Jammapuri dress, it had seemed like a good idea at the time. She'd hoped it would soften Brad up.

She wasn't sure whether it had or not, only that he'd looked his fill when she'd opened the door. She had, too, and she'd liked what she'd seen. Brad had seemed more approachable in slacks and a sweater, more relaxed and less grim. As for his face, she'd found him handsome this morning without being especially attracted to him, probably because of his constant scowl. A smile—even an ironic one—did wonders for him.

His eyes were quite extraordinary, a light, clear brown that reminded her of fine sherry. His hair was a little too short, but she liked the warm, dark color and the way it curled out of place despite his careful combing. His skin was tanned but virtually unlined, so he probably used a sunscreen when he sailed. It fitted what she'd seen of his personality—careful, sensible, conservative.

She didn't necessarily object to that. What she disliked were traits like small-mindedness, a knee-jerk approval of the conventional and an automatic rejection of anything different or unusual. Since she didn't know Brad at all, she had no idea if he possessed those characteristics.

As for the behavior she'd found so outrageous this morning, if Brad had judged Howard by Diana Fraser's account of his lecture, it was little wonder he'd been suspicious and caustic. Golden Vishnus and Harappan religious writings, indeed! How was she going to explain that when she couldn't tell him the truth about Maya?

She forced her attention to a more immediate problem—explaining why the parlor looked as if some two-bit Don Juan had arranged it for his next seduction. "I guess the waiter saw the way I was dressed and assumed I was planning a romantic dinner. He even phoned down for the candles."

He nodded thoughtfully. "I see. And why *are* you dressed that way? Were you planning to go out with Josh?"

"With Josh?" She couldn't imagine where he'd gotten *that* idea. "I wouldn't waste a dress like this on him! He has no taste whatsoever. He thinks the ultimate in desirable females is some blond beach bunny in a microscopic bikini."

She noticed his confusion and finally figured out the reason. "He's my little brother," she explained with a giggle, "my mother's son by her second husband. I'd never talk about a lover that way. It would be demeaning."

"And you don't believe in demeaning your lovers?"

"I've never actually had any, but if I loved a man enough to sleep with him I'd certainly respect him enough not to make fun of him behind his back. Little brothers are fair game, though."

He cocked his eyebrow skeptically, but merely remarked, "You have interesting ideas about male-female relationships."

She picked up the champagne. "I lived in Asia for a time and the culture rubbed off on me. People—men—have told me I'm an unpredictable mixture of East and West now."

She poured some wine into his glass, then waited. Although it took him a moment to realize why, he performed the tasting ritual with all the easy expertise she'd expected of him. He was obviously an authentic Boston Brahmin, trained from birth to be polite and discreet. After filling both glasses, his first, she put the bottle back on ice.

He picked up his fork, then hesitated. "Tell me something. If I don't start eating, will you sit there and wait till I do?"

"No, because if you followed Western etiquette and waited for me and I followed Eastern custom and waited for you, we'd wind up starving." She smiled teasingly. "Obviously you have no manners, Brad, or you'd never have picked up your fork."

"You're righter than you know," he said. "If I cared about manners, I wouldn't remind you that you never answered my question about the way you're dressed. I wouldn't ask you why you're suddenly being so nice to me, either."

The last time Sabrina had given a man such a bewitching smile, he'd picked up the salt and shaken it into his coffee. Either she was slipping or Brad Fraser was even tougher than she'd feared. Either way, it was going to be a long night.

Since she'd already admitted the dress was special, she couldn't very well claim it was some rag she'd thrown on at the last minute. "I knew half an hour ago that we'd be having dinner together. I thought the least I could do was change. After all, you're my guest."

"No, I'm not. I'm a guy who came here to talk to your father about laying off my aunt. We're on opposite sides of an argument, so why did you put on an outfit that any man in his right mind would want to take off?"

"That's a ridiculous exaggeration, but the answer is that I thought you'd like it. I thought it might make you a little—friendlier." She put a soft, demure note into her voice. "Are you insulted that I wanted to look attractive for you?"

He didn't back off an inch, much less dip a shrimp into the salad dressing rather than the cocktail sauce. "Why should you care if I'm friendly? Why should you give a damn if I find you attractive?''

"Would you stop cross-examining me? This isn't a courtroom, counselor.'' Sabrina wasn't angry, given that Brad had every reason to be suspicious, but she *was* rather vexed. She wasn't accustomed to scrambling for all she was worth just to stay even. "If you'd stop jumping down my throat and give me a chance to explain—''

"I'd love to.'' He settled back in his chair, the picture of reason and patience. "This should be riveting.''

Honesty was obviously the best policy, especially since he'd never believe a story that didn't contain at least a smidgen of the truth. "I had a talk with my father this morning. You were right about what happened at the lecture, but I suppose you already know that. Diana probably gave you a blow-by-blow description.''

She waited for him to agree, but he sat impassively, giving no hint of his feelings. "Anyway, what you don't understand is *why* Dad said the things he did. It was pure showmanship. It's an expensive tour, so people won't be interested unless it sounds really special. Not that it won't be, because the Harappan civilization is fascinating, but searching for a golden statue of Vishnu sounds so much more exciting than looking at ancient ruins. He'll give them their money's worth, though. He always does.''

Brad continued to regard her blandly. "And my aunt? Where does she fit into the picture?''

"He fell for her the moment she started lecturing him. He wanted to capture her interest and saying outrageous things was a surefire way to do it.'' All of which was true, but only partly so, and Sabrina found it hard to hide her discomfort. "He's interested in *her*, not in her money. If you don't believe that, maybe you should try looking at her as a woman rather than your aunt. She's lovely, sweet and intelligent. Why *wouldn't* he be interested in her?''

"So when he called to say he'd be late, you decided to be a good daughter and plead his case. You thought I'd be more amenable to listening if a beautiful woman did the talking."

She looked at her plate, hating all the evasions and half-truths. If there were any choice...but there wasn't. Besides, a white lie or two wouldn't hurt anybody. "Yes. I'm not going to apologize for that, but maybe I should change into a regular dress. You don't seem to approve of the one I have on."

Brad had been fighting to stay objective, but Sabrina was too damn captivating. He didn't believe everything she'd said—she looked too uncomfortable—but he was willing to accept the part about wanting to help her father. Of course, that didn't mean Lang had been straight with her. She was obviously a dutiful daughter, and people could be incredibly blind about those they loved. He hadn't forgotten the men she'd wrapped around her finger, either, and he knew for a fact that she'd slept with at least one of them, but he figured he was smart enough to avoid being her next conquest.

Gently chiding her, he said, "You know damn well I approve of the dress. Now stop staring at your shrimp cocktail and eat it, Sabrina."

He lighted the candles, an amused expression on his face. "And tell me what all that business about Harappans and Vishnu was. If you knew Diana, you'd know that she's hopeless when it comes to details. She didn't say a word about the tour your father is hustling for, and the only thing I remember about ancient civilizations is something about Egypt and Mesopotamia."

Given what Sabrina had seen of Brad Fraser, she pitied anyone who had to face him in a courtroom. "Your aunt doesn't talk to you about her work?" she asked.

"I don't read her journal articles and she doesn't read my legal briefs. I've skimmed some of her books, though—the one about the rise of Buddhism and the one dealing with Alexander the Great's invasion of India and the dynasty that supplanted him—the Mauryan empire."

Sabrina replied that those events had taken place long after the Harappan or Indus Valley civilization had declined, adding that the Harappans had built one of the four great civilizations of the ancient world. All had originated in river valleys—the Nile in Egypt, the Tigris-Euphrates in Iraq, the Hwang Ho in China, and, in the case of the Harappans, the Indus in what was now Pakistan.

Civilization had developed later there than in the other three places, about 2500 B.C., but the Harappans had spread throughout a far greater area—from the Himalayan foothills to the Arabian Sea. They'd been the first to grow cotton and the first to domesticate fowl, building large cities containing fired brick buildings, rectangular grids of streets, facilities for storing grain, and elaborate, brick-lined sanitation systems. Their houses, often built around central courtyards, had often contained indoor bathrooms. Archaeologists had found evidence of a substantial amount of trade—beads and decorated seals from Mesopotamia, and stones and metals from central Asia, southern India and Persia.

The Harappans had also attained a high level of craftsmanship and artistry. They'd used bronze or stone for everyday items like weapons and pottery, and had fashioned jewelry from gold and silver as well as from more common materials. Their artists had sculpted statues from bronze, terra-cotta, ivory and various types of stone, some of them remarkable for their sophistication and naturalism. Finally there were the seals—small soapstone rectangles depicting real or imaginary animals, humans or deities with one or more glyphs, or symbols, written along the top.

The Harappan civilization had reached its peak about 2000 B.C. and then declined, all but disappearing by 1500 B.C. Nobody knew why, but archaeologists blamed flooding or overpopulation and pointed to evidence of destruction by the Aryans, a seminomadic people who had moved across central Asia into the Indian subcontinent in great successive waves during that same five-hundred-year period.

"And that's where religion enters the picture," Sabrina said. Brad had finished both his shrimp and salad, so she stood to clear the table. He started to do the same, but she waved him back. "I'll do it. You sit and rest. You were sailing all day—you must be tired."

Brad felt a mixture of embarrassment and pleasure as he settled back in his chair. Although Sabrina wasn't his date, simple good manners dictated that he treat her as if she were. It didn't seem right that she should wait on him hand and foot, but he thoroughly enjoyed the way she refilled his glass whenever it was half empty and whisked away dishes as soon as he was through with them.

She reached into the cart's warming oven and took out two covered platters. "Which do you want? The veal piccata or the chicken cordon bleu?"

Veal piccata was one of his favorite dishes, but he said politely, "You choose first."

"We have ways of making you commit yourself, Mr. Fraser." She removed a lid and passed the chicken back and forth under his nose. He sniffed appreciatively. Then she did the same with the veal, but this time he smiled helplessly. "The veal it is," she said.

Her arm brushed his shoulder as she set the plate in front of him, making him more aware of her than ever. If the situation had been different, he might have led her to the couch after dinner and seen what developed, but he was here to talk to her father, he still smelled a setup and he was faithful to his girlfriend. "We were talking about religion," he reminded her as she sat down.

"Yes. The origins of Hinduism." Sabrina took a sip of champagne, trying to get her mind off Brad and back to the Aryans. Why hadn't she noticed how beautifully built he was? Those large, strong hands, that powerful chest, those wonderful broad shoulders... "The, uh, the Aryans spoke a form of Sanskrit but had no written language during the period of the invasion. The priestly class passed down religious stories through the oral tradition. The earliest ones, the Vedic hymns, originated between 1500 and 1000 B.C. and were finally written down around the time of Christ. The most important hymn, the *Rig Veda*, describes how the Aryans swept into the Indian subcontinent and conquered the natives there—the Harappans, undoubtedly. Some of the Harappans' beliefs found their way into the Vedic hymns and other early Hindu literature, especially their worship of a prototype of the god Shiva, or to be more precise, of his..." She paused. "That is, he's always depicted as..." She struggled to find a delicate way to put it. How had she gotten into this?

Brad suddenly looked exceptionally interested. "Yes?"

"The lingam is an important emblem in Hinduism," she finally stated. "It's a symbol of Shiva, who's one of the three main deities along with Vishnu and Brahma, and it seems to have had its origins among the Harappans."

"The lingam," he said. "I'm not familiar with the term."

Sabrina had the feeling he knew exactly what it meant but wasn't going to pass up the opportunity to tease her. Blushing, she murmured, "A stylized depiction of the male sexual organ. Shiva is always—ithyphallic."

"Ithyphallic?" he repeated, sounding lost.

There was no help for it. "Permanently erect."

Brad could identify with that. He gave Sabrina a look she couldn't possibly misinterpret and drawled, "I know exactly how Shiva felt."

There was a long silence during which Sabrina considered running into the nearest bathroom but rejected the idea as adolescent. This was a scholarly discussion. It was stupid to be embarrassed.

"Shiva was also permanently chaste," she said tartly, "so I seriously doubt it." She ignored his burst of laughter. "The point is, my father said the Harappan seals referred to the god Vishnu, but they've never been deciphered. He said he wanted to look for a golden Harappan statue, but archaeologists have only found bronze and stone statues. And he claimed the statue was of Vishnu, but Vishnu wasn't worshipped by the Harappans or even by the original Aryans. He came along centuries later. Dad was so outrageous that your aunt finally walked out, so I can see why you were suspicious this morning. I'm sorry I jumped all over you before I knew what had really happened, but he was just being a showman. Kathleen understands that.''

Brad thought there was a big difference between con artists and showmen, but didn't say so. Maybe it was the champagne, but he decided he was stuck here till Lang returned and might as well make the best of it. Besides, he enjoyed Sabrina's company.

"You seem to know a lot about Indian history," he remarked. "Did you study it while you lived in Jammapur?"

Sabrina nodded, feeling the usual quiet resignation at the reference to her past. "I've always been fascinated by Eastern religions and customs."

He started to question her, but in a gentle, interested way—about Jammapur's climate, people, cuisine and history. She found him so easy to talk to that she relaxed and dropped her guard. It seemed natural to take their coffee to the couch after dinner and continue their conversation.

He noticed the African fertility goddess on the coffee table and asked her where it was from. She told him the story about the kittens and they both laughed. He yawned and stretched, then leaned back, crossing an ankle over one knee. A little later, as he related his own cat story—a pregnant female had moved into their summer place on Martha's Vineyard and gifted them with six kittens—he tucked a thumb inside his shoe and absently massaged his arch.

"You know what they say," Sabrina remarked, when he was finished talking. "People don't own cats. Cats own people." She noticed the way he was rubbing his foot. "Why don't you take your shoes off and put your feet up on the table? You'll be more comfortable."

He reddened. "I didn't realize I was doing that. It's a bad habit—I've got rotten feet and they give me trouble whenever I sail or ski for too long."

Sabrina didn't think—she simply reacted. Her years in Jammapur had accustomed her to performing certain little rituals that the average American woman would have blanched at. "I can cure that." She smiled and stood up. "Take off your shoes and socks. I'll be back in a minute."

Brad watched her walk away, wondering what she planned to do to him. It was beside the point that he shouldn't permit her to do anything; he couldn't remember when he'd enjoyed an evening as much as this one and had no inclination to stop her. Her attentions made him feel like a sultan, and he liked that more than he wanted to admit.

Chapter Five

Sabrina returned to the parlor with a brass wastebasket filled with hot water and bath salts, some towels and a bottle of lotion. She spread a towel on the rug to protect it, put the wastebasket on top and lifted Brad's left foot onto her lap. Rolling up his trousers, touching the sinewy muscles in his calf, she was reminded that even the most routine chores in the East could have underlying elements of eroticism. The ritualistic kindness she was performing turned into a prelude to sensual pleasures, at least in her imagination.

She pictured herself slipping her hand under his slacks and running it up his leg or brushing her mouth over his instep and sucking one of his toes. The impossible, forbidden images made her pulses race with excitement. Then she remembered that he was a virtual stranger who was involved with somebody else and she was a woman who'd given herself to only one man, her lawful husband, and pushed the fantasy to the back of her mind.

She placed his foot in the water and made herself more comfortable on the floor. "Visitors on the subcontinent were traditionally given water to wash their feet when they arrived. Dutiful wives rubbed their husbands' feet after a hard day's work, something many of them still do. Most of the men I've met seem to like those customs."

"Sounds like the women got the short end of it," he said, looking a little ambivalent about the whole operation.

"I suppose so." She paused. "On the other hand, husbands were expected to please their wives, too—never to scold them too harshly and to provide them with as many luxuries as they could afford."

"Not to mention satisfying them in bed." He lazed on the couch and closed his eyes, relaxing now. "Back in college, I read the Indian books that appealed to my prurient interests—the *Kama Sutra*, for example. Now that I think about it, I remember the term lingam very well." He smiled. "An Indian friend once told me that according to one of the ancient texts, women enjoy sex eight times as much as men. Do you think that's true?"

"It comes from the *Mahabharata*, which was composed between 500 and 1000 B.C., undoubtedly by men. One wonders where they got their information from." Not to mention wondering why the subject of sex kept coming up, though Sabrina didn't mind. It injected a thrilling note of tension into the air.

"You don't agree?" he said.

She didn't answer. Her experience was limited to her ex-husband, who'd taught her to arouse him as skillfully as a courtesan while assuming, quite incorrectly, that she was trembling at his every touch.

"Sabrina?" Brad prompted.

"I'll let you know if I ever come back as a man," she finally replied.

He didn't press her. Whether she enjoyed sex or not was none of his business, but if she didn't it was a damn shame. If Indian art was any guide, she had the kind of body Eastern men love—full breasts and hips and a tiny waist. He found the combination as erotic as they did. Given the raw material, any husband worth the name should have been inspired to arouse her to the heights of ecstasy.

Neither of them spoke for the next several minutes. Eventually she lifted his foot out of the water, patted it dry and gently rolled up his other trouser leg. Her touch turned his nerves into dry kindling—an encouraging look, word or caress, and his self-control would go up in flames. He was beginning to understand why so many men had found her irresistible.

Once his right foot was in the water, she lifted the left one onto her thigh. He'd never known toes could be so sensitive. He wanted to run them up and down her soft, firm flesh, then slide them between her closed thighs and tease her into parting them. The situation was clearly getting out of control.

He was about to pull away his foot when he felt something cold and wet on his instep—the lotion she'd brought in with her. She smoothed it onto his foot and deftly kneaded it in, soothing the soreness so effectively that he sighed in relief. It hurt a little whenever she hit a spot that was especially tender, but that only made the pleasure more intense. Her fingers were both strong and gentle, and he wondered how they would feel on more intimate parts of his body than his feet.

He moaned softly and slumped down on the couch, letting the pleasure engulf him. If he'd been an Indian husband, he never would have made it to dinner after work. He would have dragged his wife to bed first. She massaged each part of his foot from the ankle to the little toe, then slipped his sock back on and went to work on the other foot.

He opened his eyes, needing to know whether she was enjoying this or considered it merely an act of mercy. Her head was bent low in concentration, a dreamy, almost abandoned smile on her face. She was enjoying it, all right.

He'd always preferred liberated women—their initiative, intelligence and independence—but this...this made him feel totally male...potent and virile. It wasn't her subservience that aroused him, because he hadn't given her any orders and wouldn't have wanted to. It was that of her own free will she was anticipating his desires and eagerly satisfying them. He closed his eyes again, thinking a little sheepishly that if she kept it up for very much longer his rapidly expanding ego would outgrow the entire hotel.

Sabrina could feel Brad unwinding but had no idea of the havoc she was wreaking. It was the nature of males to enjoy being spoiled and it was her particular nature to enjoy obliging them. Besides, it gave her pleasure to touch him and fulfillment to ease his pain.

Her fingers were a little tired now, but she wasn't going to stop if he didn't want her to. Raising her head, she saw his closed eyes and wondered if he'd fallen asleep. "Is that better?" she asked softly.

He opened his eyes halfway. "You're a miracle worker. They hardly hurt at all anymore." His voice was soft and husky, from simple fatigue, she assumed. "The rest of my body is jealous. Have you ever considered turning professional?"

"Never. You have to be a robust Scandinavian blonde who enjoys pummeling the life out of people." She slid his sock back on and stood up. "I'll be back as soon as I clean up."

"I'll help you," he said, but made no attempt to move.

"You can't. You have to sit quietly and let your feet rest for the next hour or the whole effect is lost."

"Really?"

"Really." Both of them knew she was indulging him. She picked everything up and left the room, dumping the water in the bathtub and putting the towels in the hamper. Afterward, passing by the bar in the parlor, she decided a nightcap would be nice and grabbed some brandy and a pair of snifters.

Brad had his feet on the coffee table by then, the fertility goddess in his lap. He ran his finger across her swollen belly as Sabrina poured the brandy and sat down. "I'd be careful if I were you. Her magic might rub off and you could suddenly become a father."

"Five years ago I would have dropped her like a hot potato if you'd told me that, but now I sort of like the idea." He was caressing the statue in an unconsciously suggestive way, making Sabrina feel as if he were touching *her* in those places...on her arms, her neck, her breasts. Her nipples tingled and hardened, aching to be rubbed and teased. "How about you? Do you want kids?"

She felt a familiar tightness in her throat, mingling with her desire, heightening her emotions. "Yes. Do you like the brandy? I could get you a liqueur if you'd prefer."

"The brandy is fine." He took a sip and she did the same. "Why did you change the subject?"

She knew he'd only pursue it if she didn't explain, but it was hard to get the words out. Her voice took on a thin, brittle quality quite alien to its usual throatiness. "One of my duties as crown princess was to produce an heir. I couldn't, even though I desperately wanted to. I really don't like talking about it. Would you mind putting the goddess away? Looking at her makes me..." She shook her head, overwhelmed by pain. "I'm sorry. Maybe I've had too much to drink. I don't usually get maudlin."

Brad wanted to take her in his arms and comfort her, but he was holding the goddess in one hand and the brandy in the other. By the time he put them down, she'd bolted and hurried into her room. He tucked the goddess under the couch so the sight of it wouldn't upset her.

She returned with a guitar, smiling in a forced, almost haunted way, and joined him on the couch. Her inability to have children had obviously been deeply traumatic. "Given the way my father's kept you waiting, the least I can do is entertain you," she said.

The melody she played was instantly familiar—the instrumental introduction to Joni Mitchell's "Both Sides Now," the song Judy Collins had made famous. Then she began to sing—first of clouds, then of love—in a sweet, mellow soprano that took Brad's breath away.

Moons and Junes and ferris wheels, the dizzy dancing way you feel,
as ev'ry fairy tale comes real, I've looked at love that way.
But now it's just another show, you leave 'em laughing when you go.
And if you care, don't let them know, don't give yourself away.

I've looked at love from both sides now
from give and take, and still somehow
it's love's illusions I recall;
I really don't know love at all.

Finally she sang of life, in a voice that was husky with feeling. Brad didn't say a word when she was finished—he was too moved to speak. The room was still and silent, the air thick with emotion.

The jarring ring of a telephone startled them back to reality. Brad absently answered it, then listened as Howard Lang apologetically explained that they were still waiting for Kathleen's car and wouldn't be back for at least an hour and a half. He added that he would understand if Brad decided not to wait.

Not wanting to commit himself either way, Brad thanked him for calling and hung up. He repeated the conversation to Sabrina, then dismissed it from his mind. He was alone with one of the most enchanting women he'd ever met and he wanted to know more about her.

"You have a beautiful voice," he said. "Did you have any special reason for choosing that song?"

"It fits my range and I've always liked it," she answered.

"It doesn't have any particular meaning for you?"

It had as much meaning as any song Sabrina knew. As a young bride, she'd thought she knew everything about life and love. In the years since, she'd learned she knew almost nothing. She'd fallen in love with an illusion, not a real human being, and she'd paid a terrible price for it.

"I identify with it," she said. "People aren't always what they seem. It makes you afraid—" She cut herself off, reluctant to reveal too much. "I *am* in a maudlin mood. I'm sorry."

"Don't apologize. There's nothing maudlin about honest emotion." He moved closer to her on the couch. "Maybe I've had too much to drink, too, but if I have, I'm not complaining. I feel terrific. Play something else for me."

His approval warmed and relaxed her. Suddenly giddy, she thought of the perfect song, strummed a series of chords and launched into a chorus of "What Shall We Do with the Drunken Sailor?" Brad laughed and draped his arm around her. She didn't mind; the gesture was spontaneous and friendly.

Her father had taught her some rather bawdy verses in addition to the traditional ones, and she tacked them on at the end. When she was finished, he drawled, "I take it you were describing *me*."

"If the shoe fits..." She grinned at him. "If you have a more appropriate song, you're welcome to sing it."

He drained his glass and put it down. "Not more appropriate—I'm more honest than that. Let's just say I plead guilty with an explanation." He caressed her hair, then added softly, "'Almost Like Being in Love,' from *Brigadoon*. Sing it for me, Sabrina."

Pleasure curled through her body. There were men who tossed out endearments as casually as they breathed or slept, but Brad wasn't one of them. If his concern for Kathleen was any guide, he was thoughtful and caring. "But it's your turn to sing," she teased.

He shook his head. "I'd ruin it. I never stay in key. All I want right now is to sit here and listen to *you*."

"All right." The dizzying enchantment she felt intensified with each note she sang. She didn't need pealing bells to know she was smitten, only the warmth in Brad's eyes and the possessiveness of his arms. Toward the end of the song, he bent his head and nuzzled her neck, and her voice got softer and throatier. It was hard to even think, much less get the last few words of the chorus out.

"That was perfect," he murmured. "Magical. Like being in Brigadoon." He put her guitar on the coffee table and took her into his arms. "*You're* magical. I'm afraid you'll disappear at dawn."

She'd never felt this way before—so desperate to be kissed that the room was reeling. She raised her head until their mouths almost touched. "Disappear into the mists like Brigadoon?"

"Yes." He brushed his lips across her mouth. "As if you're not quite real. As if you're part of some other universe."

She slid her arms around his waist, past logic and reason now. She wanted him with an intensity no other man had evoked, and it felt completely, absolutely right. "Then maybe you should enjoy me while I'm here."

Enjoy me.... The words ricocheted through Brad's mind. God, yes, he wanted to enjoy her...her sensuous mouth, her full, ripe breasts, her generous hips. He pulled her onto his lap and buried his hand in her hair. She tipped her head back, offering him her throat, drawing his lips like a magnet draws iron. He couldn't have said which was more arousing—her soft, sweet skin or the breathless way she gasped his name at the first touch of his tongue.

Sabrina had never felt so exquisitely responsive. Every nerve seemed to be achingly sensitive, firing wildly at the slightest contact with Brad's body—at the urgency of his loins beneath her thighs...at the tickle of his tongue on her neck...at the sudden pressure against her back as he sought and found the top button of her dress and slipped it free.

His tongue moved higher, finding her closed lips and probing at the space between. Knowing it would excite him, she turned her head away and offered only her cheek, murmuring an agonized "No." Since she was permitting him to unbutton her dress at a slow but steady pace, there was no question of him taking her seriously.

He nuzzled her ear, laughing softly. "Why not?"

"Because we've only just met. You're going too fast." He was midway down her back now. "You have to stop."

"Games from the *Kama Sutra*, hmm?" Still smiling, he cupped her chin and coaxed her mouth back to his. "Let's see how much I remember."

He grazed her mouth and drew back, then repeated the gesture. The kiss after that was firmer, accompanied by a slow back-and-forth movement of his lower lip against hers. Her arms tightened around his waist and her mouth grew softer and more pliant. He captured her lower lip and sucked it, then nibbled it with just enough pressure to make her melt closer and ache for more.

Her lips parted in surrender even as she teasingly turned away. "That's enough. As a properly raised woman—"

"You've been taught not to argue with what a man wants." Breathing heavily, he brought her mouth to his and roughly covered it, kissing her with deep, dominating thrusts of his tongue. As her own tongue danced provocatively against his, she hazily realized what a clever, sensitive lover he was. Every step he'd taken had been calculated to heighten her desire. And it had.

She was dazed and breathless when he finally let her go. "You remember a lot," she said.

"I was an *A* student." He was unfastening her buttons more impatiently now, disposing of the one at her waist and continuing downward to free her hips. The shyness she'd pretended to feel earlier became real when he slid down her dress and pants in one smooth motion. It had been years since a man had seen her naked. She reddened and looked at the floor, wishing her hips were smaller, her nipples lighter, the room darker.

Brad was so inflamed by the revealing wisps of lace on her hips and breasts that he didn't notice her uneasiness at first. He could see the rosy brown of her nipples and the dark, lush hair between her legs, contrasting delightfully with her fair, delicate skin. Her body was even lovelier than he'd imagined, a visual feast of sweet, generous curves that beckoned a man to caress them. Between alcohol and passion, he wasn't thinking too clearly, but he certainly realized his good fortune. A woman like Sabrina didn't come into a man's life very often.

It was only when he unhooked her bra and felt her shudder that he realized how nervous she was. Tenderness and protectiveness mingled with his intense desire for her. He wanted to soothe away her fears, then arouse her until she was shaking in his arms and ready to explode with pleasure.

He tilted up her chin and looked into her eyes. There was no resistance there, only shyness and quiet trust. She seemed to be waiting for him to tell her what to do, and he liked that more than he wanted to admit. She made a man feel like a leader, a hunter, a conqueror. Brad had never realized he had such a primitive streak in him.

He tossed aside her bra. "I want you to straddle me. Twist around and wrap your legs around my waist."

Sabrina didn't question him, but permitted him to gently lift up her leg, pull it across his thighs and settle her face-to-face on his lap. She hooked her legs around his back, clutching his shoulders for support even though he was holding her firmly. She felt extremely vulnerable in this position, very much at the mercy of his desires. If he let her go, she could tumble backward, and if he chose to take her, he could easily do so. Far from frightening her, the idea excited her so wildly that she trembled.

He kissed her hotly and thoroughly but made no attempt to touch her. She was clinging weakly by the time he drew away, too aroused and dazed to do anything but wait for his next embrace.

He slid her backward on his lap until her knees were flush against his sides, then brought her hands to his waist. "My sweater, Sabrina. Take it off."

She pulled it over his head and put it on the couch.

"Now unbutton my shirt, sweetheart." His voice was husky with passion. "Massage my back and shoulders for me. They ache from sailing all day."

Her hands were clumsier than she would have liked, but she managed to get the shirt off. She wanted to press herself against his naked chest afterward, to feel his hard muscles against her sensitive breasts, but when she swayed forward, he eased her back. "We'll get to that later. Do as you were told and give me a massage."

Amused, she tossed her hair and pretended to pout. "I've spoiled you. You like playing the lord and master far too much."

He grinned at her. "You're damn right you have, but I'll make it worth your while. Go on, woman, get to work."

Smiling, she rose to her knees and placed her hands on his shoulders. The muscles at the sides of his neck were tighter than she'd expected, so she concentrated on stretching and relaxing them. As she pressed and rubbed him with the heels of her hands, he cupped her breasts and lightly caressed them. She ignored the rush of pleasure she felt and kept working on his neck.

His thumbs settled against her nipples, rubbing back and forth over the erect tips until she longed for something more demanding. Her hands moved down his back, kneading his shoulder blades; he took each of her nipples between a thumb and forefinger and squeezed it just hard enough to make her catch her breath at the sheer excitement of it. They continued with their respective tasks, Sabrina massaging Brad's back and Brad teasing and rubbing her breasts. She grew more languorous and submissive with each passing minute.

Brad felt her hands grow gentler, caressing instead of massaging him, and he knew she was ready to make love. It was hard not to rush things when he was desperate to be inside her, but his instincts told him she'd be a wildcat if he could take her high enough. The thought damn near destroyed him. Maybe she'd even scratch and bite and moan, like the women in the *Kama Sutra*.

His fingers slid lower, trailing over her rib cage, hips and thighs and finally slipping under her panties. Sabrina's hands went utterly still when she felt the light touch of his thumbs between her legs. She couldn't move; the pleasure and anticipation were too intense. He caressed and teased her, finally finding the spot where she needed to be touched and lightly fondling it.

She arched her body against his fingers, wanting him to be rougher, but he grasped her hips and pulled her down on his lap instead. Then he kissed her in a feverish, shattering way that told her he was through with the preliminary love play.

They separated, silently undressed, and came together again. He probed to make sure she was ready and then teased her to the edge of madness; she stroked him until his kisses dissolved into groans of need and then guided him inside her. The lovemaking that followed was violently passionate—a quick, hard mixture of deep, fierce thrusts, frenzied kisses and nips and feverish, tempestuous embraces. The spasms that finally ripped through Sabrina's body were unlike anything she'd ever experienced...not only more intense and prolonged, but primitive, unrestrained and exhaustingly satisfying. She'd never opened up so completely before, or given herself so totally.

She wasn't the one who was magic. He was.

Chapter Six

Brad was relieved when Sabrina gathered up her clothes and went into the bedroom to change. Although he'd said and done the right thing after their lovemaking—told her how wonderful she'd been, held her and caressed her—his heart hadn't been in it. He felt as if he'd been riding on a runaway train that had careened off its tracks and slammed to a halt—dazed, disoriented and shaken. The past couple of hours just didn't seem real.

He picked up his clothes and slowly pulled them on. He wasn't capable of doing anything quickly; his brain was enveloped in a thick fog. It was an effort to even think, much less answer the question that kept running through his mind: After thirty-two years of sound judgment and rational behavior, how had he wound up making fiery, uninhibited love to a woman he should have avoided like the plague?

It wasn't just that she was Howard Lang's daughter and therefore a member of the enemy camp. It wasn't even that he disapproved of her aimless life-style and the way she

routinely broke men's hearts. The bottom line was *his* life.
He was committed to Grace Fitzsimmons. He intended to
marry her someday. He never should have permitted himself to become attracted to Sabrina in the first place, much
less have convinced himself that she was the most desirable
woman he'd ever met. Even someone with the brains of a
chimp would have known it would be a mistake to make love
to her.

While he'd drunk more than usual, he still should have
known better. Fortunately this was the twentieth century,
when an evening of intimacy didn't obligate a man to anything more than a polite good-night. All he wanted was to
get out of the suite before Lang came back. He'd compro-
mised himself enough already without Sabrina's father
finding the two of them in a state of postcoital afterglow.

He straightened up the couch, cleared away the dirty
dishes and put the decanter of brandy back on the bar.
Simple good manners required him to stick around instead
of sneaking off into the night, but he was too restless to sit
still. He finally walked to the window and stared down at the
traffic. The view made him so dizzy he had to grasp the back
of a chair for support. Maybe it *had* been the liquor. He
generally didn't experience vertigo.

He was staring at the building across the street when Sabrina returned to the parlor. One look at her and his logic
went up in smoke. She was wearing a caftan that fluttered
and clung, and smiling in such a sweet, starry-eyed way that
his hands tightened on the chair in turmoil. God help him,
but he wanted her all over again. Had the alcohol burned
away the part of his brain that controlled his common sense?

He did what any well-trained lawyer would do in such a
situation—he reviewed the facts. His first priority was to get
out of here as quickly and gracefully as possible. He could
trust neither his emotions nor his judgment, so the best al-
ternative was that old male standby, the noncommittal
good-night. On some level he knew that in the space of five

seconds he'd gone from a polite brush-off to an open-ended goodbye, but he didn't examine the implications of that.

Like any bachelor his age, he had a fair amount of experience in such matters. "I wish I could stay all night," he murmured, smiling with just the right amount of regret.

She walked up behind him and snuggled against his back. "Me too. Even the people in Brigadoon had till dawn."

He hadn't counted on having to cope with her warm, fragrant body and sweet, gentle nature. They reminded him of things he would have preferred to forget, like how virile she'd made him feel, how wildly she'd excited him and how she'd driven him to a more reckless, intense release than any woman he'd ever known. He hadn't been a bit bored, either, not since the moment she'd opened the door.

"Your father will be back soon," he mumbled. "I'm conventional enough not to want to run into him."

She laughed softly. "I guess you're right. He's awfully old-fashioned that way. It's the only time he behaves like a typical father." She slid her palms under his trousers, caressing him with the comfortable intimacy of a longtime lover. "It's obvious what we've been doing, I guess. Did I mention that he keeps a rifle in his room?"

"No." Even the ludicrous image of a womanizer like Lang playing the outraged father couldn't stop Brad from responding to Sabrina's touch. He enjoyed her affectionate possessiveness almost as much as her closeness. The only games she seemed to know were the ones in the *Kama Sutra*.

He wanted to pull her into his arms and make love to her again, but removed her hands while he still had the willpower to manage it. "Has he ever used it?" he asked.

"Only in self-defense. He goes to a lot of dangerous places." She tugged at his belt until he reluctantly turned around, then cuddled up to his chest and sighed. She was so soft, so exquisitely feminine.... He put his arms around her because it seemed caddish not to.

"I'm sure you'd like him if only you could get to know him," she said. "So much of what they write about him isn't true. It's just hype. They sell more magazines that way."

Brad stiffened, feeling an irrational sense of betrayal. How could she be thinking of her father when the only thing on his mind was her? "If you remember, I showed up tonight and he didn't. I'm willing to talk to him anytime he can fit me into his busy schedule, but in the meantime you're not going to change my opinion. I don't consider you an objective source of information."

Several silent seconds went by. He could feel the tension in her body, but her reply was quiet and appeasing. "I'm sorry. I shouldn't have brought it up."

He was sorry, too, but only that she hadn't argued; it would have fueled his anger and made it easier to leave. "Then why did you?"

"Because I know he loves Kathleen and I want them to be happy. She cares about what you think—"

"Not very much, obviously. She refused to come with me." He released her and straightened, giving her no choice but to move away.

Sabrina didn't want Brad's quarrel with her father to destroy the feelings they'd just shared, but she wasn't some mindless puppet who would agree with his every word, either. While she couldn't insist car trouble had been responsible for Howard's absence when he was really at Diana's, his remark about Kathleen was another matter entirely. "That's not fair and you know it. Anyone could see she was upset that you and Dad were fighting. She just wasn't willing to let you bully her into leaving."

"Sure she was upset," he answered. "That's why she couldn't stop laughing."

"She wasn't laughing when she told Dad not to call you names. She was very distressed." Sabrina paused, trying to remember what had happened. "Anyway, the only reason she started laughing was that you and I kept provoking each other. She could probably tell what we *really* wanted before either of us had a clue."

"Then it's the first time Kathleen's ever found anything funny about a one-night stand," he retorted.

She stiffened and looked away. If she'd thought he really meant it, she would have told him to leave and spared herself further pain. Instead, sure that anger with her father was behind his cutting words, she pretended he'd never spoken. "Let's not quarrel, Brad. You've said you'd be willing to listen to what Dad has to say and I know you'll be fair."

"Do you?" He folded his arms across his chest. "How, when all you've really learned about me is that I'm good in bed?"

Waves of hostility were radiating from his body, making her want to turn and run. She didn't understand why he was so angry, but very few people she'd met had been able to argue with quiet sincerity. "You listened to me when I explained about Dad's lecture, and later, when we made love, you were sensitive and giving. I think that's the real Brad Fraser, not the man who's deliberately trying to hurt me."

He stared at her in such a cool, appraising way that she blushed and took a step backward. He probably used that stare in court to intimidate opponents' witnesses, and very effectively, too. Lord knew it intimidated *her.*

"Just don't try to soften me up on behalf of your father," he finally said.

"I wasn't trying to soften you up. I was just trying to explain—"

"I don't care what you call it. Don't do it again."

Having deceived Brad about Howard's whereabouts, Sabrina felt too guilty to pester him about the difference between explaining something and trying to manipulate him. In a sense, she'd been doing the second all night.

"All right," she said. He still looked icy. Screwing up her courage, she put her hands on his waist and continued in a soft, unsteady voice, "This isn't the way I wanted to say goodbye—with you so angry I feel as if you'll never want to see me again. Please tell me tonight meant as much to you as it did to me." *Even if it didn't,* she thought.

Brad could no more resist the gentle plea in her eyes than a child could resist his favorite flavor of ice cream. He wasn't so much angry as confused and unsure of himself. "It meant something," he admitted hoarsely. "It meant a lot." Unable to stop himself, he pulled her into his arms and kissed her, savoring her taste while she clung to him with a sweetness and passion that made everything else in the world seem unimportant. Her kisses were absolutely perfect, and when she moved her hips so sensuously and enticed him with her soft, full breasts . . .

He wanted to drown in the scent and feel of her but somehow remembered the time and tore himself away. Her father wasn't due for another half hour yet but he could always be early. "I have to go," he said. "I'll call you."

She smiled teasingly. "Isn't that what men say when they want to get rid of a woman?"

After the way he'd kissed her, there couldn't be any doubt that he'd meant it. "Sometimes. Not in this case. I'll speak to you in the morning." He left the room before the temptation to stay proved too great.

He was still thinking about her as he crossed the lobby. Why not take a room in the hotel? Why not ask her to share it? Then he stepped outside and got a blast of cold night air on his face, and his head began to clear. Was he really considering ending a three-year relationship—a satisfying, enjoyable relationship—on the strength of a single evening? He'd never rushed into anything in his life and this was no time to start. What he needed was a day on his boat—a day to think, take stock and decide.

At the moment, though, his chief concern was getting home. He'd gone outside instead of to the garage under the hotel where his car was, and if that wasn't a sign that he was in no shape to drive, his dizziness definitely was. As a lawyer, he knew better than to mix alcohol and automobiles.

Besides, Bostonians turned into maniacs when they got behind the wheel. You were lucky to escape an accident even when you were sober.

There were several taxis by the hotel entrance, so the lack of a car wouldn't be a problem. Still, he lived out past Lynn near the yacht club where he kept his boat, and if he went home, he'd have to return here in another cab. It made a lot more sense to spend the night at Diana's Beacon Hill town house, which was less than ten blocks away, and come back for his car in the morning.

Too tired to walk, he got into a taxi, gave the driver Diana's address and leaned his head against the torn vinyl seat. Sabrina's scent was still on his skin and her taste lingered in his mouth. No wonder he couldn't get her out of his mind. Maybe he didn't even want to.

Sabrina stared at the door for several seconds and then drifted to the couch. Smiling to herself, she buried her face against a cushion and breathed in the scent of Brad's cologne. It reminded her of the passion they'd just shared. All those years of marriage, and she'd never realized what she was missing.

And to learn it from Brad Fraser of all people! How could she have thought he was bloodless and stuffy? Why had she assumed a man needed to be a corporate raider or maverick financier to be exciting? She'd run around the world for three solid years and had met dozens of wealthy, handsome men, but not one of them had inflamed her the way Brad had.

It was shocking, really. She was a woman who believed in marriage, a woman who disdained casual affairs, and yet she'd made love with a man she barely knew without the slightest protest or qualm. Even more amazing, she didn't feel ashamed or sorry. When had she become so impetuous?

She'd been engaged for two years before feeling ready to marry. And after her divorce, once she'd recovered enough to think about a new relationship, she'd always been perfectly controlled, always stopped a man before things went too far. But tonight, from the moment Brad had first touched her, she'd been ready to give herself completely. Her brain said she was violently infatuated while her heart insisted she was in love. And that was the most surprising thing of all, because she'd never believed in love at first sight.

She looked around the suite, wondering if anyone would be able to tell what had happened. Everything had been put away, even the dirty coffee cups and brandy glasses. Brad was obviously the perfect man, confident and masculine but still liberated enough to help with the housework. She was going to spoil him rotten and enjoy every moment of it.

She gazed dreamily at the items on the coffee table—an ashtray, several magazines, a bowl of fruit—and suddenly frowned. The statue of the fertility goddess was missing. Where had Brad put it?

A moment later she was checking under tables and chairs. She located the goddess beneath the couch, lying on her back with her belly grazing the underside of the seat. Picking up the statue, she settled back on the couch and cradled it in her lap. Between the goddess's magic and simple biology, there was no telling what she and Brad might have started tonight. Oddly enough, the idea didn't panic her at all.

Getting pregnant had never been a problem, only staying that way. It hadn't mattered that she'd given herself plenty of time to recover after each miscarriage; the end result had been the same. She would carry a child for a few weeks, then begin to spot and cramp. It was never especially painful and it was always over within a month or two.

After her second miscarriage, her husband had sent her to his sister Ferdoz's doctor in Delhi for tests, but he hadn't found a thing wrong with her. He'd attributed her problems to a run of bad luck and told her not to worry. She'd tried everything after that—bed rest, a special diet, even Jammapuri folk remedies—but nothing had worked.

Her anguish had been wrenching, but the knowledge that she'd disappointed her husband and failed an entire country had been even worse. It was the reason she hadn't fought to save her marriage. A man who still wanted her wouldn't have been so quick to believe the worst of her.

If she'd been sensible she would have forgotten the whole experience, but even now uncertainties haunted her. What if it hadn't been solely her fault, but some unusual biological interaction between her husband's genes and hers? Would a specialist in London or New York have found things the Indian doctor had missed? If she'd checked into one of those fancy Swiss clinics the moment she'd learned she was pregnant, would she have been able to carry to term?

She stretched out on the couch, still holding the goddess, puzzling over her own recklessness. This was the most fertile part of her cycle. She'd made love with a man who'd had every reason to suppose she couldn't conceive, so why hadn't she suggested they take precautions?

She hadn't forgotten what she'd told herself at the time— that he hadn't expected to make love and wouldn't be prepared, that she'd die if he stopped touching her, that it didn't matter in the first place because she could never bear his child. Now, sitting in an empty room with only her conscience for company, she couldn't escape the feeling that she'd been lying to herself.

Maybe she'd *wanted* to become pregnant...to see if anything had changed or prove that the problem had been partly her husband's. Maybe she'd had some sick need to satisfy her curiosity. If so, she'd used Brad unforgivably, treating him like a prize bull rather than a human being.

Restless now, she set the goddess on the table and prowled around the room. It had to be more than that. She could have had a dozen different lovers over the years, a dozen different men to experiment on, but she'd turned them all down. Brad had been special, and she'd said yes because it had felt so right. If she'd deliberately taken a chance, the reasons had to be more complicated than a simple desire to become pregnant.

She ran her hands over her flat, firm stomach, imagining that it was swollen with Brad's child. The idea made her smile. Then she pictured the two of them in a snug colonial home out in the country and smiled even more broadly. She'd traveled to the most exotic, exciting places in the world, but not one of them could compare to the thrill of Brad's embrace.

Chapter Seven

Brad could never visit Diana's Beacon Hill town house without feeling a little guilty. It had been in his family for generations and was technically his, but he'd never liked living in the city and planned to sell the place eventually. Obviously he lacked familial pride, or maybe just a sense of history.

He was surprised to hear talking and laughter as he unlocked the door. He looked up and down the street, spotted Grace's Porsche and frowned. Why would Diana invite Grace over and not include him?

Given what he'd been up to that evening, the thought of seeing Grace made him uncomfortable, but he was too curious to go away. A familiar voice boomed out as he entered the foyer, but he didn't place it until he was halfway down the hall. It was Howard Lang, telling some story about going bear-hunting in Alaska with a bunch of Eskimos. What was Lang doing at Diana's and why was he surrounded by what sounded like a dozen people?

Brad had no sooner reached the living room than Diana breezed through the archway into the hall, apparently on her way to the kitchen. She pursed her lips disapprovingly. "It's about time you got here. Where's Sabrina?"

He wasn't about to admit that he had no idea what she was talking about. "Back at the hotel. Can I help you with something?"

"You can carry in a tray of pastries. Rose is in bed with the flu." Rose was her housekeeper. "Why didn't Sabrina want to come? I was looking forward to meeting her."

"She was tired," he answered. "Jet lag, I suppose."

Diana gave a snort and continued on her way. "A girl her age should have more energy. Obviously she doesn't take after her father."

"He seems to be making quite a hit." Lang was still talking; his audience was still laughing. "Has he been at it all night?"

"Umm. He's a real charmer, that one, and outrageously handsome in the bargain. I can see why Kathleen is smitten, not that I've dropped all my objections, mind you."

She walked into the kitchen, took out a silver platter and placed a doily on it. Her usual reaction to silence was to fill the void with chatter, so Brad opened the bakery box on the counter and started arranging pastries on the tray. "I can see you're annoyed, darling, but really, this was the best way to handle things," she said, spooning coffee into a filter. "I had to give Howard a chance. Otherwise Kathleen would have married him simply to spite me."

Brad kept a bland expression on his face and continued working. "Very well, Bradley, perhaps I should have consulted you beforehand, but you were on your boat. You're positively neurotic about this solitude business. Do you realize it's after ten? How can you sail when it's dark?"

"You expected me sooner?"

She didn't notice that he hadn't answered her question. "Of course I did. You were due at Howard's at seven, so I assumed you and Sabrina would arrive by seven-thirty." She put some water on to boil. "You're usually so prompt."

Now he understood what had happened. Diana must have thrown this party to introduce Lang to some of her friends and relatives. She'd probably hoped he would make a spectacle of himself and embarrass Kathleen into losing interest, but he seemed to be charming everyone's socks off instead. Even more galling, Diana believed Sabrina had remained at the hotel to inform Brad of the change in plans when she'd actually been waiting there to stall him.

It wasn't hard to figure out why. If Brad had been at the party, Lang wouldn't have had a chance to charm anyone. He would have been too busy fending off questions. In other words, Sabrina had taken him for a three-hour ride, and with consummate skill.

He couldn't remember when he'd felt such a stinging mixture of rage and self-disgust. It was amazing how clearheaded he suddenly was. How could he have been gullible enough to fall for that Indian courtesan routine of hers? The dinner, the massage, the love song... When something looked like a setup and smelled like a setup, it invariably *was* a setup. Even a green schoolboy would have known that.

Fortunately, seven years in the courtroom had taught him how to hide his emotions. "I had some trouble with the boat. I wanted to fix it before I left."

"Sometimes I think you care more for that boat than for your family." Diana moved several pieces of pastry, then handed him the tray. "Take this into the living room. I'll be in when the coffee's ready."

He stopped halfway down the hall to compose himself and think things through. Lang was talking about running into Prince Charles at a concert and being asked to give a lecture on behalf of the Prince's Trust. Not only was he a splendid storyteller; he could drop names with the best of them.

There was only one option, Brad realized. He would have to do exactly what he would have done if he'd been here all night—politely expose Lang as the consummate bull artist he was. Throwing a tantrum about how he'd been deceived would only make him look foolish.

As he entered the living room, Lang said, "The intermission was over and people were filing back to their seats, but I could see he wanted to leave. He hates rock music. He only went because it was for charity. So I asked him if we could tour one of his projects—" He cut himself off when he noticed Brad walk in. "Brad! I thought you'd never get here. Where's Sabrina?"

Astonished by Lang's audacity, Brad set the tray on the coffee table and drawled, "She had a tough night. She was too tired to make it."

The double entendre didn't faze him, but Kathleen reddened dramatically. Brad realized she'd known what Sabrina had done and approved it in advance. In a way, her defection was the most stunning blow of the night. He'd been an idiot to let Sabrina delay and seduce him, but at least she'd done it to help the family cause. Kathleen, on the other hand, was as close to him as a sister. She owed him her loyalty and honesty.

"So how was the sight-seeing?" he asked her.

She couldn't meet his eyes. "Fine."

"And your car? Is it fixed?"

"Yes." She paused. "I know how you must feel, but—"

"But he's finally here now, and the evening isn't over," Lang said. He looked at Elliott Carberry, Brad's cousin and law partner. "Elliott, give the man your seat. He's been sailing all day and he's tired."

Rather than taking offense at Lang's casual order, Elliott smiled, relinquished his place to Brad and pulled over another chair. Brad sat down and glanced around the room, which was large enough to contain several groupings of furniture without being crowded. Diana had invited her closest friends, her sister and brother-in-law, and various members of the Fraser family, all of whom had made a large circle around the couch, where Lang was holding court.

The sole exceptions were Grace Fitzsimmons and Josh Rogers, who were huddled together on a piano bench in the farthest corner of the room. They were too absorbed in conversation to notice Brad's arrival. The last time Grace had been so spellbound, she'd been gazing at a hideous modern painting in the Institute of Contemporary Art.

Lang continued his tale of leaving the rock concert with Prince Charles and touring a trade school for underprivileged youths while Brad listened cynically. The situation had one saving note—Kathleen looked miserably guilty, and a guilty Kathleen would be a more tractable Kathleen. If he could discredit Lang at all, maybe he could persuade her to end the romance.

He couldn't accuse Lang of making the story up because it was true—*People* magazine had run a photo—but there were other ways to attack him. Brad's memory was one of his strongest assets, and he recalled not only the photograph but also the date and the accompanying caption.

"I remember seeing something about that," he remarked, when Lang had finished speaking. "It was about five years ago, wasn't it?"

Lang sighed. "Five years! It doesn't seem that long. I'll have to schedule another benefit lecture soon."

"Weren't you married to Joan Whitson at the time?"

"A lovely lady. I can't blame her for not wanting to put up with my constant running around." He smiled at Kathleen. "Of course, I've mended my ways since then. I don't go out every night anymore."

"On that particular night, weren't you out with Julia Palmer?"

"A dear friend and wonderful actress," he replied blithely, but Brad had made his point. Julia Palmer had legions of dear friends, all of them male and most of them intimate. "That reminds me of a story about Sir Oliver Page, Julia's first husband," Lang continued, "but of course, he wasn't a sir back in those days. He was an ordinary Oxford don, terrified because his first play was about to open."

Lang was a good enough speaker to hold the floor all night, but he knew also the value of sharing the spotlight. The story about Page's play led to a discussion of his career, and since this was a cultured group, everyone had an opinion. Twenty minutes went by before Brad had another opportunity to attack.

One of Diana's friends had remarked that Page's recent play about South Africa had been surprisingly mild in its treatment of apartheid; another had pointed out that Page had visited the country to do research and probably knew more about it than anyone present. "Except for Howard," Brad said. "You've led several tours there, haven't you?"

"Yes, but none recently," he answered. "Still, I'm inclined to agree with Sybil. The country is going to explode one of these days, but Page doesn't see it."

"That was your impression the last time you visited? That the black workers were becoming radicalized?"

Brad could sense the wheels spinning around in Lang's head as he tried to figure out what Brad was up to. "It's hard for any outsider to know what's really going on, but yes, that's the way it seemed to me."

"You talked to some of them, then? The diamond miners, for example?"

"I tried to. It wasn't easy to get them alone, even in those days."

"I see. You know, Howard, I've always wondered how you managed to get your hands on the Christiana diamond." Brad was referring to a diamond that had come from a mine near Christiana, South Africa, disappeared one day, and allegedly wound up in the hands of Texas oil billionaire Jim Delancey. "Did the miners help you steal it and smuggle it out of the country as a protest against the white power structure?"

"I'm sure you realize that nobody knows whether the Delancey diamond is the same stone as the one that disappeared, least of all me. I'm afraid that the only time I saw it, it was hanging around Babe Delancey's neck at the opera, and it had been cut by then.''

Brad smiled knowingly. "Come on, Howard. You were in South Africa when it was stolen and in Dallas a week before it turned up again. Two months later, if memory serves me, you purchased a rather expensive house in London.''

"True enough. Life is full of amazing coincidences.'' He put his arm around Kathleen's shoulders. "I didn't take the diamond, but I would have been sorely tempted if I'd known you at the time. It would look beautiful on you.''

"I prefer sapphires,'' she said lightly, "and I'd rather buy my own than depend on someone to steal them for me.''

Lang promptly promised that he would shop for all her gems at Tiffany's, but Brad had made his point—Howard Lang's reputation was questionable at best. During the next hour, he politely but persistently drove it home. No matter how charming he was, Lang wasn't the sort of man Kathleen should become involved with. His past was a shadowy mixture of high living, mysterious acquisitions and fast women. If her increasingly subdued behavior was anything to go by, the message got through.

The party broke up around eleven-thirty. Grace and Josh were still holed up in the corner, and it was only when Diana called them over to say goodbye to everyone that they realized people were leaving. Grace finally noticed Brad as she crossed the room and remarked with a startled smile that she'd given up hope of him ever making it.

He kissed her hello and gave her the same story he'd given Diana—that he'd needed to fix his boat. "I've been here for over an hour. You were too busy talking to Josh to realize it.''

"He was telling me about some of the trips he's taken with Howard.'' She sighed dreamily. "I would love to go on his tour of Australia. They say the light there is fabulous. I could bring along my paints and soak up the inspiration. They're visiting places that tourists don't usually see and it's going to be marvelously exciting. You have no idea how boring it's been at the museum lately."

"Then go," Brad said. "I'm sure you can get the time off."

"The hotels are completely booked up. Josh is taking a sleeping bag and bunking out wherever he can, but you know me. I can't survive without a private bathroom."

"So you want both excitement and comfort," he teased.

She sheepishly agreed. "I'm not much of an artist, am I? My idea of suffering for my muse is using a bathroom sink with separate taps for the hot and cold water."

He grinned at her, reminded all over again of why he liked her. There was nothing phony or pretentious about her. She was the first to admit to being spoiled and a little materialistic, but her honesty was part of her charm. She was also intelligent, vivacious and undemanding. Besides, he could remember meeting her when she was ten years old and thinking she'd be a knockout someday. He'd been right.

At the moment, however, the only thing on his mind was extricating Kathleen from the clutches of Howard Lang. Her troubled look indicated that she was reconsidering their relationship, and he wanted to strike before she had a chance to rationalize away her doubts.

Since he was afraid that suggesting a private meeting might make her defensive, he took her aside and asked if she and Howard could stay for a while to discuss the situation with him and Diana. Then, sensing her reluctance, he added crisply, "You owe me at least that much, Kathleen."

She nodded uneasily. "All right. I'll tell Howard. I guess Josh could wait in the den—"

"I'll ask Grace to drive him to the hotel."

Grace was musing about whether she could possibly tolerate lumpy cots and shared bathrooms and was glad of the opportunity to find out more about the tour. Brad didn't miss the kid's puppylike enthusiasm at the prospect of being alone with her, but his adolescent infatuation was of no great concern. She preferred older men.

Diana made more coffee, then sat everyone down in the parlor. "I have the oddest feeling that something is going on that I don't know about," she said sternly. "Bradley?"

Brad had already decided to level with her. He needed her on his side, but at the moment, she was dangerously taken with Howard Lang. "I wasn't fixing my boat tonight, Diana. I was with Sabrina, waiting for Howard. She told me that Kathleen's car had broken down while the two of them and Josh were sightseeing and that they would be back as soon as it was repaired. I only came here because I'd had too much to drink and didn't think I should drive home."

She frowned. "You mean you spent the evening drinking?"

"Sabrina and I had dinner together. After all, there was no point letting the meal Howard had ordered go to waste." He paused. "The champagne and candles were nice touches, Howard. So was your daughter's dress. My compliments on a slick operation."

Lang put down his coffee cup. "If you're implying that we make a habit of this sort of thing—"

"I don't give a damn whether you do or don't. The fact is, you didn't want me around because you're incapable of answering the kind of question I ask. Your solution was entirely logical, but it wasn't ethical or honorable." He looked at Kathleen. "I love you more than anyone in the world. It ties me in knots that you went along with this."

She looked away, too stricken and guilty to answer. Although Brad had meant every word of what he'd said, he immediately softened. "He's incredibly persuasive—I realize that. I know you're not used to dealing with people like him and I can understand how you let yourself get talked into this, but I wish you would stop and ask yourself what kind of person he's turning you into."

"I didn't realize I was talking to Snow White," Lang drawled. "It's a real honor to meet an attorney who's never defended a guilty client or represented a negligent corporation." He took Kathleen's hand. "All we did was arrange for a couple of hours of peace. That's hardly a crime. Your nephew is laying another guilt trip on you."

"But Brad is the most honorable man I know," she said. "He conducts his law practice with total integrity and he's always treated me with respect and love. He has a right to be angry."

Brad shifted uncomfortably. Having shaded the truth about Ted Solomon that morning and been unfaithful to Grace mere hours ago, he was in no position to apply for sainthood. "Look, Kathleen, the issue isn't whether I'm simon-pure or not; it's that you've done something that bothers you, that you're obviously sorry about, and that you wouldn't have considered before meeting Howard Lang. The fact that he thinks it was perfectly all right is symptomatic of the differences between you."

"Brad is right," Diana said. "You have to ask yourself where this is leading. What future can you possibly have with a man whose values are so different from your own?"

Disgruntled, Howard muttered, "For God's sake, Kathleen, I'm not some kind of Nazi. I admit I've been involved in a couple of shady deals in my time, but I've never deliberately hurt anyone and I've tried to be honest with the people I care about."

"You weren't honest at your lecture the other night," Brad pointed out. "You make your living by telling people highly inventive stories and call yourself a showman, but in my opinion you're a con artist. When easy money comes your way—the Christiana diamond, for example—you grab it."

Howard smiled wistfully. "If you want the truth, there was nothing easy about it. I was lucky not to get caught. By the way, I donated half the proceeds to an anti-apartheid group."

"So playing Robin Hood made it okay."

He shrugged. "It was a living, Brad. I haven't pulled a job like that in years."

"Are you claiming you've reformed?"

"Probably not. I'm just too old to handle the stress these days."

It was hard to dislike a man who could be so disarming, but that didn't change the fundamental issue. "You're one of the most interesting, charismatic people I've ever met," Brad admitted, "and I can understand why Kathleen is fascinated with you, but the two of you have nothing in common when it comes to how you look at the world. Even if you're really in love with her—which I doubt—you'll only wind up disappointing her. Sooner or later you'll do something that destroys her trust or respect, so why don't you spare her a lot of heartache and get out of her life right now?"

"Sorry, but I'm not that selfless. I'm crazy about her and I'm not giving her up without a fight." He touched her cheek. "I know I'm not a knight in shining armor, but I'd never do anything to hurt you. Come to Australia with me and give us a chance to get to know each other better."

There was a tense silence while everyone waited for her decision. Finally she murmured, "You're the most exciting man I've ever met, Howard. I've never had as much fun as I've had with you this past week, but you think what we did tonight was fine and I don't. You think it's okay to smuggle statues out of African countries and I don't. You weren't a faithful husband—"

"I was faithful to Sabrina's mother and I'd be faithful to you. Marla and Joan didn't give fidelity or expect it. As far as the other things go, I understand your point of view and I respect it. I can't promise to take as strict a moral view of the world as you do, but I won't swipe any more diamonds, either. We have something special together, Kathleen. Come to Australia and give it a chance to grow."

She shook her head uncertainly. "I need time to decide what I want. Besides, I have lectures to work on, revisions to make on my book and people to contact about getting you into the restricted areas you want to visit. If I go to Australia, I'll have to rush to get everything done." Her manner grew a little surer. "We can write and call while you're away. Then, when you come back, I'll tell you whether I'll go to Asia as your friend—or as something more."

Diana looked at Brad and shrugged. They'd obviously reached the same conclusion—that Kathleen wasn't ready to give Howard up yet and further argument would be counterproductive. Since she saw the potential problems in the relationship, they could only hope she would come to her senses once he left town.

Howard accepted her decision without a word of protest and rose to leave. He probably figured Kathleen would miss him dreadfully while he was away and want him more than ever, and maybe he was right. They left together, arm in arm.

Brad didn't try to stop her; he was dead tired and sick to his stomach, and his head felt as if it were caught in a vise. The thought of fighting any more battles was enough to make him wince. Somewhere deep inside him there was an unforgiving streak of puritanism, because he fully believed he deserved every bit of what he'd gotten. He'd behaved badly tonight and he was paying the price.

All the same, if he ever got hold of Sabrina Lang, he was going to have to restrain himself from wringing her beautiful neck. It didn't do any good to tell himself that her actions hadn't been personal—that she would have opposed anyone who stood in her father's way. He was still furious. He'd meant nothing to her. He didn't matter. It was a feeling he'd had countless times as a child, and he didn't like it any better now than he had then.

Chapter Eight

Sabrina was propped up in bed in the room she was now sharing with Kathleen, watching television. It was pointless to try to sleep; she was too happy and excited. Although it was a little unsettling to be so crazy about a man she barely knew, she wouldn't have changed a thing that had happened tonight. And tomorrow, when Brad phoned her, she was going to make him an offer he couldn't refuse. If he would take her sailing and show her around his house, she would cook him dinner, rub his feet and test him on the next couple of chapters of the *Kama Sutra*, an open book definitely permitted.

She heard the parlor door open and turned on the lamp for Kathleen. A moment later, her father poked his head in the door, saying he was surprised to find her awake. She reminded him that she was still on Pacific Time and asked how things had gone. She wasn't so lost in her own emotions that she didn't notice how drained he looked.

"Okay," he said. "I liked everyone a lot more than I'd expected to and I think the feeling was mutual. Good night, honey."

Kathleen passed him as he turned away, giving him a peck on the lips before continuing into the room. For someone who hadn't been on the hot seat that evening, she looked simply terrible—pale, tired and tense. "Did something go wrong?" Sabrina asked. "You look upset."

"It was a long day. Would you mind very much if I asked you to watch TV in the parlor?"

"Of course not. Go ahead and turn it off." Sabrina wasn't the type to pry, but she was troubled by Kathleen's ashen appearance. "Maybe it's none of my business, but I wish you would tell me what happened. You and Dad were at Diana's for so long that I assumed your family must have really warmed up to him. In fact, I expected the three of you to breeze in here in a great mood and—" She stopped and frowned. "Where's Josh? I don't hear him."

Kathleen clicked off the TV. "Isn't he back yet?"

"No. Didn't you all leave together?"

"Grace Fitzsimmons was supposed to drive him home. They left half an hour before Howard and I did."

In the exhilaration of being with Brad, Sabrina had forgotten that Grace existed. The mention of her name made Sabrina feel guilty and insecure, but her chief emotion at that moment was concern. "Could something have happened to them between Diana's and the hotel?"

"I doubt it. It's only ten blocks." Kathleen thought it over. "They spent the evening talking, so maybe they went somewhere to continue their conversation. Don't worry about him, Sabrina. I'm sure he's fine."

"I know, I know. He's a grown man, and if he wants to go off with a woman ten years older—" She saw Kathleen's smile and stopped. "Did I say something funny?"

"You seem to have the idea that Grace is some sort of man-eater. Actually she's only twenty-four, and very sweet and vivacious. Personally I think she's too young for Brad—

her parents have seen to it that she leads a very sheltered life—but he doesn't seem to have realized that yet."

Sabrina didn't want to talk about Grace Fitzsimmons. She'd unconsciously thought of the woman as a snobby socialite, and now that she knew otherwise, she was distressed to realize the pain she was about to cause. "About tonight," she said. "I can tell something went wrong, and given Dad's temper... He didn't get into a fight with someone, did he?"

Kathleen sat down on the bed. "I know I owe you an explanation—it's the least I can do after getting you involved in this—but it's just so difficult to talk about." She sighed. "What happened was that Brad didn't go home after he left the hotel. He decided to spend the night at Diana's because he'd drunk too much to drive safely and her house is so close by. To say he was angry is putting it mildly. He doesn't react well to being manipulated."

The blood drained from Sabrina's face. Her father was in one piece, thank God, but was Brad? Alarmed, she asked, "What did he do?"

"He's a lawyer, Sabrina. He's been trained to control his emotions. He never even raised his voice, just quietly and methodically chipped away at your father's character until there was very little left. He's obviously read every word that's been written about Howard and I'm afraid not all of them were complimentary." There was a long, awkward pause. "I don't think I should say anything more."

She didn't have to *say* it—it was obvious. Brad had done such an expert hatchet job on Howard that Kathleen's confidence in him was nonexistent now. No wonder she was uncomfortable—she'd hardly enjoy explaining the situation to Howard's fiercely devoted daughter.

"I know my father's no angel," Sabrina said, "but he's kind and generous to the people he loves. I tried to make Brad see that tonight, but he wouldn't listen. He won't look beneath the surface—beneath the smooth talk and slick maneuvering—to the man underneath. I hope you won't make the same mistake, Kathleen.''

She smiled. "I'm still here, aren't I?"

"Yes, but you're also very upset. You still *like* my father, but you don't trust him."

"I don't know him well enough to have an opinion. Brad made me realize that Howard and I are two very different people and that I should take things more slowly." Kathleen added that she planned to remain in Boston for the next two months but would help with the arrangements for Howard's trip to Asia and then accompany him there. "I'm just sorry that we got you involved. I never should have taken part in something I knew was wrong. Deceiving people is almost never a good idea, no matter how good your motives are."

Given what had happened at Diana's, Sabrina couldn't agree. If Brad had been there from the beginning, Howard would have had to spend every moment defending himself, Kathleen never would have seen him at his best, and she would have walked out of his life. Sabrina couldn't feel guilty about helping to prevent that.

She wanted to tell Kathleen the truth—that Howard's *real* concern was for Maya, not the statue—but she couldn't risk it. Kathleen was much too close to her family, and given how she felt about deception, much too likely to confide in them. The important thing was that she was still willing to help, although persuading her to take them into Jammapur with doctored papers might present a problem. They would have to convince her that the statue had such enormous archaeological and historical importance that the search for it, though quixotic, was worthwhile.

She could say none of that, however, so she simply murmured, "We used to debate that in college—whether the end ever justifies the means. I don't think we reached a conclusion."

"Most people seem to agree that murder would be justified if it were Hitler you wanted to kill, but things become more complicated after that." Kathleen looked troubled and ashamed. "I only know that tonight was a mistake. I won't deny that people got a chance to know and like Howard before Brad arrived, but the price was too high. Brad is hurt and angry now. The people closest to him—Diana and his parents—consistently disappointed him when he was a child. I was the only exception. It's a distinction I seem to have lost."

"But it wasn't your idea—"

"I approved it. It's enough." She wearily got up and walked into the bathroom.

Sabrina's heart went out to her. It was traumatic to hurt someone you loved; she would have felt just as guilty about disappointing Josh. But Brad was an adult, not a vulnerable child, and in time, he was bound to see the difference between the sorts of things Diana and his parents had done and the little white lie Kathleen had told.

It was only several minutes later, as she sat in the parlor staring blankly at the television, that reality hit. Dear God, had she been living in a dreamworld for the past half hour? Brad wasn't only angry with Kathleen; he was furious with *her*. After all, Kathleen had only approved the plan while *she* had carried it out.

She grimaced. Never mind the past half hour; she'd been lost in fantasy for the entire evening. How could she have overlooked the fact that Brad would eventually find out about the party—that too many people he knew had been there for one of them not to mention it? He was too smart not to realize she'd set him up and too touchy about her father not to hit the ceiling. He would have been angry in any event, but to learn about it by walking straight into it was the worst thing that could have happened.

She was still worrying about it when Josh let himself into the suite fifteen minutes later. He had the same silly grin on his face as he'd had after his first dance, when he and Jeanie Cunningham had sneaked outside and discovered the delights of kissing. Whether that was good or bad depended on how Grace felt.

"Where have you been all this time?" she asked casually.

"In a coffeehouse in Cambridge. Grace Fitzsimmons took me there. We were talking about—" he paused theatrically "—life."

Life. The situation sounded promising. "Isn't she Brad Fraser's girlfriend?"

His grin got even sillier. "Maybe and maybe not. The guy is a total stiff. Grace needs someone younger and looser, you know?"

"Someone like you," she said.

"Yup. I talked her into going to the beach with me tomorrow. If I'm not up by ten, wake me, okay?"

"Sure." Her response didn't begin to convey her enthusiasm. A romance between Grace and Josh would be absolutely perfect. "Have a good sleep, hon."

He gave a jaunty wave and sailed into his room, floating on a sea of euphoria.

Although Brad was angry, Sabrina still expected to hear from him, if only so he could demand an explanation or chew her out. She waited for his call the next morning instead of going out for breakfast with Howard and Kathleen, but the only one who phoned was Grace, to say she was canceling her beach date with Josh because of the cloudy weather. He suggested several alternatives but she turned them all down, insisting she felt a cold coming on and needed to stay in bed. Josh was crestfallen when he hung up.

So was Sabrina, but she managed not to show it. "Grace and Brad have been going together for three years," she said. "Would you really want a woman who cheats on her boyfriend that easily?"

"In general, no. With me, yes." It was exactly the way Sabrina felt about Brad. "Anyway, we're just friends right now. I wasn't going to make a pass at her."

She smiled teasingly. "Then maybe you should develop a sudden interest in art. She couldn't refuse to show a *friend* around the latest exhibit in her museum, could she?"

He admitted the idea had occurred to him. "I thought I could catch her during her lunch hour tomorrow. I just wish I'd paid more attention in Fine Arts 101. It would be nice to know what she's talking about."

"Kathleen might have some books you could study. Better yet, ask her to get you into her college library."

"So I can beat her nephew's time?" He shook his head. "I doubt she'd go along with it."

"Yes, she would. She thinks Grace is too young for Brad—she told me that last night." Sabrina ruffled Josh's hair, prompting him to draw back in affronted dignity. "Now stop looking like you've lost your dearest friend and go get packed. We have to leave soon." Kathleen had invited them to stay at her house in Brookline, an offer Howard had accepted with alacrity. She had three bedrooms and didn't charge rent.

"I've hardly had a chance to *un*pack," he grumbled, but went to his room all the same. Sabrina had some packing to do as well, but decided to shower first. It was pointless to sit staring at the phone, and besides, everyone knew it always started ringing the minute you stepped in the tub.

It didn't, though, not then and not at Kathleen's, even though Howard had asked the desk to forward their calls. Sabrina got more and more subdued as the afternoon wore on. With Josh at the library furthering his pursuit of Grace, and Howard and Kathleen at the theater, she was reduced to sitting by herself in the living room and wallowing in self-pity. Finally, disgusted with her own inertia, she went out. She visited John F. Kennedy's birthplace on Beals Street, then went to a nearby park and watched the children play.

In the past, children had always reminded her of what she'd failed to achieve, and watching them, especially the littlest ones, had torn at her heart. Now though, all she could think about was Brad—his lovemaking, the child they might have created, the way she'd deceived him, the anger he undoubtedly felt. Why did life have to turn on you the moment you dropped your defenses?

Her eyes filled with tears, but she impatiently rubbed them away. So things were a little tough. She had no right to carry on as if she'd suffered some awful tragedy. Tragedy was what she had seen in that house on Beals Street—a vibrant life, snuffed out in its prime by a spray of bullets.

She noticed a little girl toddling toward her and quickly hid her face behind a brochure. Then she slid the brochure away, called out "Peekaboo!" and savored the child's delight. Both of them giggled, playing the game several times more before the little girl lost interest.

In college Sabrina had dreamed of being a teacher, but the closest she'd come was volunteer work during her marriage. Although she'd had a lot of fun during the years that had followed, it had been an empty existence, devoid of personal accomplishment. She'd let the pain of childlessness prevent her from doing what she most loved—working with kids. Maybe it was time to revive the dream.

She waved goodbye to the little girl, then walked home. Howard and Kathleen had returned by the time she got back and were talking about his upcoming schedule. There was only one thing the rich loved more than bargains, and that was merchandise their friends hadn't discovered yet, so Howard and Sabrina ran a series of shopping trips each fall.

"Nobody's better than Sabrina at finding out-of-the-way places smack in the middle of the world's largest cities," he remarked. "Paris, London, Rome... She has contacts everywhere, don't you, sweetheart? It's the most successful part of our business."

By "successful" he meant profitable. "Flattery will get you everywhere," she answered, thinking that she probably looked depressed. Her father delivered these ego boosts whenever he sensed she was low.

"You should fly to Europe for some last-minute research. You can buy yourself some new clothes while you're
here and then meet us in Australia."

Sabrina said it sounded like fun, but the truth was that she
intended to stay in Cambridge. Brad would eventually cool
down, and when he did, she wanted to be around. She only
hoped it would be soon, because they left for Australia on
Sunday.

She excused herself and went upstairs, flopping onto her
bed and reproaching herself for being an ungrateful brat.
Her father had given her his unconditional love and support after she'd left Jammapur. He'd taken her into his
business as a full partner and taught her everything he knew.
How could she think of leaving him when he depended on
her so much?

Not only did she arrange and supervise the fall shopping
trips; she promoted tours like the one in August by lecturing about her experiences in Jammapur. People were always interested in fallen crown princesses, and although
Sabrina wished they weren't, she also recognized what an
asset that was. She'd learned to reveal exactly as much of
herself as she chose and not a bit more.

She considered herself a resilient person, and over the
years had come to pride herself on that. She could even remember the first time she'd heard the word, when her
mother had used it in a conversation with her father and she
hadn't known what it meant. Jane had assured Howard that
Sabrina was a resilient little girl and would be able to cope
with their impending divorce, and Sabrina had sensed it was
a compliment. She'd been through a lot since then—her
mother's remarriage, the birth of a brother who'd quickly
taken center stage, her father's lengthy absences and her
own painful marriage and divorce—but she'd always
bounced back.

So what if some man didn't call her? She'd live. Was her
career less than fulfilling? She'd do volunteer work so she
could feel she was making a contribution. And she'd either

rescue Maya from a hideous marriage or get thrown into jail trying.

Even Josh, who knew her better than anyone, didn't guess how upset she was. He was too wrapped up in Grace, who had drawn the line at friendship and refused to step over it. Sabrina suspected Grace was more interested than she let on, because she took a whole day off on Tuesday to show Josh three different museums. Sabrina told him to be patient.

Years of practice had taught her to seem cheerful and relaxed even when she wasn't, so nobody noticed that she jumped every time the phone rang. They didn't realize that her heart pounded in double time whenever Brad's name came up. She wasn't sleeping well, but makeup disguised it. She told herself she wasn't the first one-night stand to be dumped and wouldn't be the last.

There was only one problem; she was sure Brad would have called her Sunday morning if he hadn't gone to Diana's. He'd told her she mattered and he didn't lie. There had been something special between the two of them, and Sabrina couldn't believe he would throw it away so casually. Surely he would listen if she apologized and explained.

By Thursday she couldn't stand it a moment longer. If Brad wouldn't call *her*, she'd call him. She waited until everyone had left the house, then sat down with the phone. Five minutes went by, then ten. She couldn't bring herself to dial; phones were too impersonal. Besides, his secretary probably screened his calls and she didn't care to expose herself to the indignity of having him refuse to speak to her.

It took her another hour to screw up the courage to go see him. According to Kathleen's street map, his office was near the courthouse, a few blocks from a subway stop. All she had to do was catch a streetcar on Commonwealth Avenue and take it downtown.

Although her stomach was churning like a puddle during an earthquake, she didn't look nervous when she walked into Brad's building an hour and a half later. Princesses, even minor ones, learned to act imperious, just as secretaries in influential, old-line law firms like Fraser, Carberry and Mill learned to recognize wealth. While Sabrina had little use for the trappings of the privileged, she could mimic them when she needed to. Her white silk suit, Ferragamo pumps and elegant carriage marked her as someone important.

Heads turned when she entered the reception area, but she pretended not to notice. She wasn't asked if she had an appointment when she requested directions to Brad's office; she was respectfully shown the way. His secretary, a slender woman with salt-and-pepper hair, put aside the file she was studying and asked how she could help.

"Please tell Mr. Fraser that Miss Lang is here to see him," Sabrina said.

"He's out right now but if you'd like to wait—"

"Thank you." Sabrina ignored what the secretary had obviously intended—that she should wait in the reception area—and headed toward Brad's private office.

As she reached the door, the secretary sputtered, "But Miss Lang—you can't go in there."

She smiled serenely. "I won't disturb anything."

"I'm sorry, but I'll have to insist—"

"Don't worry. I'll make sure Brad yells at *me* about it, not you." She certainly wasn't going to return to the reception area and risk having him publicly snub her.

She opened the door and walked inside. The entire office was early American, but the furnishings in the reception area and secretary's office had looked to be reproductions while Brad's desk and bookcases were undoubtedly authentic. The whole atmosphere reeked of status and power, from the graceful old building itself to the drawings of colonial Boston on Brad's walls.

The secretary walked in a moment later, but only to offer her a cup of coffee. She'd obviously decided that Sabrina wasn't someone to trifle with. Sabrina declined the coffee and sat down on the couch, noticing distractedly that the secretary had left the door ajar. Since the secretary couldn't see the couch from behind her desk, she probably intended to keep a sharp ear open to make sure Sabrina didn't disturb anything.

Sabrina might have been a princess once, but she'd originally been a shy little girl from a broken home in rural California. She'd worked hard to look as if she were comfortable with power and privilege, but Brad was the genuine article. At the moment, she felt every bit of that difference.

Chapter Nine

Brad was in a lousy mood as he rode upstairs to his office. He'd just left a lengthy negotiating session that had accomplished absolutely nothing, except perhaps to give his opponents more time to prepare their case. He hadn't shown his impatience or his preference for settling out of court; that would have jeopardized his client's position. Instead he'd played his hand as skillfully as a poker expert, bluffing the opposing lawyers into thinking his case was stronger than it really was. Tomorrow, he hoped, the bargaining would begin in earnest.

He walked into the reception area and stopped at the desk. The receptionist, his cousin's college-age daughter, was working in the office for the summer. "Is your father here?" he asked brusquely.

The girl, Amy Carberry, made a face exactly like his own and grumped back, "No, he's not, Uncle Brad, and what difference does it make when the sky is obviously falling?"

"You can be replaced," he said, amused by her imitation but too irritable to laugh. "Where is he?"

"Having his front tooth capped." She gave him a side-long look. "A procedure, I might add, that certain people in this office will never need, because they never smile anymore. Some woman is here to see you, and if you don't smile at *her*, you need brain surgery. She's gorgeous."

"So are you," Brad said, finally unbending a little, "but I've managed not to smile at *you*. Who is she?"

"She didn't say, but she's a brunette with long hair and green eyes, maybe five foot ten in heels, and totally stacked." She paused. "Does it sound like anyone you know?"

It sounded so much like Sabrina Lang that Brad wanted to turn around and leave, but if he did, Amy would gossip about it for a week. "As a matter of fact, it does." He strode away from the desk, leaving her agape with curiosity.

The past couple of days had been brutal, and not only because he'd been grappling with a number of complicated cases. On the contrary, difficult cases were a challenge he normally enjoyed. It was just that his personal life had been one giant hassle after another. Kathleen was still chasing around with Howard Lang and, much to his annoyance, Diana had dumped the whole mess in his lap. Not only had she run off to the Vineyard on Sunday; she'd sternly instructed him to keep an eye on the situation. As for Grace, he'd seen her only once this week, on Monday night, and had wound up taking her home early. They were supposed to attend a concert tomorrow and he was already wondering how he could get out of it. The problem wasn't her, but himself; he wasn't in the mood for company, especially not female company.

In his more honest moments he admitted that his lousy mood had started Saturday night, but it wasn't something he cared to analyze. As a rational, mature man, he understood it was a waste of energy to smart about what a sucker he'd been. Sabrina had been a mistake, and it was stupid to let his wounded ego spill over into his daily life.

He made himself a couple of promises as he walked down the hall. He wasn't going to bring up what had happened on Saturday night—it was over and done with. He wasn't going to lose his temper, either—he would look like a fool. Most of all, he wasn't going to let her sucker him again. If her visit was personal, he would get rid of her as soon as possible, and if she had a legal problem, he would refer her to one of his partners.

He frowned when he walked into his office and saw that his door was partially open, but he didn't hold Carol responsible for that. When Sabrina went after something, she was almost impossible to stop. "Sabrina Lang?" he asked.

Carol looked surprised. "You didn't mention you were expecting her."

"I wasn't. Amy gave me a description of who was here. Are there any calls I need to return right away?"

"No." She handed him a stack of messages. "About Miss Lang... She was determined to wait inside, and since she seemed to be a personal friend of yours—"

"She's not, but don't worry about it. I've tangled with her a time or two myself and I didn't do any better than you did." He looked through his messages and walked into his office.

Sabrina jerked to her feet the moment he entered the room. He closed the door, thinking she looked pale and nervous. It was probably an act, not that he cared one way or the other. No matter how personal her business was, he meant to treat this as a routine legal consultation.

He crossed to his desk, aware that she was following him with her eyes. Pale or not, she was as beautiful as ever, and he found himself resenting the quick, powerful response she evoked. He didn't want to find her attractive. "Have a seat," he said, gesturing at the chair in front of his desk.

She hesitated for a second, then made her way to the chair and sat down. Brad seated himself a moment later and asked her what he could do for her.

"I wanted to apologize for Saturday night." She fidgeted with the strap on her purse. "I know what you think, but it wasn't the way it looked. That is, I did lie to you about where everyone was and I deliberately kept you at the hotel, but everything else was real."

It certainly had been, right down to the candlelight and wine, and Brad wanted to sarcastically thank her for giving him such a good time. Instead he replied coolly, "I see."

"You're angry," she said resignedly. "I don't really blame you, but if you would try to understand... I said no at first, but Dad kept pressing me, and I wanted to help him and Kathleen. Even though I realized it was dishonest, I figured it wouldn't hurt anyone. And then when we got along so well, I forgot why you'd even come. All I could think about was—" She blushed and looked away. "What I'm trying to say is, you weren't what I'd expected and it took me by surprise. Everything happened so fast that I never realized how it would look—that one way or another you were bound to find out about Diana's party and misunderstand. And then Dad and Kathleen got back and she explained what had happened and I've been agonizing about it ever since."

"So you came here to apologize to me for lying."

"Yes."

"And you want me to know you're sorry for not explaining everything on Saturday night, even though you knew I would go straight to Diana's and tear your father apart."

"You know I couldn't have explained before you left—I promised my father I would help him and I couldn't break my word. But I would have told you on Sunday." She looked up, smiling uncertainly. "Right after we'd made love a couple of times. You would have been too satisfied to be mad at me."

Brad thought that was typical of her. Her first instinct was to manipulate people, not deal honestly with them. Whatever she was after—sexual pleasure, his approval of her father, another male notch in her belt—it didn't matter. He didn't want any part of it.

"Your apology is accepted," he said briskly. "Now if you'll excuse me, I have some phone calls to make."

Her smile crumbled. "Brad, I was only joking—"

"I don't want to be rude, but I'm very busy. Enjoy yourself in Australia." He reached for the phone.

"You're still angry, but if you would listen and try to understand—"

"I've been listening for the past five minutes and I understand perfectly. You wanted to help your father and you succeeded. You lied to me in the process and you're sorry, but it was unavoidable. Does that sum it up?"

"No." She straightened, a hurt but determined look on her face. "You're denying that any feelings were involved. You're making it sound as if it were just—just sex, but it wasn't, not for either of us."

"On the contrary, that's exactly what it was—a one-night stand resulting from too much liquor on my part and a rare sense of filial devotion on yours." Although outwardly composed, Brad was seething. He hated being forced to talk about something he was ashamed of. "There's already a woman in my life, someone I care about very much. Saturday shouldn't have happened."

"You don't love Grace Fitzsimmons," she said. "If you did, you would have married her by now, and you wouldn't have responded to me the way you did. The things you whispered while we were making love—that I was magical and beautiful and exciting—you really meant them. And you would have called me Sunday morning if you hadn't gone to Diana's. I know you would have."

Brad didn't say a word. Her presumption was getting under his skin, and if he answered he was going to lose his temper. Where did she get off telling him how he felt? She didn't know a thing about his relationship with Grace and it was none of her damn business in the first place. Besides,

the woman had been around the track more times than Sec
retariat. Why didn't she find someone else to amuse herself
with and leave him the hell alone?

She leaned forward, looking earnest, hurt and nervous all
at the same time. There was no way he was going to fall for
that again. "Brad, please. I have to leave on Sunday and I
can't bear the thought of going when you're still so angry.
Can't we talk this out? I know this is a bad time, but I could
come to your house and cook dinner—"

"And rub my feet and take me to bed." Totally out of
patience now, he decided he'd wasted more time on her than
she deserved and that he wanted her out of his office. If he
had to be blunt to accomplish that, he would do it. "Exactly what do you want from me, Sabrina? A roll in the hay
to remember me by? Another shot at using your body to
convince me what a swell guy your father is?"

Sabrina flinched at his crude accusations, but even so, his
anger came as a relief. She'd steeled herself for hot fury, not
cold indifference, and his icy manner had turned her into
even more of a wreck than she'd been in the first place. His
anger proved he'd felt something that night.

"I don't want either of those things," she said. "I just
want to spend some time with you and get to know you better."

"I'm flattered," he drawled. "Might I ask why?"

Answering him honestly was one of the hardest things
she'd ever done, but beating around the bush wasn't going
to accomplish anything. "Because I'm in love with you. I
didn't sleep with you to manipulate you, but I think you
know that. We've gotten off to a complicated start, but there
has to be a way...." She swallowed hard, trying to control
her emotions. "We had something special together, Brad.
Don't throw it away without giving it another chance."

That was when Brad decided to take her apart. The rational part of him dissolved and gave way to pure, irate reaction. Nobody was going to barge into his office, feed him
outrageous lines and walk away unscathed. Dangling the

prospect of sex in front of him like a sugar cube in front of a donkey had been bad enough, but using love!... Given her history, it took an unimaginable amount of gall to even say the word. She and her father were one hell of a team, and he aimed to find out what they were up to.

He lazed back in his chair and smiled the way he smiled at witnesses he was about to crush. "Tell me something, Sabrina. Why was it so important to your father to have my family like him? After all, Kathleen doesn't need anyone's permission to have an affair."

Sabrina shifted uneasily. Brad's smile was chilling, like that of an inquisitor studying his next victim. Even more unnerving, his question, which had come out of nowhere, went to the heart of matters she simply couldn't discuss.

Still, she had to give him an answer. She had the feeling it was some sort of test—that their future together depended on whether she satisfied him. "Kathleen is very close to all of you. Dad could see your disapproval was upsetting her. He thought she'd be happier if he could persuade you to accept him."

"I see." His manner was so casual, they might have been discussing the weather. "You know, your father is an intelligent man. I can't understand why he didn't keep a lower profile and give the family a chance to get to know him. If he's as decent a guy as you claim, he would have won us over eventually."

"But there wasn't time. He had to go to Australia—"

"And pressured Kathleen to go along. That was a serious mistake, Sabrina. He should have insisted that she stay home. We don't approve of the way he rushed her. What's a few extra months apart when you're talking about spending your whole lives together?"

Sabrina didn't understand how he could be so cold-hearted. People weren't computers, for heaven's sake. "It can seem like forever when you're in love. Dad wants to be with her every moment."

"Especially in Asia." Brad hadn't forgotten the way Howard and Kathleen had met. Somehow Asia had to be the key to the situation. "That statue he's looking for—assuming it really exists, it has to be in some remote place or it would have been discovered by now. The search will be expensive. If my family was unhappy before, they'll be twice as unhappy if Kathleen decides to finance it...unless, of course, your father manages to con them into being just as interested in looking for it as he is."

Sabrina's face, he noticed, was flushed with emotion. "And that's what Saturday night was all about. Your father couldn't afford to wait—he needed Kathleen's money right away. He needed to win my family over so they wouldn't hit the ceiling when she started writing fat checks."

"That's not true!" she said hotly. "He doesn't need her money. He has plenty of his own—"

"But not enough to keep paying for the hotel suite."

"He could have afforded it, but Kathleen thought it was ridiculously expensive. She was the one who wanted to leave. Anyway, I don't see what this has to do with you and me—"

"Then I'll refresh your memory. You lied to me on Saturday night, supposedly against your better judgment, because you wanted to help your father. What was so urgent that you were willing to sacrifice your principles? You claim money wasn't the issue, and your father can be patient when he needs to be—the Christiana diamond is proof of that—so what was the big hurry?"

"The what diamond?" she asked, looking lost.

He didn't believe for a moment that she didn't know what he was talking about, but he was willing to spell it out if that was what she wanted. "The Christiana diamond. Nobody manages to steal something that well-known without being patient. If your father really loved Kathleen, he would have been equally patient about doing whatever was necessary to win her. Since he wasn't, he must need her for something right away." He frowned, trying to analyze the situation.

The statue, if it existed, was evidently in the northern region of the Indian subcontinent, but the area was notoriously unstable. Was *that* Howard's problem?

"My father used to be the ambassador to India," he remarked casually. Sabrina tensed and started to tremble, a reaction so dramatic that even Brad was taken aback. He was obviously probing a sensitive area. "He showed me quite a bit of the subcontinent, but there were areas we weren't permitted to visit. Of course, Kathleen is a very prominent scholar. She could probably get access to regions even diplomats can't enter."

Sabrina was so stunned she could hardly think. The blows had come too fast: Brad's alarmingly perceptive questions about her father's motives; his confident assertion that Howard had stolen some diamond she'd never heard of; his reference to Royce Fraser; and finally, his distressingly accurate speculation about why they'd been in such a hurry to gain Kathleen's cooperation.

As he'd guessed, they needed the access she could get them and they needed it now; even two months was a short time in which to obtain the necessary papers. But their true motive was to rescue Maya.

Dazed and frightened, she could think of only one thing to do—agree with whatever Brad said. If she told him he was right, maybe he would leave her alone. "You make it sound like it's some sort of crime to ask for Kathleen's help, but she knows we need her and she doesn't mind at all. She's already working on the arrangements."

"That won't be enough. She'll have to go to Asia. Nothing short of her name and presence will get you into those areas."

"I suppose so," she agreed.

"And that's what it's really about. Your father needs her to find the statue—"

"He happens to love her—"

"And that's why you did what he asked. *You* want that statue as much as he does, so you were willing to do whatever was necessary to keep me at the hotel Saturday night."

"All right, *yes!*" Sabrina buried her face in her hands, rattled into abject retreat now. It was better to have him think she was after the statue than to risk further questions. He was so mercilessly thorough—God knew what he would find out if he did as much reading about her years in Jammapur as he'd evidently done about her father's career.

"We want the statue and we need Kathleen to get us into restricted areas," she said, and then frantically realized that she'd dug herself even deeper into a hole by admitting they'd used Kathleen for anything at all. "That is, it started out that way, but—"

"We were talking about Saturday night. That's less than a week ago. Surely your father loved her enough by then to forget the statue and wait for her to work things out with her family."

"You're taking something complicated and treating it like it's simple," Sabrina said desperately. "Dad can want the statue and still love Kathleen, and Kathleen can want to help him without feeling he's using her. The statue has enormous historical significance—"

"She doesn't think it exists. Neither do you, if what you told me Saturday night was true."

Totally trapped now, she answered, "I lied."

Brad seriously doubted it, if only because she looked so shaken. He was almost certain she'd told him the truth that night, at least about the statue, which meant she was lying right now. "I don't believe you," he said. "You don't think that statue exists any more than Kathleen does."

She was willing to go along with anything he said. "All right, then. I don't."

"So why did you agree to stall me on Saturday?"

"Because my father asked me to."

"So even though you were madly in love with me, you decided it was more important to keep your word to your father than to be honest with someone you wanted to spend the rest of your life with."

She hadn't realized how she'd felt until he'd left, but it wasn't important. She still wouldn't have confided in him. She wouldn't have risked their chance to rescue Maya for anything in the world. "Yes," she said.

"Then your definition of love has very little in common with mine. It doesn't include things like openness, honesty and trust." Brad wasn't so much angry as frustrated now. Sabrina was still lying to him—he could see it on her face. He wanted to grab her and shake the damn truth out of her.

She flinched but didn't say anything. Deliberately goading her, he continued, "Does that statement bother you? Do you consider it unfair?"

She took a deep breath, visibly calming herself, and looked at him warily. He didn't trust the pain in her eyes, mostly because he didn't trust anything about her at all. "I know a lot about love—more than you seem to," she said.

"Do you?" He smiled cynically. "That's not what you sang the other night."

"It was only a song. I'm talking about real life."

"Are you? Who taught you? Your husband?"

Sabrina simply stared at him, her eyes filling with tears. The answer was Josh and Maya and every child she'd ever carried for a few weeks and lost, but she wasn't going to explain that. She wasn't going to admit she was a total failure when it came to love between men and women. Her pain wasn't something she paraded for other people's edification.

When all else fails, Brad thought to himself, *they cry*. He resisted the impulse to soften, to say something sympathetic, to take her in his arms. It was one more feminine ploy, one more attempt to manipulate him. "No response, hmm? Was it one of your lovers, Sabrina? Geoffrey Newhouse or Jean-Claude Miraux or Karl DeWitt?"

"They weren't my lovers, not that it's any of your business—"

"The hell it isn't! I slept with you, remember? Given the crowd you've been running around with for the past three years, I should probably see a doctor."

Sabrina was suddenly so furious she wanted to pick up a book and throw it at him. Violence, however, was alien to her nature. Instead of exploding, she grew closer to tears. "I told you on Saturday night, I've never *had* a lover. If there were any risk, I would have told you. There were no drugs, no lovers—"

"With the exception of Ved Pradham, I suppose, or doesn't it count if it's all in the family?"

She felt as if he'd slapped her. How could he possibly know about that? Ashoka had considered it one of the great shames of his life and never would have mentioned it, while Pradham would have had nothing to gain by repeating the story. There was only one possibility—that one of the servants had overheard the fight that had taken place that morning and gossiped about it, with the story eventually finding its way into the American embassy in New Delhi. It was one more reason to dislike Royce Fraser—and at that moment, the son he'd so obviously repeated it to.

The accusation was so nasty there was no possible way she could answer. Given Brad's obvious contempt, her only thought was to salvage what remained of her pride and flee. "Before you judge other people, maybe you should look inside *yourself.* There's something mean and petty and ugly in there, something that enjoys hurting other people and making them feel small. I guess I was wrong on Saturday night when I spoke about who the real Brad Fraser was, but then, I've never been very smart about men."

As she got to her feet, she noticed that he was smiling. And as she turned to leave, she heard him drawl softly, "My compliments on an incredible performance." It was the last straw.

Sabrina, who'd never struck anyone in her life, picked up the carafe on his desk, yanked out the top and swung it wildly. Brad ducked an instant before water landed all over his desk. Throwing the carafe onto the floor, she squared her shoulders, turned on her heel and marched out of his office.

Chapter Ten

Brad kept a gym bag in his closet containing athletic gear and towels, a fortuitous habit given the state of his desk and left shoulder. It wasn't until he'd retrieved a towel that he realized his face was as damp as his suit—not from the water Sabrina had thrown, but from perspiration. The last half hour had left him emotionally drained.

He dried his desk, jacket and face, then stared absently out the window at the frenetic rush-hour traffic. It was just as well it was time to go home; he wasn't going to be any good to anyone for the rest of the day. For a man who had taunted Sabrina about the quality of her performance, he was a pretty fair actor himself. Not only had he been far less cool than he'd pretended; his show of knowing all the answers had been a skillful facade.

The truth was that he was confused, angry and resentful ... confused because he couldn't figure Sabrina out, angry because her accusations had stung him, and resentful of the way she'd turned his life upside down. She was a lousy liar—he'd known that since Saturday night—so it was stupid to suppose that nothing just now had been real. She might have deliberately kept things from him, but she'd also been nervous, angry and hurt. He was sorry now that he'd lost his temper, sorry that he'd attacked her with enough firepower to kill a charging bull when she was nothing but a spitting cat.

He no longer knew what to believe. Maybe she *didn't* sleep around. Maybe she'd been as carried away Saturday night as he had. Remembering it, recalling how nervous she'd been, he felt a sharp stab of guilt. Party girls didn't tremble just because you took their clothes off. She couldn't possibly have had as much experience as he'd insisted on believing.

Still, she'd set him up that night—gotten him drunk, spoiled him rotten and aroused him until he was one big knot of need. And just now she'd accused him of things he'd never done in his life. He didn't like hurting people. He didn't enjoy belittling them. His job was to win lawsuits and he tried to do it well, but he only really relished the task when his opponents were as tough as he was or miserable bastards who deserved every bit of what he dished out. He was sure of that, wasn't he?

He gripped the windowsill, his jaw tightening in annoyance. Of course he was sure. Two stories below, he saw wavy dark hair and a white silk suit and realized Sabrina had just left the building. She started toward the corner, then stopped. He could tell she was breathing deeply by the way her shoulders moved up and down. She fumbled with the catch on her purse, then removed a handkerchief and raised it to her face. He couldn't see her eyes, but it was obvious she was crying. People looked at her curiously as they passed by, but nobody stopped to talk to her.

Brad stared at her, so full of turmoil that his fingers tightened on the sill. He hated feeling this way—so guilty and unsure of himself. All he'd ever wanted was a reasonably interesting career and a stable, predictable existence, preferably with a steady, loving woman at his side. Sabrina was nothing but trouble. Regardless of who or what she was, only a madman would have gotten mixed up with her.

Sabrina wasn't in the habit of standing on public sidewalks and bawling, but she couldn't help it. Every bit of her pride and energy had gone into walking out of Brad's building with her dignity intact, and there had been nothing left when she'd reached the street. Only once in her life had she been treated with such contempt, and that had been when her husband had found her in bed with his brother-in-law and immediately assumed they were having an affair.

She'd known then that their marriage was over; Ashoka had chosen to believe Pradham rather than her. In the years since, she'd forgotten how much it hurt to be labeled a liar and cheat, but her confrontation with Brad had brought it all back. She felt a raw, sharp pain in her chest. Dear Lord, she'd given herself to a man who considered her a cheap little tramp, had let him use her however he pleased, moaned in his arms when he kissed her and writhed with pleasure when he touched her. The memories made her skin crawl.

She wiped her eyes and blew her nose, but the tears kept falling. People stared at her, obviously thinking she was crazy or bereaved, and gave her a wide berth. Mortified to have become a public spectacle, she hurried to the end of the block. The subway wasn't far. It would be darker there, and crowded with people on their way home. She would attract less attention.

A huge truck was parked at the corner, sticking out into the cross street and blocking the right-hand lane. A driver honked impatiently, then accelerated sharply and cut off another car to get into the next lane over. Sabrina flinched at the shrill squeal of brakes and backed away from the curb, bumping into several pedestrians. One of them yelled at her to watch where she was going and all but shoved her aside.

Flustered and disoriented, her vision blurred by tears, she turned around and unsteadily retraced her steps. The front bumper of the truck was almost touching the car ahead of it, but she managed to squeeze between the two. The heat, noise and motion were making her dizzy and claustrophobic. She stepped into the street to double back to the crosswalk but saw a car barreling at her and froze. Time slowed down. She jumped back, but not quickly enough. The car was suddenly on top of her, but there was no pain, only consuming darkness.

She had no sense of time having passed. One moment the world was going black and the next she was sprawled on the hard, hot street. She opened her eyes, but everything was blurred. The picture gradually came into focus. A crowd of people had gathered around, most of them standing a short distance away but one of them bending over her. He asked if she was all right and she managed a weak "Yes." Everything seemed to hurt, but it took her a moment to sort out the pain. "My leg..." she moaned.

He pulled off his jacket and placed it under her head. He was very gentle. "Try to relax," he said. She closed her eyes and heard him ask if anyone had called an ambulance. A woman said something about her friend going to find a phone and a man shouted that his secretary had already taken care of it. His voice sounded familiar, but the pain in her leg was too excruciating to think about who he might be.

She felt a hand on her shoulder but didn't move. "The ambulance will be here any minute, Sabrina. The hospital's only a mile away."

It was the voice she'd heard earlier, the one belonging to the man whose secretary had phoned for an ambulance, but she recognized it now. It was Brad Fraser's voice. She cringed. "Don't touch me," she mumbled.

"What did she say?" a woman asked.

He answered that he hadn't been able to make out her words, but he took away his hand all the same. "She sounds dazed. I don't think she's completely coherent."

Sabrina wanted to tell him she was perfectly lucid but was in too much pain to speak. Still, she wasn't going to let him see her cry. She bit her lip and willed away her tears, vaguely aware that he'd stood up and was talking to someone in the crowd.

A siren wailed in the distance. Time passed—she had no idea how much—and then someone touched her arm. She opened her eyes, saw the blood-pressure cuff he was holding and relaxed. Now that help was here, the pain was more endurable. The paramedic examined her with gentle expertise, then asked her what had happened. "I was hit by a car," she said. "I think my leg is broken."

"I think you're right," he replied, "but other than some cuts and bruises, the rest of you seems to be okay." He and his colleague eased her onto a stretcher.

"She was in my office just before it happened," Brad said. "If you don't mind, I'd like to go along."

"You're a friend?"

"I'm her attorney."

Sabrina thought about refusing, but her initial relief at seeing the paramedics had given way to fear. She'd had enough of doctors and hospitals during her years in Jammapur to last a lifetime and associated them with arrogance and failure. Brad represented protection. Everyone knew doctors were more careful when lawyers were around.

The paramedic smiled. "Relax, buddy. Nobody's going to screw up. You can follow us inside."

Brad nodded and turned to the man next to him. Sabrina saw him jot something down on a piece of paper as she was wheeled into the ambulance. Even though she was woozy, she knew what he was doing—noting down license numbers, talking to witnesses, preparing for a possible lawsuit. His concern, she thought scornfully, was touching. That was when she remembered she didn't like lawyers any better than doctors.

She was hoping he would leave her alone, but once the ambulance got underway he leaned close to her and asked her how she was feeling. Her anger welled up, breaking through the barriers she'd tried to erect. "Just fine, counselor. There goes the fat contingency fee."

Brad heard the sarcasm in her voice and took her answer for exactly what it was—naked hostility—but the paramedic riding across from him apparently noticed only the weak, slurred words themselves. "She's still got her sense of humor. I think she'll be okay."

Brad smiled but didn't reply. It had been second nature to gather evidence for a possible trial, but Sabrina's dig to the contrary, he'd made sure she was all right first. Still, as a lawyer, he knew that problems could exist that weren't readily apparent. Their differences no longer mattered. She was a fellow human being, a guest in his aunt's home, and he meant to look after her interests.

Watching from the window, he'd thought that the car had struck her only a glancing blow, and several witnesses had agreed. Although her leg was badly swollen under the ice the paramedic had applied, the injury seemed to be the result of the awkward way she'd fallen rather than the impact itself.

On the other hand, she'd lost consciousness for a time and that was never a good thing. He paled, reliving the way she'd bounced off the car and fallen to the ground—like a rag doll. The horror and nausea of those first few moments in his office hit him all over again, but he rationalized them away. Naturally the accident had affected him. It was never pleasant to see someone almost killed. Shaken all the same, he straightened and moved away.

Sabrina took a brittle sense of satisfaction in his withdrawal. She'd put him in his place—let him know what she thought of him—and it eased her humiliation. The need to lash out at him wasn't as strong now; she could tolerate him as long as he kept his distance.

The people in the hospital seemed to accept his presence, probably because he exuded authority. She was worried there might be a problem with her medical coverage, but Brad handled the admitting process. As a lawyer, he was good at that sort of thing, and although she was too angry to be grateful, she *was* relieved.

He waited outside while the doctor examined her, returning to the room immediately afterward for a report. The doctor explained that while her only serious injury seemed to be her broken leg, he wanted to keep her in the hospital till morning as a precaution. Since she'd lost consciousness, he was recommending a brain scan, and they'd also need X rays of her leg to see how bad the break was. She stopped paying attention when she heard them discussing orthopedic surgeons. The painkiller the doctor had given her had added to her wooziness, and she didn't know one orthopedist from another.

Brad walked beside the gurney as she was wheeled down for X rays and accompanied her into the room. She groggily noticed the way the attractive blond technician smiled at him and told herself women were stupid. The packaging was nice enough, but inside...inside... She yawned and closed her eyes, unable to concentrate on completing the thought.

The technician helped her onto the X-ray table, then asked crisply, "Is there any chance that you could be pregnant, Ms. Lang?"

Sabrina had had X rays before and knew it was a routine question. "Yes," she mumbled. "Maybe...probably." Even if Brad hadn't been around to remind her, she wouldn't have forgotten Saturday night. It didn't matter that she would probably miscarry—the technician hadn't asked that.

"Then we'll make sure you're well protected." After asking Brad to leave, the technician arranged a lead shield over Sabrina's middle and went to work.

Out in the hallway, Brad was pacing up and down, trying to control his shock. How could Sabrina be pregnant? Less than a week ago she'd told him she couldn't have children. Had she lied about *that*, too?

Maybe she'd misunderstood the question. She was so woozy it was a wonder she was awake. Still, her answer had been very definite—not just "Yes," but "Maybe, probably." He ran his hand through his hair. Dear God, *probably*!

What was he going to do if Sabrina Lang was pregnant with his child? His parents would go into cardiac arrest. He'd never live down the headlines...conventional, conservative Brad Fraser, impregnating some hedonistic, jet-setting adventuress. The idea was appalling.

He stopped pacing and forced himself to think rationally. Something didn't add up. Sabrina couldn't suspect she was pregnant—they'd made love too recently. There hadn't even been time for her to start worrying.

Unless, he suddenly realized, there had been someone in her bed before him. Was that why she'd seduced him? Because she was already pregnant? Because she planned to claim the pregnancy was a fluke and then hit him up for child support?

It didn't seem possible. She was too smart not to know that he never would accept a child as his own without having a complete battery of blood tests. Unfortunately, even if she'd known what she was saying, she was in no shape to answer questions. Since she'd be busy with tests for a while, he decided to find a phone and call her father.

Howard arrived with Kathleen and Josh while Sabrina was being prepped for the orthopedist. Brad was relieved that Howard didn't ask what she'd been doing in his office—he didn't want to have to explain their relationship. Even worse, if he hadn't gotten her so upset, she might have been more careful before she'd stepped into the street. But damn it, how was he supposed to have known how she felt? She'd looked furious at the end, but not distraught.

Howard's only apparent concern was Sabrina's medical condition, so much so that he barely seemed to hear Kathleen's quiet assurance that the doctor Brad had gotten was one of the best in town. He only settled down once he'd seen her test results. There was no sign of brain injury and the break in her leg was a simple fracture of the tibia. The orthopedist appeared a few minutes later and explained that the injury would require an ankle-to-thigh cast but no surgery. He suggested that they grab a bite to eat and then return to the waiting room, promising that he or a nurse would find them and tell them how things had gone.

Brad left the hospital at that point. He knew Sabrina wouldn't welcome his continuing presence—his usefulness had ended the moment her family had arrived. When Howard thanked him profusely for his help, he replied stiffly that he hoped she would feel better soon. The man was a concerned father, he had to give him that. He shook Howard's hand and walked away, a roiling mixture of guilt, confusion and anxiety.

Despite Sabrina's dislike of hospitals, she was an easy patient, the type who did as she was told and suffered the resulting pain in stoic silence. Besides, the people who treated her were gentle and competent, and they explained what they were doing before she even asked.

She expected to see Brad as they wheeled her upstairs, but he'd apparently left. It wasn't reasonable to be annoyed when she'd repeatedly told herself she didn't want him around, but she couldn't help it. She felt deserted.

Her self-pity disappeared as soon as she reached her room and saw her father and brother inside. Kathleen was there, too, but not Brad. Maybe he'd gotten tired of playing the good samaritan and gone about his business, but if so, it was only what she'd expected of him.

The nurse got her settled in bed, then left. After hugging everyone hello, she gave her father a rueful look and said, "There goes Australia."

"Don't worry—Josh will give me a hand. He knows the place almost as well as you do. How are you feeling, honey?"

"Better than before. I was really out of it for a while, but I guess it was shock and painkillers." Even so, she remembered everything that had happened. Patting her cast, she added, "This can be replaced with a walking cast in three or four weeks, but until then, I'll be pretty much immobilized. I'll call Mom tomorrow and tell her I'm coming home."

Howard pulled over a chair and sat down. "We've been talking about that, and Kathleen wants you to stay with her."

"That's a very generous offer, but I can't possibly accept." She smiled at Kathleen. "You have work to do. You can't spend your time looking after me."

Josh rolled his eyes. "Come on, Sabrina, be serious. Mom was driving you nuts after a single week at home. Six weeks of her nagging you about your scandalous life-style and you'll be certifiable."

"We'll get you some crutches and a wheelchair," Kathleen said. "After a little practice, you should be able to get around just fine. Besides, Howard was telling me you're a terrific typist. I could use someone to help me with my notes and lectures. It usually takes me forever to transcribe them."

Her father spoke before she had a chance to. "I don't like the idea of your changing doctors in midtreatment, Sabrina. Dr. Horowitz is first-rate. Who knows what you'll get in Redding."

A perfectly competent physician, but she didn't argue. Josh was right about their mother. Jane disapproved of the unconventional life Sabrina led and never tired of saying so. The truth was that she *wanted* to be talked into staying.

"It still seems like an imposition," she said to Kathleen, "but if you're sure I can earn my keep—"

"Of course I'm sure. I'll enjoy having your company. I won't take no for an answer."

"All right, but if I'm in the way at all—"

"You won't be."

"—I'll expect you to put me on the first plane to California."

Kathleen laughed and said she would carry Sabrina aboard herself if there were a problem, but Sabrina didn't expect one. She got along with almost everyone, and according to her father, so did Kathleen. "Just be sure you don't let anything slip to Mom," she said to Josh. "She'll be hurt if she knows I broke my leg and didn't come home."

"Are you crazy? She hates the idea of *your* leading tours, so I'm not about to tell her I took your place." He grinned at her. "Of course, your unfortunate accident frees up a spot on the roster. It would be nice if Howard could fill it up and make a few extra bucks."

"And as luck would have it, you happen to know a hot prospect." She was very tired and her speech was a little slurred, but she managed to look offended. "Here I am," she teased, "suffering abominably, totally exhausted—"

"You're the most devoted sister in the world to break your leg just to make me happy. I owe you one."

"What *are* you two chattering about?" Kathleen asked.

"Grace Fitzsimmons. She wants to go to Australia." Josh paused, looking a little uneasy. "Personally, I hope she can arrange to get away. I'm sorry about your nephew, Kathleen, but if he loses her it's his own damn fault. He doesn't pay enough attention to her."

"And here I thought the two of you were just good friends!" Kathleen's sly tone indicated she hadn't thought any such thing. She knew Josh and Grace had spent quite a bit of time together during the past week and had obviously reached the right conclusion. "Although I don't suppose you care, you have my blessing. I love both Brad and Grace, but they're totally wrong for each other. Brad wants to settle down, but Grace is far too inexperienced. She needs to spread her wings and taste what life has to offer."

"You've got to talk this woman into marrying you," Josh said to Howard. "She's a gem. Maybe she could even get through to Mom."

"I'm also observant enough to see that poor Sabrina can barely stay awake," Kathleen said. "It's time we left and let her get some rest."

Howard kissed Sabrina on the forehead. "As usual, the lady is right. We'll see you first thing in the morning, sweetheart. Try to get some sleep."

Sabrina nodded and yawned. The entire day had turned into a hazy blur. Nothing about it seemed real. She closed her eyes a moment after Josh turned off the light.

Chapter Eleven

Sabrina's life settled into a comfortable routine. Rose Clauswicz, Diana Fraser's housekeeper, came over each morning to help her bathe and dress, then fixed her breakfast. A hardy, cheerful woman of about fifty, Rose turned awkward tasks into easy ones. Diana had insisted on sending her over, and Sabrina was grateful for her help.

After eating breakfast, she went up to Kathleen's office, negotiating the steps one by one on her rump. Rose generally stood and watched her, mumbling all the while about how stubborn she was, but Sabrina had drawn the line at being carried. She'd rented a wheelchair and a set of crutches and had learned to use both.

Learning to use Kathleen's computer had been a little harder, but she'd gotten the hang of it thanks to the lessons in the manual. Kathleen had put her to work copying a stack of handwritten notes into various computer files, a process that involved jumping from document to document. Sabrina lived in dire fear of accidentally erasing something, but Kathleen assured her it was almost impossible—cold comfort to someone with her innate distrust of machinery.

Kathleen left early each morning, going to her office at school or to one of the local libraries, and Rose left after lunch, so Sabrina didn't feel like a burden. She was busy, she was helping Kathleen, and nobody nagged her about eating and sleeping enough or how she lived her life.

Things would have been perfect—or as perfect as they could be given her broken leg—if it hadn't been for the existence of Brad Fraser. Being in his company even for a short time made her resentful and tense, but he and Kathleen saw each other too often for her to avoid him.

Their first meeting after the accident was at the going-away party Kathleen threw for Howard, Josh and Grace. Brad asked stiffly after her health, waited for her equally stiff reply, and turned to Diana. For the rest of the evening, Sabrina sat imprisoned on the couch while she and Brad studiously ignored each other.

The party was interesting in at least one way; it gave her an opportunity to observe Grace Fitzsimmons and her parents, who were upset about her decision to go to Australia and kept trying to change her mind. Grace had attended a local university and lived in the Fitzsimmonses' Boston home; she worked at a museum among old family friends and never traveled anywhere except with relatives or Brad. Sabrina got the feeling that Abby and Charles Fitzsimmons had handpicked him as their future son-in-law and weren't pleased that he'd encouraged Grace to go away. If anything, they'd expected him to do the opposite.

Given how overprotective they were, Sabrina thought it was high time Grace rebelled. She was bright, likable and pretty, and although she hadn't painted since graduate school, apparently had a considerable amount of talent. Now she was thinking of getting back to it, but her parents refused to take her seriously. They acted as if painting were a sweet little hobby—hardly the sort of thing a Fitzsimmons should pursue seriously.

They were lecturing her about the importance of contributing something to society when Brad declared that, in his opinion, she was frittering away her life and dreams working at the museum and should paint full-time. Her father glared at him while her mother looked as if she were about to have a stroke, prompting Kathleen to tactfully but firmly change the subject.

Sabrina noticed the grin on Howard's face and smiled helplessly. Howard had never been one to follow convention, an attitude that seemed to irk the Fitzsimmonses no end. Unfortunately, it hadn't helped his marriages, either.

Although her opinion of Brad wasn't much higher than on Thursday, he was obviously good for Grace. Far from trying to run her life, he'd encouraged her to be her own woman. His supportiveness didn't tally with the accusations Sabrina had once made, and a tiny amount of doubt crept in as to whether she'd been fair. He might have been judgmental and cruel to *her*, but that didn't mean he treated everyone that way.

Josh noticed it, too. Coming into her room after the party, he said dejectedly, "Brad is actually a pretty nice guy—kind of stiff and distant, but he cares about Grace. I pick terrific people to fall for, don't I?"

"Are you saying it's hopeless?" she asked.

He shook his head. "I'm not going to give up. I just didn't think the competition would be so tough."

She had the feeling it would be easier than he thought. "I was watching them together, Josh. They've known each other forever and it shows. There's a lot of caring and affection there, but there's no—no passion, in the emotional sense, I mean. There's no intensity. They don't seem to be involved in each other's lives."

He shrugged. "You know New Englanders. They don't show what they feel."

"True, but I think it's more than that." After last Saturday night, she knew it for a fact, but she couldn't tell her kid brother that she'd once seen Brad Fraser radiate emotion like uranium radiates alpha rays. He didn't even know the truth about her accident. She'd told everyone that she'd left Brad's office after chatting with him about Howard and run headlong into one of Boston's more demented drivers. "Remember what Grace said when Brad mentioned he was going to miss her?" she asked.

"You mean that bit about never even noticing she was gone because he'd be too busy working or sailing? She was joking, Sabrina."

"On the surface, maybe, but deep down, I think she meant it." She smiled. "Anyway, you're going to have her to yourself for the next six weeks. What's Brad Fraser compared to the heartthrob of Redding High?"

"A great-looking guy with a law degree and tons of money."

"But old," she said solemnly. "Very old."

He laughed. "You have a point. I'll see you in the morning. You will get up, won't you?"

They were leaving very early because members of the tour group were flying into New York from all over the country and Howard wanted to be available if problems arose. Sabrina assured him she would get up to say goodbye, then tried to find a comfortable position and fall asleep. Her leg, she thought forlornly, had begun to itch. It was going to be a long six weeks.

Sabrina saw Brad twice during the next several days. He took Kathleen to dinner on Wednesday and invited her to join them, but she pleaded exhaustion, and they met at a reception for a Chinese dance troupe on Sunday, an event she wouldn't have attended if she'd known he would be there. All in all, they exchanged fewer than a dozen sentences.

He was always impeccably polite, but he had a way of speaking to her that made her feel as if he were looking straight through her. She was equally distant, answering his questions about how she was doing as concisely as possible and never asking anything back. She assumed he felt the same way she did—that sleeping together had been a mistake and was best forgotten.

She was working upstairs late Monday afternoon when the doorbell rang. She was alone at the time—Rose was at Diana's and Kathleen was at the library—but she didn't attempt to answer it. Whoever was there would only lose patience and go away by the time she got downstairs.

The bell rang again but she continued to ignore it. A few seconds later the front door opened and closed. A little alarmed, she transferred the computer keyboard from her lap to the desk, then maneuvered her wheelchair to the doorway. She couldn't see downstairs, but she could hear heavy, unfamiliar footfalls. Her heart began to race. A stranger was walking around downstairs and she was helpless in the event of an attack.

She was making her way to the bathroom—the door had a lock—when he finally spoke. "Kathleen? Sabrina? Is anyone home?"

It was Brad, but the bathroom still seemed like a good idea. She resisted the urge to lock herself inside and called back, "Kathleen's at the library."

A moment later he trotted up the stairs. "Good. I came to see *you*, not her." He walked up behind her and pushed her down the hall. "We can talk in your room. You'll be more comfortable there."

If Sabrina had had any sense she would have kept her mouth shut, but her resentment got the better of her. "You scared me half to death," she said sharply. "Shouldn't you be at work?"

"I'm sorry." His tone was clipped, offended. "When nobody answered, I decided to unlock the door and look around inside. I didn't mean to frighten you."

"You might have called before you came."

He pushed her into her bedroom. "I was at a meeting in Newton. I decided to stop off here while I was driving back to my office. I'll buy a car phone as soon as possible so it doesn't happen again.''

"There's no need to be sarcastic," she said, delighted that he'd lost his temper. He was always so stuffy and controlled. "Actually, I'm surprised you don't have a car phone already. Isn't it a necessity for an important corporate lawyer like you?"

He parked the chair by her bed. "Obviously you're feeling better. You were much less spirited last week."

"Horses are spirited, not women," she sniffed. "I happen to be busy with some work for Kathleen, so if you'd say what you came to say..."

Brad felt like doing something quite different, like gagging her with his handkerchief in order to shut her up, but well-bred gentlemen didn't resort to such tactics. It was enough to make him long for the good old days when James Cagney had shoved a grapefruit into Mae Clarke's face.

It wasn't the first time she'd gotten under his skin lately; she irritated him every time they saw each other, especially since she flirted with every guy she met while treating *him* like an unpleasant substance on the sidewalk. Since he'd seen to it that she got the best medical treatment in Boston after her accident, he figured he deserved better.

It annoyed him that he still should feel so guilty—that he could remember the stricken look on her face when he'd asked her about her lovers and recall how she'd stood on the sidewalk afterward and cried. But damn it, it was mostly her fault! If she hadn't played stupid games that afternoon, neither of those things would have happened, and she was *still* playing stupid games. She'd had a week to explain that remark about a possible pregnancy but hadn't said a word.

Tired of being provoked, he lifted her out of her wheelchair and smiled complacently at the way she stiffened. She was at a disadvantage on two counts—she was injured and she was physically weaker—and he was letting her know it.

"You'll be more comfortable on the bed," he said, and gently set her down. Far from being intimidated, she looked as if she wanted to claw his eyes out. Even more irritating, he'd been acutely aware of her during those moments in his arms—aware of the softness of her skin, the scent of her hair and the warmth of her body.

He strolled to the dressing table, grabbed the chair and sat down by her bedside. "We need to discuss your insurance settlement. The truck that was parked illegally at the corner and the car that hit you happen to have the same carrier. Their attorneys want to dispose of the case as soon as possible, but I'd recommend waiting. You have some fairly serious injuries, and you should make sure there's no permanent damage before you agree to anything."

Sabrina was too mad about being scooped up like a sack of laundry and dumped on the bed to think about insurance. Brad Fraser had no authority over her whatsoever and it was time he acknowledged it. "What gave you the right to talk to the insurance company? I never asked you to represent me."

He grinned at her. "True enough. You're just lucky, I guess."

Angry or not, she knew he was right. She didn't have the vaguest idea how to sort this out on her own, and he *had* looked after her in the hospital. Sighing, she told herself it was stupid to keep trading barbs. They would never be friends, but they could at least be civil to each other.

She held up her index finger. "Your point, Brad. I'm lucky to have you looking after my interests. I'll be a good little girl from now on and listen to what you have to say."

"Then listen to this and get it through your head. I don't want any money from you. If you've forgotten what you said in the ambulance—"

"I haven't."

"Then we don't have to discuss it further. As far as the insurance goes, I want to try getting your immediate medical expenses paid as soon as possible while still leaving the door open for a future claim. That might not be possible, though, because the company has a reputation for stalling.

If the delay causes financial problems for you, let me know and I'll loan you whatever you need.''

Sabrina wanted to ask him if he provided free legal and banking services to all his former mistresses, but held her tongue. "That's very generous of you," she said stiffly. "I don't think I've thanked you properly for your help after the accident. Hospitals make me nervous, and it was—reassuring to have someone I knew there."

"It was the least I could do." He looked away for a moment, visibly uncomfortable. "Look, Sabrina, if I'd known how upset you were, I never would have let you leave. After the way you chewed me out, I assumed you were just mad as hell. I shouldn't have—that is, it wasn't exactly a fair match. I'm sorry I was so hard on you."

"Then you're helping me because you feel partially responsible."

"Maybe. I don't know."

"Well, you're not." She would never forget Brad's sickening accusations, but laying a guilt trip on him was foreign to her nature. "As long as we're being honest, I want you to understand that even though the things you said that day hurt me very badly, what happened afterward was a freak accident. The crosswalk was blocked, the people here drive like maniacs and I wasn't paying attention to where I was going. You're obviously spending a lot of time on my case so you should collect your normal percentage."

His jaw tightened. "No. Now if we could settle how you want me to proceed—"

"Why not?"

He ignored her. "As I said before, I'd recommend waiting before you agree to a final settlement. Can I have your approval of that?"

"You didn't answer my question."

"Damn it, I don't *have* an answer! It just doesn't feel right to take your money, okay?"

Sabrina stopped arguing. He was refusing the money because he felt guilty, but the feeling would fade in time and she would make the offer again once she'd gotten a check. "All right. Frankly, there's nothing wrong with me except a simple fracture and I'd rather have this settled and off my mind. All I care about is having my medical bills paid."

Brad didn't want to frighten her, but it was his duty to point out potential problems. "Things can go wrong, Sabrina. You hit the pavement with enough force to black out, and next week or next month you could start having seizures. Your leg might need to be rebroken and reset after the cast comes off, or you could find you need extensive physical therapy. I'd recommend waiting."

She thought that was nonsense. "If you're trying to scare me, you're not succeeding."

"I'm giving you the best legal advice I can." Brad wasn't surprised she was being stubborn—she'd given him a hard time from the moment they'd met. Maybe, he told himself, *he* was the real problem. "If you dislike having to deal with me, I can ask one of my partners to handle your case. Would that make a difference?"

"No," she insisted. "My feelings are exactly what I've said—that I want to put the accident behind me and I won't be able to do that until the insurance is settled. I wasn't that badly hurt, so there's no reason to think anything will go wrong."

Although Brad wasn't eager to raise the subject of her possible pregnancy—he'd hoped she would do it—he knew he had no choice. No attorney worth the name would fail to point out the possibility of prenatal damage or the fact that the resulting medical bills could continue for the entire life of the child and run into millions of dollars. "You told the X-ray technician that you might be pregnant. Suppose you are? Suppose the child has serious birth defects and has to be institutionalized? Do you have any idea how much that could cost?" He noticed the way she paled and realized he'd been as subtle as a sledgehammer. "I know this isn't easy for you to think about," he continued gently, "but you have no choice. Fetal damage might be a remote possibility, but it's one you have to plan for. If you *are* pregnant, I couldn't possibly allow you to settle until after the baby is born."

Sabrina remembered her conversation with the X-ray technician very well and assumed Brad did, too. Since he was nothing if not thorough, she'd known he'd eventually ask about it. She only wished he'd waited a couple of weeks, because the subject would have been moot by then.

She avoided his eyes and tried to stall him. "The truck hit my leg, not my stomach, and I fell on my hip. There won't be any problem."

"Then there's still a possibility that you're pregnant?"

She was two days late, but she'd been under a lot of stress recently. "Yes, but I won't stay that way. I never do." Knowing he would demand an explanation, she reluctantly went on, "I told you two weeks ago—I was a total failure at producing an heir. I had six straight miscarriages in Jammapur. Can we please drop the subject?"

He frowned. "Are you telling me that even if you're pregnant, you expect to miscarry? That you have some physical problem?—"

"I don't know. The doctors never found anything wrong, but I never carried to term no matter how careful I was or what medicines I tried." She was getting the same queasy, shivery feeling that she always got when she discussed her fertility problems. Desperately fighting it down, she said, "This won't be any different."

"But three years have gone by. Maybe there's been some physical change, or maybe you'll get better medical care in the West than you did in Asia." Now that Brad understood the real meaning of what she'd said that night, he felt like a heel for thinking she might have lied. Even so, he wanted to be clear about what they were discussing. "We *are* talking about my child, aren't we?"

To Sabrina it was one more horrible attack. As much as she hated putting her emotions on display for the likes of Brad Fraser, she couldn't stop her eyes from filling with tears. "I don't know how you can even ask me that. Didn't you listen to anything I said last Thursday?" She blinked and turned away. "Oh, God, what's the use? You're determined to think I'm a tramp, so go ahead and think it. It doesn't matter."

"I'm sorry. I just wanted to make sure...." Brad grimaced and stopped talking; Sabrina didn't seem to be listening. She'd buried her face in the pillow and was sobbing softly. He reached out a hand to comfort her, then pulled it back. She cringed every time he touched her.

He waited until she quieted, then said awkwardly, "I was confused, Sabrina. On Saturday you told me you couldn't have children and less than a week later you said you might be pregnant. I didn't know what to think."

She didn't answer, but she certainly must have heard. He was so stung by her low opinion of him that he wondered if she understood that he would do the right thing. "If you *are* pregnant—and if it turns out differently this time—I want you to know that I'll take full financial responsibility for the child."

How noble of you! Sabrina thought bitterly. *A Boston Brahmin to the core!* She felt like a giant open sore and wished Brad would just leave. Then she could curl into a tight little ball and pretend the outside world didn't exist.

She heard him move closer. "Sabrina? Are you okay?"

"I'm fine." Her voice was husky with tears, tears she would have done anything to take back. Brad was even more unfeeling than she'd thought, and it was mortifying to have broken down in front of him.

"You don't sound fine," he said. "You don't look fine, either."

She felt his hand on her shoulder and abruptly lost control. Why didn't he leave her alone? What in hell did he want from her? Jerking up, she yelled, "And is the child your moral responsibility, too? Are you going to publicly acknowledge it? Be a father to it?"

"Sabrina, you've got to calm down—"

"I didn't think so." She could see it in his eyes—the idea appalled him. "There probably isn't a chance in a thousand I'll actually bear a child, but if I do, you're not having anything to do with it. I don't want your money and you're not my idea of a father. Now get out of here before I—before I..." Her anger collapsed with humiliating swiftness, turning into agonizing, numbing pain. "Please—just get out of here."

Brad wasn't about to do any such thing. Sabrina was far too upset, and besides, he wasn't going to be able to live with himself until his rather tattered honor was restored. He was suddenly deeply ashamed that he'd been embarrassed by the thought of acknowledging an out-of-wedlock baby. A child was a precious thing, and you didn't punish it because of how it had been conceived.

"I seem to keep apologizing to you, but I don't know what else to do." He paused, struggling to put his feelings into words. "I wouldn't ignore my own son or daughter. When I was a kid... My parents dumped me on my grandfather and Diana when I was only seven, and for the next ten years, nobody paid any attention to me but Kathleen. It was a terrible way to grow up." He was shaken by the power of his emotions, emotions he'd scarcely realized he had. "I would never repeat that with my own child. It would kill me to cause anyone that kind of pain—to be separated from someone who was a physical part of me, someone I was supposed to love and take care of. Things just happened so fast.... What I'm trying to say is, I'm not a very adaptable person. When something happens that I'm not prepared for, I push away what I feel and then ignore it, or else analyze it to death."

Sabrina had been sure that nothing Brad could say would make a difference—that her contempt was too strong, her pain too deep—but his words were those of a desolate child. They'd been wrenched from his heart and soul. Having learned about his childhood from Kathleen, she could understand how it might have affected him, made him reserved and wary, set him at war with his emotions. Both of them had been rejected as children, but he'd coped by withdrawing while she'd tried to win over everyone she'd met.

She was as stuck with her fundamental nature as he was; she couldn't ignore someone else's pain, much less pour salt into his wounds. "I didn't mean what I said," she murmured. "I was just angry. I'm sure you'd be a wonderful father." She swallowed hard. "But not to this child. A few more weeks and there won't be any child."

"Maybe you should see a doctor—"

"It wouldn't make a difference. It was always the same— the cramps, the blood…" She shook her head. "There's no point."

"I'm sorry," he said.

She nodded, accepting the fact that he probably really was. Unfortunately, you couldn't always have what you wanted. Life didn't work that way.

He stood up. "About the insurance—I still think you should wait."

"Sure." She managed a weak smile. "You're the lawyer." The truth was that she didn't have the energy to argue.

Brad took a step forward, then paused. Sabrina's eyes were puffy from crying and her clothes were wrinkled and disheveled, but he could hardly tear himself away. There seemed to be depths to her that he'd never imagined existed, and he suddenly felt an overwhelming sympathy and tenderness. "If there's anything I can do, call me," he said, and leaned down to kiss her on the forehead.

For the first time in two weeks, she didn't recoil. Her willingness to let him come close felt like a victory, but he wasn't sure why. After all, he was still committed to Grace and Sabrina was still the wrong sort of woman to become involved with.

All of that was perfectly clear, so it didn't make sense that he should feel so confused. Faced with emotions he didn't want to have, he did what he always did—shoved them aside and thought about something else. Maybe he would check Grace's itinerary when he got home and give her a call. He'd never been to Australia and it would be fun to see it through her eyes.

He let himself out of the house and walked to his car, his thoughts already on the next day's court appearance.

Chapter Twelve

Sabrina got used to seeing Brad around town. On Friday she and Kathleen sat next to him and his cousin at a concert; the following Tuesday they attended a benefit dinner in Cambridge for his pet charity; the Sunday after that, they went to a political fund-raiser at a downtown hotel and walked in just after him.

They were more comfortable with each other each time they met, discussing everything from her leg to the upcoming mayoral election. The only hint of a deeper relationship was the protectiveness he exhibited. Having helped her after the accident and learned she might be carrying his child, he'd apparently decided it was his duty to watch over her.

By Saturday, when Kathleen insisted on taking her to one of Diana's dinner parties, she would have been surprised *not* to run into him. The doctor had replaced her original cast with a walking cast and she was looking forward to showing him how well she could get around. One glance at him and she knew he'd been sailing that day; he was smiling, relaxed and windburned. The slender redhead he was talking to was gazing at him admiringly, and with good reason. Any woman would have.

Sabrina got a warm, fluttery feeling in the pit of her stomach as she hobbled up to him, but she ignored it. She had too strong a sense of self-preservation to become involved with him again. "What do you think?" she asked. "Am I ready for the Boston Marathon?"

"Maybe next year." He introduced her to the redhead, a ballet dancer, and told her that the insurance company was being surprisingly cooperative about her claim and would pay her bills within the next month.

Diana drifted over a moment later, smiling mysteriously. Pecking the air beside Sabrina's cheek, she said, "I have a surprise for you, dear. Guess who's coming to dinner?"

It had to be someone Sabrina knew. "Good grief, not my mother!" she groaned.

"Of course not. I have more sense than that." Diana's smile widened. "I'll give you a hint. It's a he."

"A friend of mine?"

"Umm. Here's another hint. He's about five foot ten."

"That narrows the field enormously," Brad drawled.

"With dark hair and eyes."

"Another solid clue," Sabrina said.

"An English title? A polo fanatic?"

"Geoffrey Newhouse is coming? I didn't even know he was in America!" Sabrina was delighted—Geoffrey was an old riding buddy whom she hadn't seen in ages. "How—"

"I do read the gossip columns, dear, and you and Lord Newhouse were quite an item last year. When a friend mentioned he was in town for a charity polo match I called his hotel and invited him to dinner. Personally I've never met the man—until tonight, of course—but I suspected you would enjoy seeing each other."

"You mean he's already here?"

She nodded. "My sister is showing him around the house. He was interested in the antiques."

"He collects them. Of course, something isn't an antique to Geoffrey until it's three hundred years old. I used to tell him he was a terrible snob—" Sabrina heard her name and glanced over her shoulder. Geoffrey was trotting toward her, a big grin on his face.

He swept her up in his arms and kissed her on the mouth, paying no attention to her laughing protest. "For heaven's sake, Geoffrey, be careful! I don't want to have to wear this thing for another month."

"You're lovelier than ever, if that's possible." He nibbled her ear. "Ah, Sabrina, if only you'd broken your leg *last* year! You wouldn't have been able to run so fast and I would have had a sporting chance to catch you."

She put her arms around his neck. "You'd caught more than your share by then, milord. You didn't need me."

"But I did—desperately." He looked at Diana. "She was maddeningly elusive. I used to dream about having her at my mercy on a desert island, but it wasn't to be. Would you mind terribly if I carried her up to that splendid Georgian bed of yours and ravished her?"

"I certainly would. I'm ready to serve dinner." Diana took Brad's arm. "Of course, what you do afterward is your own affair. Brad, dear? Shall we?"

Brad escorted her into the dining room and seated her at the table. Sabrina was still in Newhouse's arms, he noticed, giggling like a schoolgirl. Watching them irritated the hell out of him, a feeling that grew stronger as dinner progressed. Not only was Newhouse annoyingly witty and charming; he was doing his best to convince her he couldn't live without her. His agenda couldn't have been more obvious; he'd never slept with her and meant to remedy the oversight. It didn't matter that her leg was in a cast; he probably would have dragged her to his hotel and made love to her all night if he thought he could get away with it.

The idea made Brad want to slug him. He'd be damned if some titled English lounge lizard was going to take advantage of the fact that Sabrina was in a strange city without friends or family nearby and felt isolated and lonely. Somewhere along the line, Brad had developed a feeling of protectiveness toward her.

He understood that Newhouse must be special in some way—Sabrina never would have dated him otherwise—and it worried him more than he wanted to admit. He kept a close eye on them during the rest of the evening. They exchanged some private jokes and traded looks only the two of them understood, but remained with the other guests and took part in the general conversation.

Newhouse edged closer to Sabrina as the evening wore on, finally draping his arm around her and nuzzling her hair. Fortunately, Kathleen was ready to leave by then. "I've got an early meeting tomorrow," she said to Sabrina. "We should probably be going."

"So soon?" Newhouse looked crushed. "Listen, darling, why doesn't Kathleen drop us at my hotel? It's only three blocks. You can come upstairs for a nightcap and I'll bring you home in a taxi."

She smiled at him. "I'd like that, Geoffrey. Kathleen, do you have an extra set of keys with you? I'll probably be late and I don't want to wake you."

"I don't, but Brad can give you his," she said.

Brad knew Kathleen would only suggest taking Diana's if he didn't hand them over, so he pulled them out of his pocket. He couldn't stop Sabrina from going with Newhouse, but he could let her know what she was in for. "I need a few minutes alone with you," he said. "We can talk in the den." He handed the keys to Kathleen so she could remove the ones to the front door.

Sabrina seemed to assume he wanted to discuss business, saying apologetically to Newhouse, "Brad is handling my insurance settlement, Geoffrey. I'm sure this won't take long." Brad didn't give Newhouse a chance to help her up; he did it himself, then led her into the den.

He didn't mince words once they were seated on the couch; they'd been through too much together for that.

"Newhouse has a lot more than a nightcap on his mind. He wants to take you to bed."

Far from being offended, Sabrina was thoroughly amused. Her tactful excuse to the contrary, she'd known what Brad wanted to say. Given how closely he'd watched her all evening, his protective instincts had obviously charged to the fore.

"I'm almost thirty years old," she replied. "I do know when a man wants to sleep with me."

He frowned. "Then why are you going back to his hotel with him? You'll only have to fight him off."

"We have a good time together. Besides, maybe I've decided to say yes."

"If you'd wanted to say yes, you would have done it last year," he retorted.

She was pleased he finally realized that. Of course, Geoffrey had made it quite clear that she'd repeatedly eluded his grasp. Unable to resist teasing Brad, she said, "Maybe I've changed my mind."

There was a long pause. Sabrina thought he looked rattled, as if the conversation had taken a different course from the one he'd expected. Finally he said, "I was wondering about—about your, uh, condition." She was astonished to see he was blushing. "Are you pregnant?"

She sobered. This was a serious matter, not something she would joke about. "Probably. I'm three weeks late and I feel queasy in the mornings."

"And the other—symptoms? The problems you've always had?"

"They haven't started yet. It could be a few more weeks." She'd gone this long only once before, but she didn't want to get her hopes up. Most of the time she managed not to think about it.

"If there's a chance you could be okay—what I'm trying to say is, I don't think you should take any risks."

He didn't have to spell out what sort of risk he meant. "I wasn't planning to."

"But Newhouse is going to pressure you—you'll be alone together in his room—"

"In his suite, actually, and we won't be alone. He travels with a valet and groom."

"You're sure you can handle him?"

"I've always managed to in the past."

Brad stared moodily at the floor. He didn't like the idea of Sabrina and Newhouse being alone together, but there was nothing he could do. He struggled to find something to say—to express his concern, to tell her to take care of herself—but nothing seemed right.

"Brad?" she finally murmured.

He raised his eyes. She looked vulnerable and solemn, as if his anxieties had become her own. "What?"

"I don't want you to worry. Besides, I'm more tired than I realized. I should probably go home to bed."

He felt a strong surge of relief, then an almost painful tenderness. He'd forgotten how sweet and gentle she could be, or maybe he'd convinced himself he'd only imagined it. For five weeks now, he'd been telling himself that the Sabrina he'd made love to was an illusion, but suddenly he wasn't so sure. He only wished he knew what to do about it.

Sabrina knew exactly how long her longest pregnancy had lasted before problems set in—thirty-seven days—so when the thirty-eighth day came and went with no sign of trouble, it was impossible not to start hoping. Other than a little morning sickness and some soreness in her breasts, she felt fine. Her appetite was good, she seldom felt tired and she hadn't had anything resembling a cramp in months.

Even so, when Kathleen invited her to go to a movie on Wednesday night, she declined. She'd spent the day with Geoffrey Newhouse, attending a charity luncheon and polo match, and she thought she should probably rest. Besides, there was a Boston Red Sox-Oakland Athletics game on TV and she wanted to watch it.

She made herself some popcorn and carried it into the den. The game had just gotten underway when the doorbell rang. She paused for long enough to see one of the A's belt a home run to right, then hobbled into the living room.

She looked through the side window, saw Brad outside, and opened the door. "Still didn't get that car phone, I see," she teased.

He shook his head. "No. Is Kathleen around?"

She took a good look at his face. His features were pinched, his expression grim. "She's at the movies, Brad. She won't be home for hours."

He nodded, apparently at a loss for words. Concerned now, she asked, "Is somebody in your family ill? You look upset."

"Everyone's fine. Tell Kathleen I stopped by, okay?"

"Why don't you come in? I was watching the ball game." Since it was common knowledge that the average Bostonian was a fanatical Red Sox fan, she added airily, "The A's are so much better that it's obvious they're going to win, but I'd still enjoy some company."

He looked startled at first, then scornful. "The A's aren't better than the Red Sox. The Sox are in first place in the A.L. East by four games."

"Maybe so, but your star pitcher just gave up a home run to our first batter. You don't have a prayer."

"Since you're so sure of that, how about a friendly bet? A hundred bucks say the Sox win."

"I'm not that much of a gambler. Let's make it ten."

"So much for your confidence," he drawled, finally cracking a smile.

Pleased that she'd cheered him up, she informed him that her bank account wasn't as inflated as his and led him into the den. Unfortunately, before even five minutes had gone by, he'd stopped watching the game and started staring vacantly at the wall.

She picked up the remote control rod and switched off the sound. "If you feel like talking, I'm a pretty good listener."

"Thanks for the offer, but in this case..." His voice trailed off.

Sabrina had a hunch about what might be wrong. Her last few letters from Josh had been full of Grace's name, and their tone had been almost exultant. While he hadn't spelled out what was happening, it obviously included more than sight-seeing and conversation. Brad must have found out what was going on, with the rejection hitting him like a cannonball in the gut.

She wasn't surprised that he didn't want to discuss it. Not only was the "other man" in the affair her kid brother, but Brad was too proper to spill out his feelings about Grace to a woman he'd once slept with.

Neither of those things bothered her in the least. "You got a Dear John letter from Grace today," she said bluntly. "She told you that she and Josh have been seeing each other in Australia."

"How did you?—" He grimaced. "Stupid question. You must have heard about it from the other side."

"Yes. *Now* do you feel like talking?"

The truth was that Brad had never *not* felt like it. While he'd told himself he was coming to visit Kathleen, deep down it had been Sabrina he'd wanted to see. He'd been thinking about her a lot lately—about how badly he'd misjudged her, about how sensitive she was to his moods, about how exciting she'd been in bed. As soon as the shock of receiving Grace's letter had worn off, it had struck him that she was the perfect person to cheer him up. She had a knack of saying the right things.

Still, he hadn't consciously sought her out. Between the accident and her pregnancy, he'd caused her more than enough grief already, and he hadn't wanted to dump his personal problems on her. But since she'd asked...

He leaned back on the couch and mumbled, "The funny thing is, I don't even miss her that much. I enjoyed her letters and I was glad she was having a good time, but I hardly ever thought about her. Then I got *this*—" he pulled the letter out of his pocket "—and I felt terrible. Hurt, rejected, depressed..." He shook his head. "I thought I was in love with her once, but I probably haven't believed that for a long time. Staying together was a habit—it was comfortable and even enjoyable, but on any given day there were two or three things I would rather have done than be with Grace. Sooner or later we were bound to split up, so why do I feel so lousy?"

"Because you're human. You've known her since she was a child, you've been her lover for the past three years—"

"Two," he corrected. "We didn't... That is, she was very—inexperienced at first, and I wanted to be sure in my own mind...." He reddened. "Hell, this is embarrassing."

It wasn't to Sabrina. Moving closer to him on the couch, she said, "I understand what you're trying to say—that you were the first man in Grace's life and you wouldn't have made love to her if you hadn't intended to marry her. Obviously you still did, but something was holding you back. You must have felt things weren't all they should be or you would have proposed. Once you got her letter you were forced to deal with your feelings, but it isn't easy to do."

"Why not? If what you're saying is true, I should be relieved."

Sabrina's heart went out to him. He looked so tense and miserable that she wanted to wave a magic wand and banish his emotional pain, or at least massage away the tightness in his muscles. The first was impossible, the second seemed too intimate, so she settled for doing something about the way he was dressed. Touching his tie, she said, "Nobody can relax when they're all trussed up this way. Take off your jacket and tie and unbutton your collar." He absently complied, and she continued, "You haven't had time to feel relieved. The hurt is still too new. You cared about Grace in a lot of different ways and you need to mourn the end of the relationship. Besides, nobody enjoys being rejected. My marriage was over long before my ex-husband found me with his brother-in-law and threw me out, and I still felt as if somebody had scraped me raw inside."

Brad was so startled that he almost forgot about Grace. Just when he'd decided the rumors about Sabrina were false, she admitted they were true! She *had* been in bed with Pradham, but there had to be more to it than that. She simply wouldn't have been unfaithful to her husband.

He would have given anything to ask what had happened that morning, but she might have interpreted it as another attack. He quashed his curiosity and thought about what she'd said. What had really hurt him? Losing Grace or something else?

"In a way, it was easy to be with Grace," he admitted. "I was older and more experienced than she was, so my basic role was to advise and encourage her. She made very few demands on me. As long as I took her to the right places and gave her the right presents, she was happy. She once told me she'd had a crush on me from the time she was fourteen, so maybe just dating me was enough at first. But somewhere along the line, she decided she needed more."

"And Grace?" she asked softly. "What was she to you?"

"Somebody pretty, bright and enthusiastic... Someone I've liked and cared about from the time she was ten... Someone who looked up to me and made me feel important and wanted..." He sighed and closed his eyes, feeling drained. He and Grace had had fun together, but they'd never really talked—not like this. So what had kept him around for three years? His childhood hang-ups? "Hell, I don't know. The more I think about it, the more neurotic the relationship sounds."

Sabrina smiled to herself, wondering if there was any other kind. "I came to the same conclusion about my marriage. When I was growing up, I thought of Jane, Sam and

Josh as the real family in our house, with me as Cinderella—the stepchild, the outsider. The only way to get my mother's approval was by being conventional and staying at home and the only way to get my father's was by trekking all over the world, so I couldn't win. I think it wasn't Ashoka I loved so much as his country and his family. They were supposed to become my anchor, to give me the sense of belonging I'd never had as a child."

Listening to her, Brad felt about two feet tall. Maybe he'd had a rotten childhood, but at least there hadn't been a sibling around to constantly remind him he was everyone's second choice. Grace might have left him, but he hadn't been rejected by an entire country and way of life. And he'd never come close to facing anything as anguishing as those six miscarriages.

"Translation," he said dryly. "'Welcome to the real world, Mr. Fraser. You're just like me and everyone else—just as blind, just as mixed-up—so stop feeling sorry for yourself and get on with your life.'" He sighed and rubbed his eyes. "I'm sorry to be such a pain. I'll get out of here and let you watch the game."

"You aren't feeling sorry for yourself and you're not being a pain. You're just confused, hurt and tired." While Sabrina couldn't take the sting out of Grace's rejection, she could make Brad feel better. The intimacy of the situation no longer troubled her; he needed human contact and comfort too much. If he misunderstood, she'd set him straight.

She leaned over to unbutton his shirt. As she'd expected, he didn't even move, much less respond romantically. "I'll bet you have a splitting headache," she said sympathetically.

"Yeah, I do." He raised his hand, groped for her face, stroked her cheek. "Are you as good with sore heads as you are with sore feet?"

"Absolutely. I can put you straight to sleep if I want to." She pulled his shirt out of his slacks and unbuttoned the last few buttons. "Of course, you would only wake up, check the score of the ball game and get tense all over again, so I'll just relax you and send you on your way. I know it's a terrible cliché, but things really will look brighter in the morning.''

Brad felt her tug at the lapels of his shirt and sat up so she could get it off. She pulled off his undershirt, then lightly grasped his shoulders. ''Turn your back to me. That's it. Now breathe deeply and picture yourself on your boat on a perfect summer day.''

Her thumbs slid up his backbone, strong, gentle and soothing. A sense of gratitude mixed with anticipation suffused him. His head would stop pounding, his muscles would uncoil and Grace would stop mattering. He folded his arms along the back of the couch and buried his head in them. Sabrina was working at the muscles in his shoulders, pressing, kneading and stretching them, and it felt wonderful. When he pictured himself on his boat as she'd asked him to, she was beside him.

At first he felt only relief, but other sensations gradually intruded—the distinctive scent of her, a spicy, erotic fragrance he associated with the East...the feel of her skin, so smooth and soft...the heat of her body, which warmed his back when she bent over him to put the full strength of her arms and shoulders into her work.

She massaged the small of his back with her fingertips, then applied pressure with the heels of her hands and slid them slowly upward. Her thumbs found the muscles at the back of his neck, moving firmly back and forth, again and again. He moaned and slid lower, marveling that she could be so mobile when her leg was in a cast. She was so close he could feel her breath on his neck and hear the soft grunts she made when her efforts were especially taxing. Fatigue had put him into a sort of fog, but his senses were crystal clear— and focused entirely on her.

His body was stretching, slackening, melting. He was conscious of a warm, low ache as well, but it was pleasurable rather than painful. He wanted to touch her, to caress her hair and face, but the need wasn't intense. The things she was doing were too soothing to interrupt. He sat there like a docile child, letting her massage him into a state of blissful relaxation, so enervated and content that even moaning with pleasure was eventually beyond him.

"Are you still awake?" she finally whispered.

He nodded. "Umm."

"Do you feel better?"

He looked over his shoulder. Sabrina was propped up on one knee, her broken leg trailing behind her at an awkward angle. "Much better." He sat up, slid one arm beneath her knees and the other around her back, and resettled her on the couch in a more comfortable position. "With very little coaxing I could let you go on all night. Where did you learn to do that?"

"It's part of being a good Jammapuri wife, and I wasn't finished. I haven't done your temples or scalp yet. The benefit is lost if you don't receive the full treatment."

Brad mumbled that she really didn't have to, but when she placed a pillow on her lap and pointed, he stretched out on his back without a murmur of protest. He still had a headache and her fingers were absolute magic.

He started to watch her, but she claimed it made her self-conscious. "Close your eyes and think about your boat. If you're cold—"

"I'm not." If anything, he was warm, becoming more so when she placed her thumbs on his temples and traced a pair of firm, gentle circles. If this wasn't heaven, he didn't know what was, unless... "Sing to me," he said thickly. If she wouldn't let him look at her, he wanted everything else—her scent, her touch, her voice.

He didn't recognize the lively, lilting melody she chose, and even the words were in a strange language. "What is that? A Jammapuri folk song?"

"A love song." She'd finished with his temples and was working on his scalp. He hadn't known that anything not connected to lovemaking could feel so good.

"What did the words mean?"

"It's about a mouse who falls in love with a cow, begs her to marry him and gets crushed in the act of consummation. It's the Jammapuri way of warning people not to violate the natural order of things."

He smiled. "You made that up. What's it *really* about?"

"A god who develops a passion for a married woman. He kidnaps her and takes her to his castle in the mountains. He slips on the ice and drops her, and she breaks her neck and dies. Same moral."

He didn't believe *that*, either. "You have a morbid sense of humor," he said. These quirky tales of mismatched lovers were having an uncomfortable effect on his libido.

"Okay, then. It's about a shepherd and his goats. The winters are long and cold in the mountains, and it gets lonely—"

"A morbid sense of humor and a dirty mind," he interrupted, laughing now. "I'm not going to bother asking you again. You'd only come up with another crazy story— maybe a sculptress who falls in love with her chisel—"

"Now who's being perverse? Anyway, I got a laugh out of you, didn't I? See? Life isn't so terrible."

As far as Brad was concerned, it wasn't terrible at all. On the contrary, blind luck had embraced him as her personal favorite and brought him to this particular spot, to this particular woman. He couldn't imagine why he'd been so depressed about Grace, not when someone as enchanting as Sabrina was part of his life. If he'd had any brains, he would have trusted what he'd felt the first night they'd met instead of letting his paranoia almost destroy it.

He turned onto his side, his face only inches from her belly. "Could I talk you into rubbing the back of my neck?"

"Sure. By the way, the A's are ahead four to nothing. You can give me the hundred bucks before you leave."

"It's only ten, but I'm not going to argue. God, that feels good." He understood that the massage was purely therapeutic—her only goal was to ease his pain—but his arousal was difficult to ignore. Besides, he didn't see why he should. They'd enjoyed each other physically in the past and his intentions were strictly honorable.

He raised his hand, slid it along her hip to her waist, and slipped it under her cotton sweater. Instead of flesh, he felt silk. "What are you wearing?"

"It's a teddy—"

"A what?"

"A teddy. Everything's one piece. Now behave yourself and put your hand back where it belongs."

"Cast out of paradise," he said sadly. "If it's all one piece, how do you get it on?"

"Over my head. There are snaps on the bottom. With the cast, it's easier that way."

"Fascinating." The thought of the snaps was so erotic that his hand strayed back to her waist, pushing up her sweater so he could nuzzle her belly.

Sabrina was patient and understanding, so Brad's maneuvers didn't fluster her. She realized he'd received a painful rejection this evening and was emotionally vulnerable; she'd been touching him for close to thirty minutes and had unwittingly aroused him. Since he found her attractive, it wasn't surprising that he would turn to her for reassurance about his masculinity.

The problem was to find a balance between her needs and his—to let him know that a physical relationship was out of the question without bruising his ego. "My teddy is going to get wet if you keep doing that," she joked.

"Then take it off." He cupped one of her breasts and pinched the nipple through the lace and silk of her teddy, rolling it between his finger and thumb until it hardened. The physical pleasure made her feel warm and a little lightheaded, but she knew she had to stop him. He was making love to her for all the wrong reasons.

"That wouldn't be a good idea," she said, and tugged at his hair. He paid no attention, teasing her other nipple until it was tingling and erect. She wasn't just warm now, she was hot—and in places she preferred not to think about. "You have to leave now," she insisted. "When I offered to relax you, I didn't mean like this."

"I know you didn't, but I'm enjoying it all the same. Your breasts are fuller." He nuzzled them. "I like that."

"For heaven's sake, Brad—" Sabrina gasped softly as his mouth closed over a nipple and sucked it hard. Erotic excitement scorched through her, playing havoc with her defenses. All she could think about was having his mouth directly on her breast, without the silk of her teddy in between.

She stopped tugging at his hair and caressed it, arching against his lips. He was fondling her with one hand and holding her tightly around her back with the other, arousing her with such an electrifying mixture of possessiveness and passion that she lost the will to resist. Her husband had never made love to her this way—as if he'd go crazy if he couldn't have her—and the sensation was intoxicating. To Ashoka, one woman had been as good as another, but Brad wanted *her*.

The thought brought her up short. Was she crazy? He didn't want her at all, but solace, reassurance and physical relief. She was a generous woman, but not *that* generous.

She pushed at his shoulders, but weakly, uncertainly. It was one thing to tell herself she was making a mistake, another to fight down the needs he'd aroused. "I meant what I said before. I want you to stop."

The sharp little nip he gave her made her shudder. He kissed his way to her neck, murmuring, "If you had any idea how much that turns me on..." He found her mouth a moment later, just as she realized what he'd meant. Her arms were captured in both of his and pulled around his neck, her lips nipped and stroked with a teasing expertise that left her breathless. She wanted to tell him it wasn't a game from the *Kama Sutra*—saying stop but meaning go, telling him no when the answer was really yes—but nothing would come out. The plain truth was that she wanted to be talked into this—wanted him to ignore her objections and arouse her until she was too excited to stop.

She dug her nails into his back and pulled her mouth away. "You're confusing me. I didn't want you to touch me ever again—"

"That was a month ago." He turned her face back to his and toyed with her lips until she gave in and parted them. He was good at kissing—very good—and the things he was doing with his tongue and teeth made her feel languorous and hot. She clung to him and kissed him back, silently surrendering to his demands. The pure, wild pleasure he'd given her had aroused a fiery need for release, leaving her stunned and vulnerable.

When he pulled his mouth away, she opened her eyes and looked at him dazedly. He was staring at her as if he owned her. "I'm going to make you feel good," he said, "very good."

He pulled off her sweater, pushed her teddy to her waist and began to make love to her again. She felt like a puppet, responding helplessly as he pulled all the right strings—kissing her deeply, then playfully...caressing her teasingly, and then, as her excitement mounted, more roughly...slipping his hand under her skirt and finding the snaps of her teddy, but not unfastening them until he'd fondled and stroked her into feverish submission. Then flesh touched flesh, and she turned into something hungry, savage and frantic.

She felt as disoriented as she had after her accident when it was finally over. After wiggling out of his arms, she saw what she'd done to him with her teeth and nails and wanted to sink through the floor. His bottom lip was puffy and there were fine, light scratches on his shoulders. He was also visibly aroused, and holding himself in check only with an obvious effort.

She touched his lip. "I'm sorry."

"Don't apologize. I loved every minute of it." His voice was hoarse, his smile strained. "I've read about this stuff in books, but it's never actually happened to me before. If that's how they make love in Jammapur..."

It was, but with her husband she'd done it because it was expected of her, not because she'd been carried away by passion. She'd learned her lessons well, though, and Brad was obviously very uncomfortable. He started shaking when she reached for his belt, watching her intently as she unbuckled it and zipped down his fly. Neither of them said a word, but the moment she actually touched him, he pulled her into his arms and urgently took her mouth.

Brad couldn't have spoken even if he'd wanted to. He was so aroused he figured he'd explode within seconds, but Sabrina was applying pressure in a confusing, unfamiliar way, inflaming him and slowing him down at the same time. If torture and bliss could be combined, she was doing it. He stroked her breasts and kissed her more deeply, desperately seeking the satisfaction he needed in the curves of her body and the sweetness of her mouth.

She fondled and caressed him, using her fingertips, her palms and even her nails, causing pleasure to mingle with pain, ecstasy with frustration. He finally stopped fighting and let her have her way—let her tease him, manipulate his responses and drive him into a frenzy of longing. When release finally came, he thought he would shatter into a million pieces.

When the pleasure had eased off and he could move again, he grinned from ear to ear. Reaching for his shirt, he teased, "So that's what they do in the mysterious East. My, uh—lingam—may never be the same."

Sabrina blushed and lowered her eyes. She didn't regret what had happened—it had given both of them a great deal of pleasure—but the situation hadn't changed. Things had been said that could never be taken back, hurts inflicted that would never heal. She was willing to be Brad's friend, but she would never again trust him enough to be his lover.

He helped her dress, then put his arm around her. "Check out the score, sweetheart. It's six to four, Sox. Where's my hundred?"

"It was ten. Listen, Brad, we have to talk—"

"I know." He stroked her belly. "It's been five and a half weeks since the first time we made love. I want you to see Kathleen's doctor. He's an old friend of the family so I should be able to get you in before the end of the week."

Sabrina had been thinking the same thing—that she should really see a doctor—and Kathleen's was sure to be a good one. She was willing to see him, and even willing to acknowledge Brad's right to come along, but that was where her obligations ended. "All right, but you seem to be assuming we'll have some relationship besides sharing a child. And we won't."

Brad figured she was still angry with him, and not without reason. "I don't think I've ever really apologized for the things I said to you in my office. I acted like a prize jerk that day. I'm sorry."

"So you don't think I've had a string of lovers."

"I know you haven't."

"And you don't think I was ever in bed with my brother-in-law."

"Obviously you were, but not because you were having an affair. You'll tell me about it when you're ready."

"And you don't mind that I set you up just to help my father? That I put him first even though I was supposedly in love with you?"

Brad frowned. He didn't want to quarrel with her, but he wasn't going to lie, either. "If you want the truth, it would bother me tremendously if I thought you'd really done that, but something else was going on that night. You just won't tell me what it was."

"And you can live with that."

"I don't have much choice," he said evenly.

Sabrina was surprised by how patient he was being, but that didn't mean anything had changed. His contempt and distaste had been deep-seated and strong; one little mistake on her part, one inadvertent slipup and they'd resurface. Besides, his low opinion of her wasn't the only issue.

She reminded him that only two hours before he'd been devastated because Grace had rejected him, then added, "You turned to me because you needed reassurance that you were still desirable, and because Grace has been gone for a month and you're a healthy human male with all the usual instincts. You once lectured me about love—that it included things like honesty and trust—but all we have together is physical compatibility. I want more than that in a relationship."

"I could have called a dozen different women if all I'd wanted were sex and reassurance," he retorted, "and I wouldn't have had to limit myself to fooling around on the couch, either. I talked to you because you're sensitive and sympathetic, and I made love to you because I care about you. You wouldn't have responded if you hadn't felt the same way."

Sabrina sighed. She knew he cared, but it wasn't enough. "You feel guilty about the accident. I'm carrying your child. It's only natural for you to be concerned about me, but that has nothing to do with wanting me as a person. And I responded because I'm physically attracted to you, which has nothing to do with wanting *you* as a person."

"So why do we enjoy being with each other and talking to each other? For God's sake, Sabrina, only a month ago you told me you loved me. I'm still the same man."

"But not the one I thought you were." She folded her arms across her chest, physically withdrawing, and he reluctantly moved away. "I'll never forget the way you treated me. Never."

"I was frustrated. You wouldn't tell me why Kathleen was so important—what you wanted in Asia—and I lost my temper. If you'd only be honest with me—"

"I thought you weren't going to question me."

Brad stood up and strode across the room. This conversation was getting him nowhere. Sabrina hadn't forgiven him yet, she had the most cockeyed notions about his feelings that he'd ever come across and she simply didn't trust him not to hurt her. Maybe he deserved all that, but he'd finally figured out what he wanted—her—and he wasn't giving up till he got it.

"You once told me I was mean-spirited and petty. Maybe you still think so, but if you do, you're as wrong about me as I was about you. Both of us were hurt and angry that day, and both of us lost our tempers. That's *all* it was—not some deep, meaningful exchange of basic truths about each other's characters. We have a lot going for us, including a child—"

"Which I'll probably lose."

"Not this time, you won't. You're going to the doctor as soon as I can get you an appointment and you're marrying me before you go to Asia."

Sabrina began to seethe. Who did he think he was, to tell her what she was going to do with the rest of her life? "I'm sorry if it bothers you to have a bastard around, but I'm not marrying you. I've made one mistake in that department already and I'm not about to make a second."

"We'll see," Brad said. This was going to be harder than he'd thought, but he could be patient when he needed to be. Sabrina was obviously going to require some intensive courting before she'd agree to marry him, so he'd have to rearrange his schedule in order to go to Asia. The trip was only two weeks away, but it could be done. Besides, he'd be able to keep an eye on Kathleen that way.

He returned to the couch and gently took her hand, earning himself a decidedly suspicious look. "I'd want to marry you even if you weren't pregnant, but since you are, will you let me take you to the doctor?"

Sabrina had no legitimate reason to refuse, especially since he'd asked rather than ordered. "All right, but I don't want you talking to him about our personal situation."

"Not a word. I promise. I'll call you after I arrange an appointment." He pecked her on the forehead, grabbed his jacket and tie, and left the room.

Sabrina stared irritably at the television, then saw the score flash on and smiled. "Hey, Brad, the A's are winning seven to six!" she yelled. "Bring that hundred bucks with you when we go to the doctor."

"The game isn't over yet!" he yelled back. Somehow she had the feeling he wasn't talking about baseball.

Chapter Thirteen

Brad didn't mention the ball game when he phoned Sabrina on Thursday about her doctor's appointment, but Boston had lost in the tenth inning and she had no intention of letting him forget it. The best way to handle him, she'd decided, was to refuse to take him seriously—to treat him like a casual friend. Eventually he was bound to realize that lust, being on the rebound and wanting to avoid gossip were hardly sound bases for a marriage.

She greeted him the next day with an open palm. He looked frazzled, maybe because it was almost five and he'd been fighting the rush-hour traffic. "In case you didn't hear the final score—"

"I heard it. The A's won thanks to good luck and bad umpiring, but I always pay my debts." He removed a small box from his inside jacket pocket and handed it to her.

If he'd bought her an expensive piece of jewelry she wasn't going to accept it. She ripped off the wrapping paper and opened it. There were six tickets inside, two box seats to each of the three Red Sox–A's games scheduled for mid-September. She might have been impressed by his originality if she hadn't noticed the perforations along the edges.

She rolled her eyes. "I see I can add cheapness to the list of your many faults. These came from a sheet of season tickets. I'll bet they didn't cost you an extra cent—you probably already owned them. You probably even expect me to take you along."

"I'll have you know I had to negotiate for those seats," he said. "Every one of my partners wanted to go to those games." He put his arm around her waist and helped her outside, closing the door behind them. "Besides, ball games are expensive nowadays. There's gas, parking, food—"

"Thirty-three dollars a game will buy a lot of hot dogs and peanuts."

"That's three dollars and thirty-three cents, and if the *Sox* had won on two bad calls and a bloop single, you probably would have said it was highway robbery and refused to pay."

"Of course I would have paid." She grinned at him as she got into the car. "In pennies, maybe, or one-cent postage stamps."

He slid into the driver's seat but didn't start the engine. "I did bring you something else."

"I can't wait! What is it? A complete set of Red Sox baseball cards?"

"Nothing so valuable." He pulled out another box, the kind that usually held a ring. Even so, Sabrina was taken aback by the large pear-shaped diamond inside.

She snapped down the top and handed it back to him. "It's very nice, but I prefer round ones."

"You mean you're passing up the chance to marry me?"

"I'm afraid so, but thanks for asking." She peered outside. "Traffic is awfully heavy. Shouldn't we be going?"

He tucked the box in his pocket and pulled away from the curb. "You're making a big mistake. You should accept the

ring and pawn it, then spend the profits on things you can't
afford because your trip to Asia isn't fully subscribed."

"There are only three open spots, and that translates into
a very nice profit. We won't starve."

"Two open spots," he said. "I'm coming along."

Sabrina hadn't expected that particular ploy—Brad was
a busy attorney—and was momentarily nonplussed. Good
grief, she couldn't have him trailing around after her in
Asia, watching her like a hawk and brandishing his ring! She
and her father had arrangements to make about Maya, none
of them with model citizens.

She was tempted to tell him she'd marry him if he'd
promise to stay home, but he would only wonder what she
was up to. "How exciting for you," she said. "Have you
told your law partners about this?"

He nodded. "They understand completely. If *their* aunt
were running around with your father, they'd want to keep
an eye on her, too. By the way, I called Kathleen in her office this morning and spoke to her about those papers she's
been working on. I've decided to join you on the side trips,
too."

"Oh?" Sabrina stifled a groan, thinking that things had
gone from bad to worse.

"Is there something wrong with that? You look pale."

She looked out the window. "It can be difficult to get
visitor's permits and visas on such short notice..."

"That's what Kathleen said, at least until I informed her
that if *I* don't go, nobody does. My father may not have the
influence to get people *into* restricted area, but he can certainly keep them out. All he has to do is make the right re-
quests to the right officials." He touched her cheek, then
added gently, "It would make it easier on both of us if you
would tell me why the idea of having me along worries you
so much."

"It doesn't worry me. I just don't want to have to keep
fending off you and your proposals."

"You won't have to do either. My only concern is for your safety. You don't find ancient statues by requesting information at the national museum; you do it by dealing with art thieves, smugglers and fences. Your father can do what he wants, but you and Kathleen aren't getting involved."

Sabrina didn't reply. His presence was going to complicate matters immeasurably, but there was nothing she could do about it. The more she objected, the more suspicious he would get.

Confiding in him was out of the question. If he thought searching for the statue was dangerous, he would go through the roof if he found out about her plans for Maya. And then he'd go straight to his father and have their passports revoked.

Taking her silence for compliance, he switched on the radio and changed the subject to Kathleen's doctor, Bob Wheeler, whom he'd known all his life. He assured her that Wheeler was an excellent doctor—a good listener and uncanny diagnostician whose patients adored him.

Sabrina realized he'd picked up on her fear of doctors during their conversations about her leg and was trying to reassure her. She was grateful for that, and impressed by Wheeler's gentleness and intelligence, but Wheeler was also extremely thorough. He questioned her at such length about the tests she'd had in Delhi and about her six miscarriages that she wound up in tears.

Brad finally told him to stop, then took her in his arms and promised her that everything would be all right—that *this* pregnancy would be different. His words were so confident and compelling that she couldn't help believing them. Suddenly his insistence on going to Asia wasn't so terrible at all.

After the examination, Wheeler walked back to his office with her and told her and Brad that everything had looked normal. In view of her history he wanted her to have some additional tests, but the fact that she'd gone six weeks without the usual problems was a good sign. He made some suggestions about her diet and cautioned her about staying away from alcohol and certain medications, then set up a schedule of prenatal visits. He added that he strongly recommended Lamaze classes, and finally, to her embarrassment, informed her that, although she and Brad might want to wait until after her test results came back, they could enjoy intimate relations as long as they were reasonably restrained.

Afterward he asked them if they had any questions. Both of them said no, but the minute they reached the car Brad claimed he was worried about the definition of "reasonable restraint." "I wonder exactly how excited I'm allowed to get you. Is panting okay? Thrashing and moaning? Biting and scratching?"

Sabrina knew she'd never hear the end of it if she took him seriously. "All you have to do is look at me and I lose control of myself. Touching me is out of the question."

He pondered that for a moment. "Maybe I could tie you to the bedposts—for your own protection, of course. You can't hurt yourself if you can't move."

"No chains could possibly contain my passion for you," she said tartly. "You'll have to make the supreme sacrifice and embrace celibacy."

He flashed her a smile and pulled into traffic. She didn't trust that smile; it was too damn confident, the kind that said he could change her mind within five minutes of getting her alone in bed. That question wasn't *if* he'd eventually try it; it was when.

It took her a full week to realize that he'd been teasing her that day, not proclaiming the inevitability of her seduction. Her first clue came when he joined her and Kathleen for dinner on Saturday and didn't lay a finger on her, not even when Kathleen went out to buy coffee and left them alone on the couch. On Monday he accompanied her to the hospital for her tests and on Wednesday he drove her to have her cast removed, but his manner remained gentle, protective and platonic. And when Howard returned from Australia on Friday and Brad stopped by Kathleen's to give him a check for the trip to Asia, his only apparent concern was the condition of Sabrina's leg. She accused him of being disappointed that it had healed so well, thereby denying him the opportunity to sue, but he only laughed. He claimed he had more than enough to do before their departure on Wednesday without scheduling another meeting with the insurance company.

She looked at Howard and Kathleen, who were immersed in a private conversation. "If you're really that busy, you should skip the appointment with Dr. Wheeler," she said softly. They were seeing him on Monday to discuss her test results.

"I've already blocked out the time. I'll pick you up at ten-thirty." He walked her into the hall, then continued, "I wouldn't let you go to Bob's without me. I want to be there to share the good news."

"You're sure it will be good news," she murmured.

"Positive." He kissed her for the first time in a week, but it was only an impersonal peck on the forehead. "Between the fertility goddess and my astonishing virility, there's no other possibility. Good night, Sabrina."

She wished him good-night and watched wistfully as he walked to his car. There was a time when he would have called her sweetheart instead of Sabrina, but he hadn't said anything romantic in a week. He was treating her exactly the way she wanted, so why did she feel so lonely and restless?

Chapter Fourteen

Things weren't going at all the way Brad had planned, a state of affairs that was doubly frustrating in view of how well they'd gone at first. Eight days ago he'd expected to have his ring on Sabrina's finger before they reached Pakistan, but now, squatting five feet away from him in a bunch of godforsaken ruins in the arid province of Sind, she was farther from his grasp than ever. Their relationship had gone backward instead of forward, but he had no idea why.

Their final few days in Boston couldn't have been more perfect if he'd written the script himself. On Sunday they'd had dinner with Grace and Josh, an evening that had started with awkward pleasantries and ended with comfortable laughter. Brad had been brilliant that night, admitting to Grace that their relationship had lacked something vital and taking full responsibility for it, expressing just the right amount of regret at their parting, and wishing her and Josh well. Then—the pièce de résistance—he'd offered to help them in the future in any way that he could. Sabrina had been dazzled.

On Monday, after Dr. Wheeler had assured them that everything looked fine, Sabrina had thrown herself into Brad's arms and sobbed against his shoulder. Holding her, he'd been overcome by emotion. He hadn't known it was possible to feel such tenderness for a woman, such heady exhilaration simply because she needed him. He'd wanted to propose again on the spot, but had driven her back to his house for a quiet celebration instead. There had been a moment when he'd been sure she wanted him to kiss her, but he'd deliberately held back. He'd wanted her to come to him, and had been confident it wouldn't take long.

Maybe it was the weight of her responsibilities, but as soon as they'd reached Asia everything had changed. They'd flown from New York to London to pick up the European contingent of the group, then continued on to Karachi, Pakistan. Everyone was exhausted by then, so Thursday was lightly scheduled—a bus tour of the city and a visit to a local tailor, where each woman in the party ordered several *salwar kamis*, the loose pants and flowing shirts that the natives wore. The costumes helped eliminate problems with Pakistani men, who were notorious for pinching Western women and making suggestive comments to them.

The next day, Friday, was the Muslim day of rest, so almost everything was closed. They rested, then listened to the lectures Lang had arranged on subcontinental history and culture. By Sunday afternoon, when they left Karachi, Brad understood why a Howard Lang tour was special. He didn't herd people to the same old monuments and museums; he took them behind the scenes and to places where only natives went, then educated and entertained them. Sabrina even taught them how to bargain, then led them through a local bazaar and helped them shop. Since Pakistan had no nightlife to speak of, they made their own entertainment—

special speakers and dinners or sing-alongs that Sabrina led with her guitar.

They spent Sunday night and Monday in Hyderabad, then continued north to Larkana, the town nearest Mohenjo-daro, one of the major cities of the Harappan civilization. The monsoon had started to blow, adding a sticky feeling to the air, but nobody complained. They were bused to Mohenjo-daro early Tuesday morning and spent the day trekking around the stark, treeless site. It contained ancient buildings that had been excavated and restored by archaeologists, a Buddhist *stupa*, or bell-shaped shrine, dating to about 200 A.D., and a modern museum.

Brad wasn't happy that Sabrina was tramping around in humid, ninety-degree air—he was damp with sweat by early afternoon—but there wasn't anything he could do about it. They hadn't been alone for a week now and their relationship had grown disturbingly distant. Besides, her father had disappeared to God only knew where the previous evening and the group was now her responsibility.

She looked tired and hot as she trudged to the bus, and they still had a full schedule ahead. After returning to their hotel to pack and eat, they traveled up to Sukkur, which turned out to be greener and cooler than Larkana. When there was no sign of Howard at their new hotel, Brad forgot his decision not to interfere with how Sabrina did her job and asked in a nettled voice where her father was.

She glanced around at the other people in the group, then said with a strained smile, "In Quetta. He had to see a man about a statue."

Brad seriously doubted it. Howard planned to follow up rumors that the statue was in a Buddhist monastery, but Quetta, a city near the Afghan border, had been founded by Muslims in the tenth century and had no tie to Buddhism whatsoever. Something else was going on, but Sabrina didn't want to talk about it.

Questioning her would be a waste of time—she would only keep lying—so he asked when Howard was due back. "He's meeting us in either Multan or Lahore," she replied.

They would reach Multan on Thursday, Lahore on Friday. "You're talking about two or three days without his help—"

"A Pakistani professor—a colleague of Kathleen's—will be joining us in the morning and traveling with us as far as Peshawar." She turned to a middle-aged couple from England, who'd asked a question about the Sukkur barrage, the largest irrigation project in the world.

Brad was muttering to himself about how evasive she'd become when Kathleen strolled up to him. "I could use a cold drink. Will you keep me company?"

The soda, however, was only an excuse. The moment they were seated in the restaurant, she asked baldly, "What's going on between you and Sabrina?"

"Me and Sabrina?" He looked at her ingenuously. "I don't know what you mean."

"I think you do, but since you insist on playing dumb... You watch her every minute and she pretends she doesn't notice. Whenever you're in the same room, the tension is so thick you could cut it with a knife." She paused. "Howard says you're having an affair. Did you have a fight?"

He wasn't admitting a thing. "Suppose I asked what was going on between you and Howard? Would you tell me?"

"No, but only because you disapprove of him so much. I don't disapprove of Sabrina."

In reality, Brad's opinion of Howard had improved, at least until he'd taken off for Quetta. Howard was the best tour guide he'd ever met, and, more important, treated Kathleen like a queen. Not only did he talk to her in a special, gentle way, he continually checked her reaction when he was speaking to the group as a whole, obviously seeking her approval. Much to Brad's astonishment, Howard really seemed to care for her. Of course, he could love her deeply and still be involved in schemes she knew nothing about.

"Maybe I was a little rough on him at first," he said. "He has his good points."

"And his bad ones, too, but that isn't what we were discussing. About you and Sabrina . . ."

"She's a beautiful woman and I'm a lonely, rejected man. Why *wouldn't* I watch her?"

"Because only a boor would do that, and you were raised to know better. Anyway, you don't just watch; you brood, as if you're afraid something terrible is going to happen."

"Do I?" He looked amazed. "How extraordinary!"

"Obviously you're not going to explain why." She sighed and shook her head. "At a minimum, dear, could you try not to be so obvious about it?"

Brad said he would do his best and summoned their rather sleepy-eyed waiter. It surprised him to learn he'd been obvious; as an attorney he prided himself on his subtlety and finesse. It just went to show what could happen to a guy when he fell as hard as Brad had.

He thought about stopping by Sabrina's room that night, but he wouldn't have known what to say. He couldn't order her to get more rest; she had a job to do. He couldn't upbraid her for her father's absence, either; it wasn't her fault. In the end he did what he always did—swore to keep a close eye on her in case anything went wrong.

Their next stop, Kot Diji, was the site of ruins even older than those at Mohenjo-daro, and an archaeological dig was currently in progress. Howard had arranged for the group to help out, but the work was so exacting and exhausting that they would probably leave by noon.

Brad positioned himself close to Sabrina and sifted through some sand. Fifteen minutes went by, then thirty. People were enjoying themselves enormously despite the heat and humidity, savoring the opportunity to do something important and unusual. Somebody spotted part of a terra-cotta animal and shrieked; somebody else dug out a shard of pottery and waved it at Dr. Mirza, Kathleen's historian friend, who'd met them at the site.

Brad kept looking at Sabrina. Rivulets of sweat were running down her cheeks, which were flushed and splotchy in the midmorning heat. Like all the women, she was wearing a Pakistani scarf over her head, and she grabbed one of the ends every now and then and wiped her forehead. Suddenly, to Brad's alarm, she took a deep breath and closed her eyes, then sat motionless in the sand with her hands clenched into fists and the color draining from her face.

He tensed. Obviously she wasn't feeling well, but he hated to embarrass her by dragging her away. He was resigning himself to the tongue-lashing he would probably receive when she looked straight at him. It wasn't the sort of look he was used to, the kind that said he was just another member of the group, but an intimate plea for help.

"I don't feel well," she whispered. "Please..."

He practically trampled the person next to him in his haste to reach her side. She was panting now, and so weak and limp that when he lifted her into his arms she could barely hold on. Dr. Mirza hurried over with his car keys, telling Brad to get her a soft drink from his ice chest and then drive her back to the hotel. He and Dr. Carlisle, he added, would supervise the group for the rest of the day.

Mirza's Jeep was only a few years old, and, much to Brad's relief, air-conditioned. He got Sabrina inside, then wrapped some ice from Mirza's cooler in his handkerchief and sponged off her face. She couldn't manage the bottle of soda by herself—it almost slipped from her grasp—so he held it to her lips. After a minute or so the color returned to her face and she was able to drink it on her own.

She fell asleep as soon as she finished the soda, only awakening when they reached the hotel and he gently shook her shoulder. Although she looked much better, he couldn't stop himself from scolding her. "You weren't just sick from the heat; you were exhausted. Are you getting enough sleep?"

She opened her door. "I'm fine, Brad. This sort of thing can happen to anyone. It had nothing to do with being pregnant."

She hadn't answered his question, but he let it pass. Obviously she *wasn't* fine, because she waited for him to lift her out of the Jeep and allowed him to put his arm around her as they walked into the hotel. He stopped at the desk to ask that some hot tea be sent to her room and then carried her upstairs. While she didn't feel like dead weight anymore, her arms were limp around his neck.

It wasn't until he'd closed her door and set her on her feet that he saw the panic in her eyes. "I need to use the bathroom," she said. "I'll just be a minute."

He swallowed a stab of fear. "Is something wrong?"

"I don't know."

"Can you manage by yourself?"

She nodded and walked away, more slowly than she probably would have preferred. Brad watched the door close behind her, then made himself comfortable on the bed. There was a black binder on her night table and he distractedly picked it up. It contained information pertaining to their tour—on hotels, restaurants, shops, museums and so on. He began to thumb through it, but he was much too worried to concentrate on anything it said.

Inside the bathroom, Sabrina slipped off her clothes, her heart pounding out of control and her hands shaking convulsively. She'd felt something awful in the bedroom—a dampness between her legs—and she was terrified to find out what it was. It had happened so many times in the past...the sensation of wetness, the sight of blood, the cramping that inevitably followed. But when she finally screwed up her courage and looked, she saw only normal body fluids. There wasn't even a tinge of pink, much less the awful red of fresh blood.

She sat down on the floor and buried her head in her hands. She'd felt so good during the past few weeks that she'd convinced herself there was nothing to worry about, but it hadn't taken much to yank her back to reality. Dr. Wheeler's assurances to the contrary, she had a miserable history behind her. Maybe she'd been pushing herself too hard.

Between Brad's constant scrutiny and the situation with Maya, she could barely sleep at night. She couldn't do anything about Maya—not yet—and Brad would be even more protective after what had happened at Kot Diji, so how was she going to stay sane? She wished her father were back, if only to handle the dozens of little problems that arose even in a group as congenial as this one.

Taking a deep breath, she dressed and opened the door. She wasn't eager to face Brad, but he deserved an explanation. He'd looked almost as worried as she'd been.

When she saw the black binder on his lap, sheer instinct took over. Without thinking, she rushed to the bed and snatched it out of his hands, so agitated she almost knocked over the pot of tea on the night table. Then, realizing how strange her behavior must have seemed, she laughed uneasily. "You shouldn't look at that. You'll find out about the surprises we've planned."

He laced his hands together behind his head and studied her. "There's something in that binder you don't want me to see."

"I told you, if you find out about our plans—"

"Not that. Something else. Don't lie to me, Sabrina. You're lousy at it."

She clutched the binder harder, reddening now. There was no point arguing; he had her pegged. "I think you should leave," she said.

"I disagree. You look as nervous as a mouse in a roomful of hungry cats. It's bad for you and it's bad for the baby. You need to relax." He sat up. "If you don't want me to look through the binder, I won't, but I want you to do something for me in return. Give me the binder and let me put it away, then get into bed and drink your tea."

He was asking her to trust him, but she couldn't do it. Trembling now, she shook her head and took a step backward.

He got up. "Sabrina, before I met you I made certain judgments about you based on what I'd read. I freely admit I should have known better; I can't even begin to count how many of my clients have had inaccurate information published about them. But I didn't, and during a time when I was feeling really burned, I said some very hurtful things to you. I'm deeply sorry about that, but I can't change it. Now you're convinced that my initial opinion was somehow fundamental, and that if we disagree about something I'll throw it up to you, but that's simply not true. I've been wrong enough times in my life to realize I make mistakes and learn from them. Except for that day in my office, have I done anything to violate your trust? Have I made a single promise I didn't keep?"

Sabrina knew the answer as well as he did. It was no. On the contrary, he'd taken her to doctors and hospitals even when he was pressed for time and he'd lifted her spirits when she was worried about her pregnancy. "You've been good to me," she admitted.

"I certainly hope so, since I happen to love you." He turned back the covers on the bed and held out his hand. "Give me the binder and get into bed."

As she debated what to do, an earlier conversation came to mind—the first one with Dr. Wheeler, when she'd broken down and Brad had taken her in his arms and promised her everything would be all right. The force of his personality had been so great that day that she'd believed him, just as she believed him now. Feeling as if he'd cast a spell over her, she handed him the binder and let him tuck her into bed.

He walked to the bureau, put the binder into a drawer and returned to her bedside. "About that dash into the bathroom—"

"Everything's fine." She explained what had frightened her, then picked up her tea.

Looking relieved, he sat down at her side and put his hand on her belly. His touch was reverent rather than sensual, an expression of his awe at the life that was growing inside her. There had been a time when she'd longed for a different sort of caress, but the erotic part of her had died. Anxiety and passion didn't mix.

That was just as well, because even if his opinion of her had changed, even if he really loved her, his determination to protect her—and his child—made it impossible to trust him. He was the type of man who did what he thought best, regardless of whether people agreed.

She finished her tea and set down the cup. "I want you to drink the whole pot," he said. "You lost a lot of fluid this morning."

"I will. You don't have to watch me."

"I like watching you. You're beautiful." He touched her hair. "Very beautiful. I feel as if we haven't been alone in a month."

He didn't have to tell her what he was thinking; the look in his eyes said it for him. Every muscle in her body tensed, but with anxiety rather than arousal. "Please—don't touch me again. You've been very nice, but that doesn't give you the right to sleep with me."

"I do have some principles, Sabrina. I've never seduced a dehydrated woman in my life. Now calm down and listen to me." He poured her some more tea and handed her the cup. "When you realized you were sick enough to need help, you didn't turn to Kathleen or Dr. Mirza. You turned to *me*, and I refuse to believe it was only because nobody else knows you're pregnant. You care for me, Sabrina. You depend on me. And in a lot of ways you trust me, although it doesn't extend to whatever's in that black binder."

He took her face in his hands, and she stiffened in alarm. "I dream about you, sweetheart." He brushed his mouth across her lips. "I go to sleep wanting you and I wake up the same way."

He was shaking now, but so was she. She couldn't understand how it had happened so quickly—the sudden rush of excitement, the intense surge of desire. When he nibbled her bottom lip in a way she'd never been able to resist, the tea wound up on the night table and her arms found their way around his waist. She wanted him to kiss her, wanted to be held and caressed. He lifted his mouth and stared solemnly down at her, but she couldn't meet his eyes. "This is crazy. There's no future—"

She never had a chance to finish; his mouth came down on hers for an intimate, searching kiss. There was no anxiety now, only pleasure. She wanted to block out the rest of the world and hold onto the moment forever.

She'd never had a man enjoy her mouth so thoroughly or arouse her so fiercely with only a kiss. By the time he pulled away, she couldn't imagine why she'd told him not to touch her. As he unbuttoned her blouse, she said dazedly, "I thought I had to drink my tea."

Brad slipped off Sabrina's blouse and eased down her pants. His self-confidence had taken a beating this week, but it was finally on the upswing. He'd proved two things to her just now—that she trusted him at least a little and that she was still attracted to him—and he wasn't going to blow it by pushing her too hard. Frustration hadn't killed a man yet, and neither had curiosity.

"You almost fainted in that desert," he said. "You're in no shape to make love, and besides, you'd accuse me of seducing you afterward and you'd be right. I can wait until you realize you love me—until you trust me enough to tell me what's going on and give yourself instead of just letting me take you." He tossed aside her clothes. "Of course, I may go crazy before then."

Sabrina looked at him in bewilderment. "If you're not going to make love to me, why did you take off my clothes?"

"To give you a massage—to relax you."

"I *am* relaxed." She was aroused, too, but she could see Brad's point. She'd done it once before—made love with him, enjoyed it thoroughly and then blamed him for seducing her—and doing it again would be unforgivably hypocritical.

She turned onto her stomach and buried her face in the pillow, sighing with pleasure as he rubbed her back. If only she could trust him...if only she could be sure he wouldn't go to Royce...but she couldn't. She couldn't even fall asleep, because in the very back of the binder, tucked into the vinyl pocket, was a letter from Maya, and she was afraid he'd sneak a look at it.

The moment he left the room, she crossed to the dresser and pulled out the letter. She knew she should destroy it but couldn't bring herself to do it. It would have been like destroying a tiny, precious part of Maya herself.

It was dated July twenty-third and had been enclosed in a note from Ranjeeta Singh that had been waiting for Sabrina when she'd reached Karachi. She barely needed to look at it to know what it said:

Dear Sabrina,

How I wish I could see you, or even speak to you! Ranjeeta tells me you will be in Delhi next month, so perhaps I shall be able to visit her when her husband is out and phone your hotel. She will have to pretend the call was to someone else, but she is willing. She has been like a mother to me this past month. I hope I shall be allowed to see her after my marriage.

The astrologers are still quibbling about the date, speaking one moment of August twenty-eighth, the next of the twenty-ninth or thirtieth. The king has made me see reason, although Ranjeeta, bless her courage, roundly scolded him for it. I fear her boldness earned her the same treatment from her husband that I received from the king, but she says there are ways to get

around a man and has told me to use them. Still, Mr.
Muhmar is not like Mr. Singh. There is no admiration
in his eyes when he looks at me.

I try to remember the teachings of the Buddha. The
cause of suffering in this life is craving, and once we rid
ourselves of all cravings, we shall experience peace,
tranquillity and, ultimately, nirvana. Since there is no
objective reality to our existence, my marriage will not
really exist, and neither will my prayers to Allah. Neither, of course, do you and I, but even so, my dearest
Sabrina, I miss you.

Love,
Maya

Every time Sabrina reread the letter she felt an uncon-
trollable mixture of rage and helplessness. She'd never accepted all that Buddhist mumbo jumbo about the world not
really existing, not even after long discussions with her father-in-law's spiritual adviser, a greatly revered monk named
Nagasena, and she didn't see how Maya could, either. From
where she sat, Maya's fears were very real, and so was the
beating Ashoka had apparently inflicted. For the only time
in her life, she felt capable of real violence.

She folded the letter in half and tucked it under the false
bottom of her jewelry case. *Dear God*, she thought, *August twenty-eighth!* There was so little time.

Chapter Fifteen

It took the better part of a day for the group to reach the city of Multan, an agricultural center in the Punjab known for its mosques and shrines. A series of ancient civilizations had arisen in this fertile, strategically important region, which had later been conquered by a succession of invaders: Persians led by Cyrus and Darius; Greeks led by Alexander the Great; Moguls, Sikhs and British. The Punjab had been split between India and Pakistan when colonial India gained its independence in 1947, and Sikhs, Muslims and Hindus had been fighting over it ever since. At the moment, however, things were relatively quiet.

The group left Multan early in the morning and traveled to Harappa, the first of the Indus Valley civilization sites to be discovered and excavated by scholars. The ancient brick buildings had been in poor condition by then, victims of extensive quarrying. After a brief tour, the group continued north to Lahore.

The major city in the Punjab, Lahore had had a series of foreign occupants who had left reminders of their dominion everywhere—in the walls, forts and gardens of the Moguls, the temples of the Sikhs and the government buildings and museums of the British. There was a lot to see and only a weekend to see it in, so their stay was tightly scheduled. Sabrina had hoped her father would rejoin them in time to help her, but there wasn't even a message from him when they checked into their motel that evening.

It made her wonder if he wasn't doing something in Quetta besides tracking down Ali Sayyid, a former Jammapuri officer and palace aide who she hoped would agree to help them. Quetta was a center for smuggling operations that extended south through the desert to the Arabian Sea and north through the mountains into Afghanistan. Sayyid, who resided in Pakistan now and made his living running everything from guns to motorcycles, wasn't the type of man she normally dealt with, but there was no question that he knew his way around Asia.

Howard arrived the next day, walking into the hotel as the group was gathering for a tour of the Shalimar Gardens, which had been built by the Moguls in the 1600s. He assured Sabrina that things had gone well, promising further details when they were alone. She pleaded tiredness and begged off going on the tour, mostly because Brad felt she'd been working too hard and she hoped that resting for a few hours would placate him.

It did, but it also puzzled her father, who took her aside that evening and asked if she was feeling ill. She mumbled something about being under the weather, then spotted Brad and Kathleen and waved them over. Within minutes, Howard was wrapped up in Kathleen and Sabrina managed to slip away.

Brad started to follow her, then decided to let things ride. She was taking better care of herself these days and her manner was less distant, so he was inclined to be patient with her. The same wasn't true of her father, whom he wanted to drag outside and give hell to for disappearing for so long. Unfortunately, it would have meant explaining things he didn't want to explain.

"I can't put my finger on it," Howard mused to Kathleen, "but she just doesn't seem like herself these days. Have things been going as well as she says?"

"Everyone seems happy," Brad said quickly.

Kathleen looked at him uneasily. "Brad, don't you think—that is, sooner or later someone from the tour is going to mention Kot Diji, and—"

"What about Kot Diji?" Howard interrupted.

Brad shook his head. "Let her tell him herself."

"Tell me what?"

"About Sabrina..." Kathleen looked apologetic. "She almost fainted there, but it was very hot and humid and she'd been working awfully hard—"

"None of that ever bothered her in the past."

Kathleen took his arm. "Calm down, darling. Brad drove her back to the hotel and saw to it that she got some rest. She's been fine since then."

Howard muttered that she still looked different—a little puffy, maybe—but his attention had been diverted by Kathleen's touch. He gazed at her with thinly veiled desire and she smiled and fiddled with his collar. Brad didn't miss the significance of that—she usually stepped away or changed the subject. Resigned to the fact that the two of them were about to become lovers, he excused himself and went to his room.

He spent the evening watching a movie on television, some incomprehensible Indian epic that was nonetheless colorful and diverting. Still wide-awake afterward, he considered checking the coffee shop for his favorite tour members—a British linguistics professor and an eccentric New York millionaire—but decided they were probably in bed. They had a full day ahead of them tomorrow.

He was thumbing through his guidebook to find out what it said about the next leg of the trip when somebody

pounded on his door. He opened it to find a scowling Howard Lang outside, wearing a wrinkled sweat suit that looked
as if he'd just pulled it on. He'd evidently added two and
two together and gotten four.

Amused by the sheer explosiveness of the man, Brad invited him inside and lounged against the dresser. "Is something wrong, Howard?"

His eyes narrowed. "I just realized what was different
about Sabrina. She looks—riper. Especially her bust line."

"Must be all those kabobs and *samosas*," Brad said.

"Dammit, Fraser, don't adopt that obnoxious drawl—"

"But I'm as much in the dark as you are. By the time I got
her back to the hotel last Wednesday, she was fine, and she's
been fine ever since."

Howard started pacing around the room. "I've noticed
the way she avoids you, and so help me, if you've hurt
her—" He stopped and glared. "Did you force her?"

"Force her to do what?" he asked, and knew at once that
he'd gone too far. Howard was hotheaded under the best of
circumstances and playing the innocent had triggered his
temper. He stalked forward and grabbed Brad by his shirt,
then repeated his question more forcefully. Rather than
subject himself to a possible mauling, Brad gave him a
straight answer. "Of course I didn't force her."

"So you admit she's pregnant? You admit you seduced
her?"

"Actually, it was the other way around."

"You little bastard—"

"Think of Kathleen," he said, resisting the urge to point
out that Howard was coming on a little strong for a man
who'd just made love to his aunt. "She'd be upset if you put
me in the hospital, and vice versa. The fact is, you told Sabrina to distract me ten weeks ago and she did an excellent
job. Congratulations on your first grandchild."

"If you're trying to provoke me—"

Brad grinned at him. "It doesn't take much, Howard."

Howard gave him a hard shake, then pushed him away, muttering, "I'm going to kill him. So help me, the kid'll be an orphan before it's even born." He raised his voice. "I expect you to marry her, Fraser—right away."

Brad nodded. "Somehow I expected you to say that. I understand you keep a rifle in your room."

"True, and unless you want to find yourself looking down the business end of it, you'll do what a man with any integrity would do and give your child your name. Being from some snooty Boston family doesn't give you the right to use my daughter and then throw her away."

Brad was hard-pressed not to keep goading him—his fits of temper provided such excellent entertainment—but he was, after all, Sabrina's father, and for some odd reason she loved him. To his credit, the reverse seemed to be equally true, although Brad had to wonder what Howard would do if he were forced to choose between Sabrina and one of his schemes.

He took a jewelry box out of his pocket and flipped it open. "Two and a half carats, Howard, and she won't accept it. What am I supposed to do?"

Lang gaped at the ring. "You mean you asked her to marry you and she refused?"

"Twice. I even told her I loved her. There are times when I question the woman's sanity."

"But she's a levelheaded girl. She wouldn't—" He stopped abruptly. "You must have done something to her— lied to her or slapped her around."

Brad barely had time to deny it before Howard's temper flared up again. "Dammit, Fraser, what did you do to her? So help me, if you laid so much as a finger on her . . ."

It was too good an opening to resist. "Obviously I laid more than a finger on her, Howard—she *is* pregnant—but I swear she loved every minute of it."

He was bracing himself for another assault on his shirt when Lang shook his head and laughed. "It's about time she made me a grandfather. I could never understand why

she didn't have a kid with that wimpy prince she married,
unless the guy was shooting blanks.''

Brad was astonished that Sabrina hadn't told him. The
situation was more complicated than he'd imagined; either
he could protect Sabrina's privacy or he could safeguard her
health, but he couldn't do both. He didn't have to think
about it for more than a moment. ''You and I have a lot to
discuss,'' he said. ''Let's do it over a cup of coffee.''

By the time they finished talking, he'd actually started to
like Howard Lang. He could be perceptive when he wanted
to be, and even more unexpectedly, calm and sympathetic.
Brad couldn't ask him to cooperate unless he knew about
Sabrina's miscarriages and understood why she was reluctant to get married, so he wound up saying a great deal more
than he would have preferred.

His opinion of Lang rose another notch when he wished
Brad well and told him he and Sabrina would have to work
out their problems on their own. ''To be honest, I would
have punched your lights out, but Kathleen told me how you
reacted at Kot Diji. I knew you had to care about Sabrina if
a little heat exhaustion panicked you that way.'' They
walked out of the coffee shop. ''One piece of advice, Brad.
When we get to Delhi, look up that doctor Sabrina saw. A
bribe here and a threat there, and maybe he'll show you her
test results. If they were normal, I'm Mahatma Gandhi.''

Brad told Howard the idea had already occurred to him.
''The last time we saw Bob Wheeler, he told us he'd been
worried about a possible hormone imbalance, but that her
tests had come back normal. It made me wonder if anything like that had shown up on the tests in Delhi. The
politics in this part of the world are so damn By-
zantine...somebody could have had the results suppressed—''

''Exactly. Sabrina was a political innocent. She did what
she felt was best for Jammapur regardless of whether India
or China or Pakistan approved, and sometimes that an-

noyed people—people like your father, for example, although I'm not accusing him of anything."

Brad was offended that Howard would suggest Royce would even be capable of such a thing, but he let the comment pass. Howard was his future father-in-law and he wanted to get along with him. He checked the time, then stepped into the elevator. It was eleven-thirty, a little late to disturb Sabrina in view of how early she had to be up, but he couldn't bring himself to wait. If they were going to quarrel, he preferred to get it over with.

She asked who was there, then opened the door. Ignoring her sheer nightgown and soft, sleepy eyes, he apologized for disturbing her and told her to get back into bed. He didn't sit beside her but remained by the door.

"Your father came to see me this evening," he began, and told her about their conversation.

She listened impassively, then said evenly, "Thank you for being honest with me, Brad. Good night."

"That's it? You're not going to curse me out or throw things at me?"

"How can I, when your behavior was so totally in character? You were worried about my health so you did what you thought was necessary to protect me. I imagine it's the Boston Brahmin in you. You were raised to think you know best, even about what's right for somebody else."

He sighed. "You *are* angry."

"Not really. Believe it or not, if you'd consulted me I probably would have agreed with you. I don't want Dad to worry about how tired I get at times. In any event, I have no reason to want to change you."

"Because you're never going to have to live with me," he mumbled, disgruntled.

"Exactly."

"Every time you say something like that I want to make love to you until you give in, and sometimes I even wonder if that's *why* you say it—to provoke me into forcing the issue, because you love me but you're afraid to admit it. A child should have two parents and a stable home, Sabrina."

"I agree completely," she said lightly, trying to jolly him into a better mood. "I'll get myself a place in Boston and we'll share custody. He'll have *two* stable homes."

Brad stared at her for a moment, then shook his head and walked out. Sabrina could be emotional and unreasonable, but she was also sensible and honest. Sooner or later she would come to her senses; he only hoped it was before the baby was born.

During the late Stone Age, migratory tribes had cut trade routes across much of Asia that later became part of the famous Great Silk Trade Route between Rome and China. Marco Polo had traveled the Silk Route in the thirteenth century and people still used it today, but it was known by a variety of other names now. The section from Lahore to Rawalpindi, part of what locals called the Grand Trunk Road, was a double-lane highway these days, and heavily trafficked with buses, ornately painted trucks and private vehicles. The arid, dusty countryside outside Lahore quickly gave way to grainfields, and then, as the group climbed higher, to lush rolling hills bordered by rugged mountains.

Although Rawalpindi was one of the oldest settlements along the Silk Route, there wasn't much to see there beyond a park and a few bazaars. Only twenty miles away, however, lay Taxila, one of the most important archaeological sites in Asia. First settled about five thousand years before, Taxila had been the locale of three distinct ancient cities. The Harappans had come there first, then the Aryans, then the Greeks followed by a series of invaders from central and western Asia. Shortly after the time of Christ, Taxila had become the center of the Buddhist Mauryan empire, remnants of which were scattered through the region today.

Despite its altitude—about two thousand feet—Taxila was flat, dusty and warm, and since the ruins covered a large area, it took the group an entire day to see them. They trekked through temples, monasteries and *stupas*, then joined Howard and Kathleen in the museum. It was noted for its spectacular collection of Buddhist artifacts and sculpture, but the two of them had gone there to talk to a curator who was an expert on ancient art.

Howard later told the group that the curator had heard the same stories about a golden statue as he had and made inquiries throughout Asia, but discovered nothing concrete. He hadn't asked about monasteries because the statue was pre-Buddhist, but he felt perhaps he should have—many monasteries owned magnificent collections of religious art. If the statue existed, the monks were surely hiding it from public view, but the curator thought they might be willing to show it to Kathleen. She had an international reputation as a scholar and her book about the Mauryan empire had endeared her to Buddhists everywhere. He'd given Howard some leads and Howard had promised to pass on any information he got.

Sabrina recognized the glow in her father's eyes as he related this conversation; it meant he was itching to get to work. She wasn't surprised when he rented a Jeep and took off with Kathleen; several of the monasteries he wanted to visit were located in isolated areas, along rough back roads. Dr. Mirza replaced him as their expert commentator while Sabrina took charge of everything else.

After another night in Rawalpindi, the group took a half-day tour of Islamabad, Pakistan's new capital, and continued north to Murree, a lovely, verdant resort in the southern Himalayas. They spent all of Thursday there, enjoying the first comfortable weather they'd had on the trip and accustoming themselves to the altitude.

The area they were about to enter, Pakistan's Northern Territory, was a spectacular mixture of soaring mountains, luxuriant forests and exquisite valleys. Once largely isolated, the region had become more accessible with the completion of the Chinese-built Karakoram Highway from

Islamabad to the Chinese border in 1986. The road wended
its way through an archaeological treasure trove, passing
ruins, rock carvings and inscriptions dating to the Stone and
Bronze ages, and monasteries, *stupas* and engravings from
the era when Buddhists had controlled the region.

On their first day out of Murree they came to one of the
most famous of the engravings: the moral edicts of the great
Buddhist emperor Ashoka, for whom Sabrina's husband
had been named. Carved into three large boulders, they
condemned wars and killing and stressed compassion and
good deeds. The message, unfortunately, was often ignored; so many different cultures and religious groups occupied this rugged, remote area that rivalries and clashes
were inevitable.

The next several days were a combination of hard travel
and thrilling sight-seeing as they followed the Karakoram
Highway north, studying the relics of long-dead peoples en
route. Howard rejoined them in Gilgit, the most important
town in the territory and a major archaeological site. His
explorations had proved a disappointment and he was hoping for better luck, but nobody in Gilgit could tell him a
thing.

The group stayed two nights, then doubled back to the
south and continued west. It was a grueling journey that
took them to the Swat Valley, a hundred-mile-long strip of
emerald bisected by a meandering river and bordered by
terraced grainfields and towering, tree-dotted hills. The
valley had been a center of Buddhist civilization during the
same period as Taxila and was littered with the ruins of
thousands of monasteries and *stupas*, but only a trace of
those days remained.

The people in Swat were easygoing, the place was relaxed
and the climate pleasant. Sabrina was extremely tired by
then and needed some rest, but she doubted she would get
any. Ever since Taxila her father had been obsessed by the
search for the statue. When problems arose—late buses, lost
hotel reservations, upset stomachs—she had to solve them.

On the morning after their arrival in Swat she came down to breakfast to find Brad sitting with her father and Kathleen, threatening to handcuff Howard to the nearest bus if he tried to take off again. There was a time when she would have objected to somebody else fighting her battles for her, but her sense of independence had taken a back seat to her concern about the baby. *Somebody* had to get through to Howard—she certainly hadn't been able to.

He dismissed Brad's arguments with an impatient wave of his hand. There was a handful of surviving monasteries in this area and he meant to visit them all. Kathleen listened thoughtfully, then remarked, "Sabrina looks tired and pale. Obviously she isn't feeling well, and she shouldn't be expected to carry the entire burden of the tour by herself."

He gave a snort. "The next few days will be easy. Brad and Mirza are helping her—there's no reason she can't handle things without me."

Brad hated to violate Sabrina's privacy but felt he had no choice. "Sabrina is pregnant with my child," he said to Kathleen. "Between the pace of this trip and the responsibilities Howard keeps dumping on her, she's totally exhausted. He needs your credentials to be taken seriously. If you stop helping him, he'll have to stop looking."

She was startled at first, then amused. "I assume you've asked her to marry you?"

"She refused. She says I'm bossy and judgmental."

"It's a common male failing, Sabrina, but you can reform him if you put your mind to it." She looked at Howard. "There's no point being angry with you—you're so obsessed with that ridiculous statue that you've lost all sense of perspective—but I won't be a party to it any longer. If you want my help, you'll have to take it on my terms. I'm willing to go to the monasteries on your list, but *you'll* have to stay with the tour group."

"But you're a woman—you know the monks will object to you when we first show up—"

"I'll take Brad along."

That was fine with Brad, whose only concern was Sabrina. Kathleen kept lecturing him about his "male chauvinist mind-set," but other than that, the next few days were fascinating. They even got a solid lead—an elderly monk in southern Swat had seen a golden statue some thirty years before in a Tantric Buddhist monastery in the Ladakh region of India, although he couldn't remember which one. That in itself wasn't exceptional—a number of monasteries owned golden statues—but this one didn't depict the Buddha or one of the Tantric deities. It was very old, perhaps a rare early Hindu work, and appeared to be a *yaksha*, a sort of spirit or demigod. Though apparently not a Harappan statue of Vishnu, it might very well be the work Howard was looking for.

Brad didn't doubt that Howard would disappear again the moment they reached Ladakh, but Sabrina wouldn't need him as much there. Their schedule was far easier, with planes transporting them from city to city instead of buses and longer stays in each location.

First, however, they visited Peshawar, literally "frontier town," the capital of the North West Frontier Province and the nearest city to the Afghan border. Much of the surrounding area was under tribal rather than government control and, as such, closed to foreigners. The best known of those tribes, the Pathans, were a swashbuckling group of warriors that nobody from the Moguls to the British had been able to conquer. Even today, one saw them swaggering around town in their pajamalike robes, rifles slung over one shoulder and ammunition belts over the other.

Howard was in top form, leading the group through bazaars and mosques in the old part of the city, arranging access to Bala Hissar Fort, a military post normally closed to tourists, and getting permission for a trip out the Khyber Highway to the border. He'd promised them a great feast that evening, but they wound up running over an hour late. Their Pathan chef was pouting when they finally arrived at his restaurant, but Howard placated him with some extra money.

The dishes were served one by one at a leisurely pace, each more delicious than the last. Since Howard seemed to love Afghan food—he ate an enormous amount—Brad was surprised when he pleaded exhaustion and left early. He hadn't looked tired, and the chef had told them that the best was yet to come.

Brad's curiosity was aroused. He left the restaurant, walked back to the hotel and put his ear to Howard's door. Somebody was moving around inside, so he slipped out of sight and waited. Howard eventually emerged wearing the baggy pants and long flowing top of a native, a turban on his head and a rifle slung over his shoulder.

Brad followed him downstairs, reaching the lobby as he opened the front door. A moment later a Jeep pulled up and he got inside. The driver greeted him warmly and drove away.

Brad returned to the restaurant for the rest of dinner, but his mind wasn't on eating. As Sabrina led the group back to the hotel, he drew her close and said softly, "An hour ago I saw your father leave his room dressed like a Pathan tribesman. The guy who picked him up was wrapped in enough ammunition to wipe out half the city. What's going on?"

She started to shiver. "I have no idea."

"Don't you? According to my guidebook, the area near the border is a smugglers' paradise. He wouldn't be up to his old tricks, would he?"

"He's probably arranging something special—maybe a visit with one of the local tribes." She removed his arm from her waist. "Excuse me, Brad. Mrs. MacKenzie wants to speak to me."

Mrs. MacKenzie could talk an elephant's ears off without half trying, but Brad let Sabrina go. He had the feeling she knew a lot more than she was willing to admit and was worried about making a slip. It didn't take a genius to realize *she* was up to something, too.

He decided to keep an eye on her that night, and since her room was just down the hall from his, it wasn't difficult. At about ten past eleven, two of the largest men he'd ever seen strode out of the elevator and knocked on her door. Like her father's friend in the Jeep, they were armed to the teeth. She let them in almost immediately.

Brad did his best to eavesdrop but couldn't hear much of the conversation. They were speaking a mixture of English and some other language, so even catching a word now and then didn't help. Twenty minutes later the Pathans strode out of her room and left via the stairs.

Brad promptly knocked on her door. She opened it so quickly that she must have thought the Pathans had returned. "Interesting company you keep," he said. "Are *you* arranging a visit with one of the local tribes, too?"

"No. I'm really very tired—"

"You've had a busy night." He brushed past her and closed the door. "Who were they, Sabrina?"

"Nobody you need to concern yourself with," she said.

He suddenly felt as tired as *she'd* just claimed to be. "What do I have to do to convince you I'm on your side? Write an oath in blood? For God's sake, Sabrina, those men are dangerous. If you have a legitimate reason for needing them, tell me what it is and let me help you. I won't argue or pass judgment. I love you. I simply want to protect you."

She looked at the floor, visibly shaken. "Please don't worry about me, Brad. I'll be fine."

"I'll worry about you every minute. You're scaring me to death." He grasped her shoulders, but she didn't look up. "You're afraid to level with me—I understand that—but there's no reason to be. I have no choice but to do what you want. If I don't, I'll lose you."

It was several seconds before she answered. "I'll think about it."

"That's all I'm asking." He kissed her cheek and left, praying that he'd finally made some progress. Something frightening was going on here, and he wasn't going to have a moment's peace until he found out what it was.

Chapter Sixteen

Delhi was a city of memories for Sabrina, some painful, others unbearably sweet. It was where the East had first enchanted her and where she'd fallen in love; where she and Maya had discovered bazaars, museums and gardens together—and also each other. She'd had D & Cs here after two of her miscarriages, fled here after her marriage had failed and met Maya for bittersweet reunions that had ended far too soon. In Gilgit, she'd stared across the border at the mountains of Jammapur and felt a poignant longing for the early days of her marriage, the busy, happy times before she'd lost her innocence, but in Delhi the past tore at her heart.

It was an ancient city, already a center of culture and power in an age when Bombay and Calcutta had been mere villages. At least eight cities had been built on this site, not one on top of the other in the usual archaeological fashion but side by side. Hindus, Muslims and Moguls had ruled vast empires from here, as had the British, who'd established trade ties to India in the seventeenth century and had conquered the subcontinent by the middle 1800s. The huge buildings of their capital, New Delhi, had been constructed in the early 1900s and now housed the Indian government.

The group had stopped here to rest and shop; most of them had been to the city before and had visited the major shrines and monuments. Howard led tours for those who hadn't while Sabrina took some time off. A week ago she would have welcomed the break, but rest was impossible now. All she did was worry.

She'd been agonizing about Maya since Karachi, but her fears were stronger than ever now. It wasn't so much that she feared their rescue plan wouldn't work as that she no longer trusted her father to carry it out. Why had he stayed in Quetta for nearly a week? It couldn't have taken six days to contact Ali Sayyid. And why had he disappeared with a Pathan tribesman for twenty hours, barely returning in time for their flight out of Peshawar? He must have been doing something besides what he'd claimed—arranging to get Maya to Pakistan and then Nepal—because he'd asked Sabrina to meet with a pair of Pathans on Friday night and finalize those arrangements herself.

Only one possibility came to mind: his interest in the golden statue went far beyond photographing it. He meant to steal it and sell it, probably to a wealthy collector. If she could believe Brad—and she was beginning to—it wouldn't be the first time he'd taken something valuable. It distressed her to have such doubts about a man she loved and admired, but she was troubled about what he was up to. He was too obsessed with the statue for his interest in it to be purely academic.

Never in a million years had she imagined she would ever spy on anyone, but when they checked into their hotel in Delhi she tracked down the manager and gave him a story about her father having a heart condition and needing to be watched constantly. Then she paid him a handsome sum to report on Howard's comings and goings and monitor his calls. If she had her way, he wouldn't even be able to summon a bellhop without her knowing about it.

The next morning, hoping to hear from Maya, she told everyone she planned to rest in her room all day. Kathleen phoned her at noon to invite her to lunch and Brad stopped by before dinner to ask her how she was feeling, but otherwise she was left alone.

The weight of her suspicions and fears was so heavy by then and her emotional equilibrium so precarious that she would have told Brad everything if he'd pressed her hard enough, but he didn't. He was waiting for her to come to him, and she both loved and hated him for that. The Western half of her needed him to respect her enough not to ride roughshod over her and the Eastern half simply wanted to be protected. She was so confused and ambivalent that she thought he was crazy to even want her.

She didn't eat or sleep that day. She could barely even concentrate on the TV. Mostly she sat staring at the phone, and finally, late that evening, it rang.

She lunged for it. "Hello?"

"Sabrina? Is that you?" The voice on the other end was thin, unsteady.

"Maya, are you all right?"

"Yes, fine. I am at Ranjeeta's house. Her husband finally fell asleep." She giggled nervously. "We gave him so much *chang* he finally passed out."

Chang was the local beer, and Mr. Singh had a decided weakness for it. Relieved that Maya still had the spirit to laugh, Sabrina said, "It's wonderful to hear your voice. You sound amazingly substantial for somebody who doesn't really exist."

"But, Sabrina, Nagasena Rimpoche says it is necessary to deal with appearances." She sighed. "If only it were not!"

"Then nothing has changed?"

"Only the date. Now it is the thirty-first. Since the stars are fixed in the heavens one wonders why it is so complicated to settle such a matter, but the king was adamant that the date must be propitious. I asked what difference it could make when I was to be married as a Muslim, but he did not reply."

Sabrina couldn't decide whether Maya's impudence had been foolhardy or incredibly brave. "You wrote that you were resigned, but you don't sound it."

"I shall be free eventually," she replied.

"Yes, eventually." *But nirvana can be a long time coming,* Sabrina thought.

"Perhaps sooner than you can imagine. My value to Mr. Muhmar is in the dowry I shall bring him and sons I shall bear. The first he will have shortly, and the second..." She paused. "Two years if I am lucky, eight or ten if I am not. He has no great liking for me, so surely he will allow me to enter a nunnery once I have served my purpose. Please don't worry about me. I am content enough."

Maya's adolescent fascination with religion to the contrary, she wasn't meant for life in a nunnery. She was bright and full of life, a girl who should be marrying a boy she loved and making her mark on a world she kept insisting didn't exist. Saddest of all, she had too much love in her to abandon any children she might bear. She didn't realize it, but she would be stuck with Muhmar forever... unless Sabrina could arrange to save her.

She didn't want to upset the girl, so she teased, "I suppose you'll meditate day and night until you turn into a tiny puff of smoke and disappear."

"You know perfectly well that the Buddha did not describe nirvana for us, but I imagine it is like—like floating on a raft in a quiet sea, with nothing at all on your mind except perhaps how good the sun feels on your face." She sighed again, then said wistfully, "I long for that, Sabrina."

"And you'll have it eventually, darling. Until then, remember that I love you." She cleared her throat, fighting back tears. "May I speak to Ranjeeta for a moment?"

"I love you, too, Sabrina. Here she is."

Their conversation was brief. Sabrina thanked Ranjeeta for her help and told her to be careful, and Ranjeeta promised to look after Maya as best she could and call Sabrina if Muhmar allowed her to leave Jammapur. Neither, thank God, seemed to suspect that she planned to interfere. There was no possibility of a slip.

Despite the emotional turmoil she felt, the call lifted her spirits. With the wedding set for the thirty-first, they would have some leeway about when to attempt the rescue. She stopped by her father's room the next morning to pick a date and was relieved when he seemed determined to follow through with their plans. Of course, that didn't mean he wasn't scheming to steal the statue as well.

After telegraphing her Pathan contact in Peshawar with the date they'd agreed on, the night of August twenty-ninth to thirtieth, and requesting confirmation by return wire, she went to the hotel coffee shop for breakfast. She was crossing the lobby on her way back to her room when Brad walked up to her. "What was the name of the doctor you saw here?" he asked.

"Rajiv Bannerji."

"And his address?"

"He was on Asaf Ali Road. Why?"

"I don't believe you were told the truth about your test results. I'm going to see him this morning. Do you want to come along?"

It was typical of him not to consult her. "I notice you're not asking my permission," she said.

"You notice right. I'm sorry if you don't approve, but I want some answers." He led her to a quiet corner by the elevators. "I'm trying to be patient, Sabrina, but when we reach Ladakh . . . That's where the statue apparently is, and my instincts tell me things are going to start happening there. I'm taking my own houseboat in Srinagar and you're going to share it with me. I want you where I can keep an eye on you. Now about Dr. Bannerji—"

"I'd rather not see him again. I didn't like the man." She turned away, half annoyed and half relieved that he'd finally put his foot down. "If you'll excuse me, some of the women asked me to take them to the bazaar in the old city this morning. I need to get an umbrella."

He led her into an empty elevator. "You can be as angry as you want, but it's not going to get you anywhere. By the way, you look beautiful in a sari. Why don't you invite me upstairs and show me how you put one of those things on?"

"Because I'd have to take it off first, but I suppose that's the general idea." It wasn't an unappealing one, either; Sabrina wore saris in India to fit in, but they also made her feel graceful, feminine—and receptive.

He smiled. "Would you believe me if I claimed the thought had never occurred to me?"

"No."

"I didn't think so. Aren't you going to argue with me about staying on my houseboat?"

She was relieved when the doors slid open. It was one thing to long to lean on him, another to actually do it. "No, but I haven't agreed to it yet, either." He didn't follow her to her room, but laughed and told her to have a good time shopping.

As she walked inside she noticed that an envelope had been slipped under her door. Amazed that the reply to her wire had come so quickly, she picked it up and slit it open. It wasn't from the Pathans, however, but the manager:

Mr. Lang received a telephone call late last night from a gentleman with an English accent. He told the gentleman that the prize was within reach and the gentleman replied that he wanted to demonstrate the sincerity of his employer's interest. They agreed they shared a desire for some good whiskey and arranged to meet in the Lotus Bar at five o'clock this evening. If you wish, I shall have their conversation recorded.

Sabrina understood what was expected of her. She put a thousand rupees—sixty or seventy dollars—into a hotel envelope and added a brief note: "Thank you for your excellent suggestion. S. Lang." Ten minutes later she handed it to the manager and went to the lobby to meet the women she was taking shopping.

They returned at a quarter of five laden with ivory, silver, textiles and pottery. Sabrina couldn't stop herself from going into the bar, but chose a small booth in back in the hope that her father wouldn't spot her. Less than ten minutes later Brad walked in, zeroing in on her like a homing pigeon. "I've been looking everywhere for you," he said. "If you were trying to hide, you should have changed first. You're the only woman in the place with a sari on."

She grimaced, hardly able to believe she'd been so absentminded. Since Hindus didn't drink, Indians didn't come in here alone—they wouldn't have gotten served even if they had. Alcohol was difficult to obtain in India, even for foreigners, and that was probably why her father and his friend had agreed to meet here—they wanted whiskey, and a bar in a big hotel was the best place to get it.

"I wasn't hiding out," she said. "I felt like having a beer and I forgot how I was dressed."

He sat down across from her. "A beer? Are you sure that's okay?"

"I'll only have a little." Actually, she couldn't stand the stuff.

"Don't you want to know what I found out today?"

"Found out? Oh, you mean from Dr. Bannerji." She'd forgotten all about it. "Yes, of course."

"Preoccupied, aren't you, sweetheart," he drawled.

"It was a long day. I suppose I'm tired." In a way, Brad was good camouflage. Her father would never imagine she was spying on him if Brad was at her table.

He gave their orders to the waiter, then took some papers out of his pocket and put them on the table. Sabrina could see they were medical reports but couldn't make head nor tail of what was written on them. "Bannerji was surprisingly cooperative once he found out who my father was. Dad still has a lot of influential friends in the government and he didn't want any trouble. Of course, I did provide him with a minor financial incentive first."

"Oh? How much?"

"Five thousand rupees."

Hotel managers obviously came cheaper than doctors. "What do all those numbers mean?" she asked.

"Basically, that your hormone levels were too high. Somebody must have been slipping you the equivalent of morning-after pills, but at a dosage that took a few weeks rather than a few days to induce a miscarriage."

Sabrina wasn't so much surprised as pained. "I don't know whether to be horrified or relieved. The thought that somebody could hate me so much . . ." She shook her head. "Was he sure that it couldn't have been—natural?"

"Why would somebody bribe him to keep quiet about a condition that was natural? Do you have any idea who might have been behind it?"

She had a very good idea. "Didn't he tell you?"

"He claimed he didn't know—that it was done by mail and phone. You didn't answer my question, Sabrina."

"No, I didn't, did I? Aren't those our drinks?" The waiter set her beer and Brad's espresso on the table. "The coffee looks good. I'm sorry I didn't order one."

"In other words, you're not going to tell me. I don't know what could have possessed me to think otherwise." He frowned. "Who's the man with your father?"

She looked furtively at the door. Her father's companion was Chinese, and very nattily dressed. They sat down by the side wall, ordered drinks from a waiter who'd materialized by their table with a dish of nuts, and began to talk animatedly. "I have no idea," she said. "I've never seen him before in my life."

"Except maybe a dozen times."

"No, really—I haven't. What did you do today besides browbeat a defenseless doctor?"

Conceding defeat, he told her about his sight-seeing and asked about her shopping. Her father was facing the other way and didn't seem to notice her, but she had a clear view of him. After about fifteen minutes he accepted an envelope from his companion and briskly walked out. His companion paid the tab and followed.

The table was cleared immediately, the waiter picking up the dirty glasses and nut dish and carrying them away. Sabrina suddenly realized the nut dish must have been bugged. She didn't want to rush out—it would have looked suspicious—so she continued to tell Brad what she'd done that day.

She was describing an ivory carving she'd bought when a man in a crisp tropical suit approached with a small basket of flowers. He waited to be acknowledged, then gave a little bow. "It's always a pleasure to have you stay with us, your highness. Please accept this with our compliments." He handed her the basket.

She thanked him and slipped him a bill, then excused herself and went to the ladies' room. Inside the stall, she probed beneath the flowers and felt something plastic at the bottom of the basket—a microcassette tape. Brad couldn't have known why she was in the bar so the exchange wouldn't have been as obvious to him as it had been to her, but she tucked the cassette under her sari just to be on the safe side. She didn't have a recorder this size, but she could buy one as soon as the shops opened tomorrow.

Brad was standing and waiting when she returned to the bar. "I'd like to see the things you bought. Will you show them to me?"

"Maybe later. I thought I'd lie down—"

"Fine. I'll walk you to your room."

There was no graceful way to refuse, so she smiled and let him escort her upstairs. He took her key out of her hand and unlocked her door, then pushed it open so she could go inside. She was about to thank him for the drink, which she'd barely touched, when he strolled in after her.

He removed the basket from her hand and tossed out the flowers. "Hmm. Empty. Now I know why you went to the ladies' room."

She gave him a blank look. "What are you talking about?"

"Take off your sari."

"If you think I'm going to fall into bed with you—"

"Maybe later, darling." He grabbed the end of her sari and pulled. She clutched the fabric to her breasts and backed away, and as they struggled, the tape she'd tucked into her bodice dropped out and fell to the floor. Brad snatched it up before she could react.

"I'll be damned," he said. "Do you have a recorder to play this on?"

"No." She was red-faced with embarrassment and anxiety. "Give it back to me. It's none of your business."

"It is, actually, because whatever Howard's up to is going to affect you and Kathleen, but I'm willing to give you a little more time." He tossed the tape onto the bed. "If you're smart enough to bug your father, you're smart enough to know you need my help. Think it over, Sabrina. We'll talk about it in Srinagar—on my boat."

He walked out of the room, leaving her paralyzed by indecision. She was terrified to listen to the tape and terrified not to. The world was closing in on her from all sides—Maya, her father, Brad—and all she could do was stand in the middle of a hotel room in Delhi and tremble.

Chapter Seventeen

Srinagar was an hour from Delhi by plane, but Sabrina barely noticed the spectacular Himalayan peaks and exquisite Kashmir valleys they flew over. She was in shock. She'd listened to the tape of her father as soon as she'd gotten back with a recorder that morning, and his words were still echoing in her mind—an ugly mixture of cynicism, egotism and greed. She couldn't even bring herself to look at him now, much less speak to him.

The man in the bar had represented a Hong Kong *taipan* who'd offered to pay twenty million dollars for the golden statue, assuming it turned out to be genuine. He'd been delighted by Howard's cleverness in locating it, but no more so than Howard himself, who'd gloried in the man's assessment that it had taken a master to come this far. It was one thing to hear the same rumors everyone had heard, but to take them seriously...to think of looking in Buddhist monasteries... *That* had required an act of genius. And se-

ducing Kathleen Carlisle had been the most brilliant move
of all!

Howard had agreed, boasting that nobody could have
been more perfect for his needs than she. Once he'd made
love to her, he'd joked, she'd been able to refuse him nothing, although he wondered how he'd get rid of her once
she'd served her purpose. The man had laughed and suggested that he keep her around; there were other rare treasures in the world, not the least of which was Howard's own
daughter Sabrina.

The *taipan* was a happily married man, his agent said, but
he'd met Sabrina at a diplomatic reception once and fan-
cied her very much. Could Howard persuade her to become his mistress? Howard had replied that she'd been
trained in the art of love by a very demanding husband and
would expect to be treated like a queen. Despite his serious
tone, Sabrina had been sure he was joking—until they'd
started haggling over the finder's fee. Joking or not, though,
a man with any decency wouldn't have spoken about his
daughter that way. She'd felt violated, defiled.

Brad, she realized, would never have behaved so crudely.
He was a gentleman; when he was angry, he either said so to
your face or kept his mouth shut. He didn't gossip about
you behind your back, crack cheap jokes at your expense or
take the easy way out when it came to making money. He
was gentle, protective and principled, and if that meant he
was also a little arrogant, it went with the territory. If she
didn't love him she was a total dope, but persuading him to
do what she wanted was another matter entirely.

By the time she stepped off the plane, she was steeling
herself to confide in him. She desperately needed someone
to talk to and he'd finally worn her down. Still, it was difficult. Not only was Maya's future at stake; she would have
to play him a tape that was miserably humiliating in view of
how staunchly she'd defended her father in the past. And
while she appreciated everything Brad had done for her and
trusted him to take care of her, she wasn't sure she loved

him. She felt detached from him, more like a stranger than a woman who'd once made love with him.

Their first day in Srinagar was so hectic it was easy to postpone their conversation. The group wasn't staying in a hotel, but in houseboats on Dal Lake, each of which had a veranda, living and dining room and two to four bedrooms. Several boats shared a kitchen boat, where the cooking was done and the servants stayed, and a *shikara*, a graceful, canopied transport boat often called the gondola of the East, just as Srinagar was called the Venice of the East.

She helped everyone get settled, then returned to the dock to look for Brad. Since there were a hundred-odd houseboats in that area of the lake, finding someone could be difficult. She finally heard him call to her from a *shikara*. "Get in. My houseboat's on Nagin Lake."

Nagin Lake was about two miles to the north and much quieter than Dal Lake, where tourists were subjected to the colorful but constant chatter of floating merchants touting everything from jewelry to toilet paper. If Brad had wanted privacy, he'd chosen well.

It would have been the perfect time to talk—enveloped in his embrace on the couchlike seat of the *shikara* with the boat's silky curtains billowing in the breeze—but she didn't say a word. She was wondering if he would kiss her—he didn't—and worried about the number of bedrooms on the boat—there were two. Although he didn't suggest that one should remain unoccupied, the boat's quiet intimacy unnerved her.

They rendezvoused with the rest of the group at the south end of Dal Lake, then took a *shikara* tour along the nearby Jhelum River. It was a lovely way to sightsee—floating peacefully along, stopping now and then at a mosque or tomb, and continuing on. After eating dinner in town, they crossed Dal Lake for the nightly sound and light show in the Shalimar Gardens on the north shore.

By the time they got back, Nagin Lake was utterly still and the other houseboats were dark and quiet. Brad helped Sabrina out of the *shikara*, then followed her up the steps onto the veranda. "It's beautiful here," he said. "Maybe that's the real reason people fight over Kashmir. It's Kashmir itself they love, not its strategic importance."

"That's a very romantic view of it." She wanted to drop the small talk and get down to business, but didn't know where to begin. "I'm glad you're enjoying yourself."

"This trip was worth every penny. Your father puts on a good show when he's not running off to Buddhist monasteries."

"Yes, he does." She was so disillusioned with Howard that it was hard to keep the anger out of her voice. "I guess I should go to bed. We have a full day tomorrow."

She hesitated, waiting for him to object. "Well, good night, then." Tense now, she walked inside, half expecting him to stop her. He didn't.

She changed into her nightgown, then stared out at the lake. Despite its altitude, Srinagar was quite warm—too warm to sleep, or perhaps she was simply too keyed up. She returned to the veranda. Although Brad had closed the curtains, a slight breeze was fluttering through the boat, and it was lovely and peaceful out here.

She took a deep breath, relaxing a bit, then heard footsteps behind her and abruptly jerked around. The sight of Brad in his bathrobe made her nervous all over again.

"You can play me the tape, you can show me what's in the binder, or you can make love with me," he said. "By morning you'll have done all three, so the only question is which you want to do first."

Her heart started racing. "It's nice of you to give me a choice."

He smiled. "I'm a reasonable man, sweetheart. Not infinitely patient, but reasonable."

She looked at the floor. "I don't feel close enough to you to make love."

"That leaves the binder and the tape."

"The binder has to come last." Telling him about Maya would be the hardest part of all.

"Then play me the tape."

"But it's so humiliating. I was so wrong about my father—"

"Just play it." Brad wasn't so much impatient as realistic. Sabrina *wanted* him to tell her what to do; it was obvious from the way she'd responded to his demand about the boat. He simply had to be careful not to cross the line from firmness into bullying.

She nodded and left the room, returning a moment later with a tape recorder. They sat down on the sofa and he turned on the machine. Fifteen minutes later he was smiling wryly, relieved that the tape hadn't told him anything he didn't suspect. Then he saw Sabrina's expression and sobered. Her face was a study in anguish and embarrassment. Obviously she had a lot to learn about men and the way they talked.

He put his arm around her and cuddled her to his chest. "Your father is an expert hustler, sweetheart. You can't take the stuff he said seriously. He was playing a role—the cynical, sophisticated adventurer. If we're lucky there won't *be* any golden statue and that will be the end of it."

"But the things he said about Kathleen—"

"I've watched them together, Sabrina. Either he loves her or he's a better actor than Olivier. Three months ago I thought she needed protecting, but I was wrong—she knows he has a streak of larceny in him but she loves him anyway. I'm willing to bet she reforms *him* before he corrupts *her*."

"And it doesn't bother you that he used her? You were so angry with him in Boston—it's so embarrassing to remember the way I defended him...."

"Kathleen once told me he had his good side and his bad side, and she was right. He may be a con artist, but he's also smart, knowledgeable, amusing and probably the best damn tour guide there is. I can see why she likes him. I do, too."

He stroked her cheek. "It's their future. Let them decide it together."

Sabrina had imagined many different reactions from Brad, but not this one. She could see his point—that her father had been playing a role and she should judge him by his actions rather than his words—but it was hard to accept. They were talking about a criminal act. "But what about the statue? Suppose he finds it and tries to steal it?"

"Why worry about it until we have to? If it turns up, we'll make sure it stays where it belongs." He grinned at her. "Aren't you going to say anything about his plan to sell you to the *taipan*?"

"It was disgusting. I don't see how you can smile—"

"Come on, honey, admit it—you're annoyed because a lousy statue is worth more than you are. The guy offered your father a mere half million bucks for you—hell, I could scrape up that much myself. I think I'll get in the *shikara* and go have a talk with him."

"That's not funny. He made me feel like a whore."

"My God, Sabrina, you didn't take him seriously!" Brad took a good look at her and realized that she had. "The man was ready to castrate me when he found out I'd gotten you pregnant. He might not worry about your health as much as I think he should, but you're his little girl and he loves you. It's just that face is important in the East—you know that. If he hadn't pretended to consider the offer, the *taipan's* agent would have been insulted."

Sabrina was chagrined that she'd been so dense. She relaxed against Brad's chest, thinking that he was really quite extraordinary—perceptive, patient and levelheaded. She was grateful he'd put things in perspective for her. "I guess I overreacted. The tape isn't really that bad. I just didn't see my father realistically before. The past few days have been a shock to me."

"That's understandable. You're his daughter and you grew up idolizing him." He paused. "Are we finished with the tape?"

"Yes." She knew what was coming next, and it terrified her. He didn't just want sex, he wanted *her*—freely and eagerly, without secrets or barriers.

"Does the binder still go third?"

"Yes, but I don't think I'm ready—"

"You're not. You're wearing too much." He started to unbutton her nightgown. "Look at it this way, darling. I'm better than some adulterous old *taipan*." He slid the gown to her waist, cupped her breasts, and ran his thumbs back and forth over her nipples until they were erect. "Very nice. Are you excited or just cold?"

"Excited," she admitted, and shivered. "I'm just so nervous, Brad. I know it's stupid, but I can't help it."

"I'll be careful." He lowered his mouth to her breasts. "I want this baby as much as you do."

She didn't bother explaining that he'd misunderstood her. He was sucking one of her nipples, sending a tingling warmth through her, and it didn't seem important. She didn't want him to stop. She just wished she could relax.

He nipped and kissed her breasts, shaking uncontrollably and breathing unevenly. This wasn't just empty passion; it was deep emotion. An overwhelming tenderness enveloped her. She'd been blind not to realize how hard the past few months must have been on him—blind and selfish.

"Let's go into the bedroom," she whispered.

He straightened slowly, dazed with arousal. She unknotted his robe, pulled it off, and ran her fingers down his chest to his loins, teasing him a little. Then she stood up, letting her nightgown fall to the floor, and walked provocatively into his room.

Brad followed her to the bed, his eyes on her swaying bottom, so wildly excited that it hurt to move. He wanted to slow the pace but she outflanked him, nuzzling his belly the moment he lay down, then suckling and nibbling and refusing to move away. Helplessly aroused, he let her do as she pleased. She found his mouth and kissed him deeply, took him in her hand and caressed him until he lost control. From start to finish, it took twenty seconds.

He felt emotionally empty afterward—disappointed and resentful. "I wish you hadn't done that," he said quietly.

"It was either that or throw you into the coldest part of the lake." She smiled. "Obviously you've been faithful."

It took him a moment to answer. "What I said before still goes. I want to make love to you. What happened just now doesn't count."

"Of course it counts. I'm keeping score." She traced a teasing circle on his chest. "You owe me one." Her hand moved lower. "And to think you had the nerve to compare yourself to Shiva! Ah, that's better... *much* better."

"I don't know what the hell is going on here," he muttered. "Why are you doing that?"

Sabrina wasn't nervous anymore, just amused. Obviously he'd misunderstood her actions, and he was very put out indeed. "I want you to make love to me but you aren't quite prepared. Things are looking up, though." She snuggled into the crook of his neck. "I'm still kind of tense, Brad. If you could take your time... I'm not quite as—as explosive as you are. Please, just hold me for a while."

He smiled sheepishly and put his arms around her. "You have no idea how stupid I feel. I really thought—"

"I know you did. This time, both of us can enjoy it." She closed her eyes. "You're so warm. You make me feel so safe."

He answered that she'd feel a lot more than safe by the time he was through with her and covered her lips with his mouth. Their lovemaking was everything she'd hoped for— a gentle, tender exploration that slowly intensified to ardent desire and exhilarating pleasure. The satisfaction they shared went far beyond the physical. It was like the first time they'd been together—pure magic.

He held her close afterward and massaged her back. "You should have put your foot down a long time ago," she mused. "To think we could have been doing this for weeks..."

"Are you saying I should tear off your clothes and throw you on the nearest bed whenever you give me a hard time?"

"Absolutely. It sounds exciting."

He laughed. "You'd hand me my head on a plate. We still have some unfinished business to discuss."

"Let's make love again." She fondled him until he responded. "How long do you suppose it would take me to—"

"Not long at all, and stop stalling. What was in the binder?"

He was right—she'd been stalling. "A letter from my former sister-in-law. Her name is Maya." She sighed deeply. "Please don't make me choose between you and her. She would win. She was like a daughter to me."

She told him everything—how close she and Maya had been, how Ashoka was forcing Maya to marry, about her determination to rescue the girl and how it had forced her to lie to Brad the first time they'd made love. "I know you could stop me with a single phone call to your father," she added, "but if you do, our relationship will be over. I mean that."

He didn't doubt it for a moment; otherwise he would have made the call. "I assume you have some sort of plan?"

She briefly sketched it out. She and her father were persona non grata in Jammapur, so they'd cross the border with doctored papers under the guise of being Kathleen's assistants. Ali Sayyid was already in the capital, visiting relatives and making preliminary preparations. He would go to the palace in the middle of the night dressed in his old military uniform and bring Maya out through her bedroom window. Howard would accompany him and wait for them in a Jeep, then drive Maya to a prearranged spot on the border.

Palace, she added, was a rather grandiose term for the place; it was actually a spacious but unpretentious two-story building located on a hillside above town. There were no fences and only a few guards, the latter lackadaisical about their duties except on the rare occasions when there was civil unrest. Maya would be met by Pathan tribesmen who would take her to Skardu and fly her into Nepal. They had contacts there who would hide her for as long as necessary.

"And then?" Brad said. The plan wasn't as screwy as he'd feared and he was relieved Sabrina wasn't directly involved, but he still didn't like it.

"I'll try to get her political asylum in the States. I thought maybe you could help."

"Dad's language will probably short out the local communications satellite, but I'll call him as soon as she's safe and start working on him." Royce was nothing if not pragmatic; when faced with an unfortunate fait accompli, he concentrated on turning it to America's advantage. "I think you should stay in India, though. There's no reason for you to go to Jammapur."

"Something could go wrong. I might be needed. Besides, I don't trust my father."

He shook his head. "Those medical results—somebody had them suppressed. The obvious conclusion is that he—or she—didn't want you to bear a son. His goal was to destroy your marriage and get you out of Jammapur. You've got a dangerous enemy somewhere, Sabrina."

"In the palace." It should have occurred to her a long time ago, well before Brad had told her about her test results, but she couldn't conceive of anyone being so coldly, schemingly evil. She reddened, finding it hard to talk about. "I never did tell you about Ved Pradham."

Brad didn't need any reminders about who Pradham was. He'd been living with the unforgivable accusations he'd made for months now. "Your former brother-in-law," he said. "The guy who tried to rape you."

"That's what *I* thought, too, but now..." She started to tremble. "I'd felt sick the night before—exhausted and woozy. I didn't so much fall asleep as pass out. And when I woke up... He was on top of me, trying to—to..." She couldn't go on. Even thinking about it made her skin crawl.

Brad held her close. "It's okay. I understand. You're saying he set you up."

She nodded. "My husband came in...Pradham said we were lovers and my husband believed him. I think he was glad to get rid of me by then. My miscarriages...my political blunders...the fuss I'd made about Maya's marriage—I was a liability." She took a deep breath. "Pradham's wife—the king's older sister—they were married a month after we were and she took over the household. She said I was too intelligent for it, that I should spend my time working to improve Jammapuri education and promoting native handicrafts overseas. So I did, and wound up offending just about everyone."

"Pradham's wife could have put hormones in your food."

"Yes. She was in charge of the kitchen, the servants, everything. The doctor I saw in Delhi—he was *her* doctor, and she and Pradham recommended him. The king is married to Pradham's younger sister now. He's a very powerful man in Jammapur. Maya's fiancé is one of his business contacts."

Brad was so enraged he wanted to strangle the bastard with his bare hands. He'd always been cynical about international politics, believing there was precious little morality on that level and accepting it as a fact of life, but this was different. The woman he loved had been the victim. He caressed her until she stopped trembling, swearing to himself that no one would ever hurt her again.

Chapter Eighteen

Sabrina reluctantly opened her eyes, saw that she was alone in bed, and went to look for Brad. He was eating breakfast out on the veranda. "Don't you ever nag me again about how much rest I get," she said. "Not after last night." He'd woken her twice during the night to make love, arousing her until she'd wanted it as much as he had.

He pulled her onto his lap and nuzzled her neck. "I was making up for lost time. Besides, you said I was a wimp compared to Shiva, and I had to prove—"

"I take it back." She tried to squirm out of his arms but he wouldn't let her go. "Stop kissing my neck. I'll be late for the tour."

"Your father doesn't need your help to visit a bunch of gardens." He slipped his hand under her robe. "I wasn't at my best last night. I was still getting used to the altitude."

"If you found it hard to perform in Srinagar, we might as well get separate rooms in Leh." Leh, the capital of the Ladakh region and their next stop, was 11,600 feet up, twice the altitude of Srinagar.

"On the contrary," he said with a grin, "I'm sure you'll inspire me to new heights."

She groaned and pushed away his hand. "A sex maniac who makes bad puns! This relationship is never going to work."

"Of course it is. In fact . . ." He whisked the pear-shaped diamond out of his pocket and slipped it onto her finger. "You're going to marry me as soon as we get back to Boston."

"What a charming proposal!"

"You're giving me a hard time, Sabrina. Does that mean I get to strip you naked and drag you to bed?"

"As soon as I eat." He was only joking, but she would have let him if he'd really wanted to. The physical attraction between them was as strong as ever, she was grateful for his help, and she respected him enormously.

Easterners would have considered that an excellent basis for marriage, but Sabrina was American enough to worry about love. Brad was a talker in bed, repeatedly telling her he loved her, and she longed to reply in kind. What stopped her wasn't so much distrust as fear. Suppose something went wrong in Jammapur? Suppose she needed his help? It was asking a lot of a man to put a woman's wishes above his own best judgment and the safety of his unborn child. She could return his engagement ring with relatively little trauma, but if she committed her emotions completely and he failed her, she'd be devastated.

They ate and dressed, then took a *shikara* to Howard's houseboat. It was deserted, but one of the kids who hung around the docks called to her and waved a piece of paper.

She read it and handed it to Brad. It was a letter from Howard saying that he and Kathleen were flying to Leh that morning. There were dozens of *gompas*—Tantric Buddhist monasteries—in the area, and he needed more time to visit them than the two days he'd originally planned to spend. He would meet them at the Leh airport the next day, then take them to some *gompas* west of the city.

Sabrina was furious, Brad philosophical. "Kathleen will keep an eye on him. She might love him but she'd have to be crazy to trust him. Come on—let's round everyone up and get going."

Fortunately they had an easy schedule that day. The group circled Dal lake in *shikaras* and visited each of the Mogul gardens along the shore, toured a fort normally closed to visitors, and strolled through the city's shopping areas. Then they had dinner, watched a folk dancing show in Nehru Park and asked Sabrina to come to one of their houseboats and sing to them. It was an excuse to get her to the party they'd planned; they'd noticed her engagement ring and ordered cake and ice cream from some shops in town.

The trip back to Nagin Lake by *shikara* was marvelously romantic. Sabrina and Brad cuddled and kissed like a pair of kids while the *shikara* men pretended not to notice, then hurried into their boat and made love. The next morning she teased him about slowing down—he'd woken her only once—but he claimed it was for her own good. They had to get everyone off their boats and onto buses in time for the plane to Leh.

It was a spectacular flight—directly across the Himalayas on a path that took them due south of K2, the second highest peak in the world, and then down through blustery winds onto a pitched runway in Leh. Howard was waiting at the airport as promised, a little irritable because their plane had been late and he was in a hurry to get going. He and Kathleen had seen numerous golden statues the day before, but not the one they were after.

Ladakh is the most remote region in India, a mountainous, nearly rainless area often called Little Tibet because its religious and cultural practices are so much closer to those of Tibet than of India. The group visited three *gompas* that day, all quite large, all centers for the smaller *gompas* in their regions and all housing splendid collections of religious art...wall paintings, painted cloth hangings called *tankas*, wooden and golden statues, and jewel-encrusted *stupas*. Certain rooms in each of them were closed to the public—the oldest prayer rooms, for example, or the head lama's chapel—but Howard and Kathleen managed to talk their way into all of them. They saw many exquisite treasures, but no ancient golden statue.

The first *gompa*, Lamayuru, was the oldest in Ladakh. The monks there were busy in the fields, but Howard induced them to offer a tour by giving them a picture of the Dalai Lama, whom they revered as the living incarnation of Chenrezig, the patron saint of Tibet and a manifestation of the Buddha. The second, Rizong, housed such a splendid library of ancient books that Kathleen hated to leave; at the third, Lekir, an elderly instructor at the *gompa*'s monks' school told them he'd seen the golden statue twenty years before in the monastery at Spitok, where the head lama kept it covered by a cloth in the holiest prayer room. While they might be allowed to see it, he remarked, they would never be permitted to photograph it.

Spitok, about six miles southwest of Leh, was on their itinerary for the following afternoon. Howard was so eager to get there that he rushed them through their tour of Leh the next morning, but nobody seemed to mind. His obsession with the statue had infected the entire group.

Kathleen asked the head lama about it as soon as he'd shown them around his *gompa*. A well-educated man, he represented Ladakh in the Indian parliament and spoke excellent English. "Ah, yes," he said with a smile. "The statue is priceless, you know. It was discovered about a hundred years ago amid the ruins of an ancient village in Jammapur. We believe it depicts the Buddha in one of his early incarnations, before he was reborn as prince Siddhartha, but it is difficult to be certain."

Sabrina thought in disgust that her father was practically
salivating on the *gompa* floor. "It must give you great joy
to have such a priceless relic entrusted to you," he said.

"Indeed, but we were simply its temporary custodians.
Ten years ago the Machulu Rimpoche visited us and asked
if he might take it back to Jammapur. Naturally we were
honored to grant his request. He was quite correct that the
statue belonged in the land of its origin. He displays it during the *gompa*'s annual festival in June, but only to very
special guests and only during the year of the snake."

Howard looked inquiringly at Kathleen, who murmured, "I'm afraid we've missed it by two months. This *is*
the year of the snake."

"We've come a very long way to see it," he said, oozing
disappointment and sincerity. "Are exceptions ever made?"

"Perhaps for a scholar of Dr. Carlisle's reputation. The
decision, of course, would be Nagasena Rimpoche's."

"Of course," he agreed.

Brad was totally lost—he had no idea whom and where
they were talking about. "This Nagasena Rimpoche..." he
said to Sabrina as they left the *gompa*. "Have you ever
heard of him? And where is Machulu?"

"It's north of the capital, and every devout Buddhist has
heard of Nagasena Rimpoche. My father-in-law studied
with him to become a monk. 'Rimpoche' is a title—it's given
to the holiest and most learned lamas who are revered as
incarnations of the Buddha himself and who come to earth
again and again to lead others to enlightenment." She
smiled. "Nagasena Rimpoche tried valiantly to lead *me*, but
I'm afraid I was a hopeless case."

She had the feeling that had it been up to her father, he
would have flown the group back to Srinagar that day and
left for Jammapur immediately afterward, but the high afternoon winds made it impossible to get in and out of Leh
except in the mornings. Faced with no choice but to spend
another night there, he made the best of it and gave everyone a unique afternoon. They saw some extraordinary

treasures—a golden, blue-haired Buddha, three hundred years old and forty feet high; ancient books printed in gold ink on black lacquered paper and decorated with hand-painted Buddhas; stunning frescoes and ancient inscriptions—but the highlight of their day was their encounter with the Shey oracle.

An ordinary layman during most of the year, the oracle went into a trance during the village's annual harvest festival and traveled around Shey prophesying the future. He told Sabrina she would bear a healthy son soon, and then, in the years to follow, three beautiful daughters. Although Brad claimed he didn't even want to contemplate how big the clothing bills would be, he grinned like a kid for the rest of the afternoon.

A local tour operator met the group at the Srinagar airport and took them to Pahalgam, a hill resort about sixty miles away, while Howard, Kathleen, Sabrina and Brad shopped for supplies in town and rented a Jeep for the trip to Jammapur. Pahalgam offered hiking and riding, tennis and golf, and rest and relaxation. The group would stay there through Wednesday, when Howard and his party returned to escort them home.

The trip to Machulu wasn't long in terms of distance—about two hundred miles—but the first leg of it was through stark, towering mountains and high, barren plains. In some places, avalanches and landslides had eaten away chunks of the roadway, leaving only narrow tracks that repair crews were still trying to shore up; in others, the road soared and plunged over steep passes or snaked along rocky ledges. Sabrina's stomach was heaving by the time they stopped in Kargil, which mercifully was situated in a green peaceful valley a mere 8,700 feet above sea level. Since she wasn't generally prone to motion sickness, she blamed her queasiness on being pregnant.

Brad had a different theory. He attributed Sabrina's problem to nerves—anxiety about Maya and fear that he couldn't be trusted. He figured he'd probably earned that,

ut it hurt to say "I love you" over and over and never hear
ie words back. She was so wrought up he never consid-
ed making love to her that night; he simply held her in his
rms and soothed her until she fell asleep.

The road from Kargil to Machulu followed a series of
vers and was less hair-raising than the one from Srinagar,
ut some long stretches were unsealed and others were so
arrow there was barely room for two Jeeps to pass. Be-
ween the need for a special travel permit and the condition
f the road, very few people came up this way. The offi-
ials at the border were glad to have some company but less
ian diligent about checking their papers. Since their chief
uty was to catch spies from other countries in the region,
n American professor and her assistants held little profes-
onal interest for them.

Sabrina's worst moment came when they rode past Kha-
alu, the capital of Jammapur. It was a lovely town, built
to the gently sloping hillside of the Shyok River Valley and
urrounded by reddish plateaus and rocky peaks, and being
ere again made her feel as if someone was squeezing her
eart. Even worse, Khapalu was small enough that a strange
shicle might attract notice and be stopped. Although they
rived so late at night that the town was dark and quiet, she
as terrified she might be recognized.

Her gaze locked onto the palace and wouldn't let go. It
as higher than the buildings around it, with nothing above
but a Jeep track and mountains, and she could see lights
urning in the upstairs windows. She shuddered, knowing
iat Maya was inside—alone and afraid.

Then they rounded a curve and the town disappeared
om view. Machulu was ten miles farther on. The *gompa*,
stone and timber building that clung to the hillside, was
achable only on foot. They left the Jeep in the small
arking area by the roadside, then grabbed their sleeping
id duffel bags and started climbing. It took them about ten
inutes to reach the entrance to the monastery.

Brad and Howard were welcomed inside, but as women Sabrina and Kathleen had to backtrack down the hillside and spend the night in a nearby nunnery. Their room was spare but clean, and so eerily tranquil that it was impossible not to be affected by it. Still, Sabrina was too nervous to really sleep. In twenty-four hours her father and Ali Sayyid would attempt to rescue Maya. She hadn't quite believed it would happen until she'd seen the lights of Khapalu Palace, but the situation was real to her now.

Like the nuns, they rose at dawn, returning to the gompa after prayers and breakfast. Sabrina had hoped the Rimpoche would be away, but he was sitting in his private room on the third floor, talking with Brad and Howard. Not only did he recognize her; he'd obviously expected her.

He smiled and patted her cheek. "My dear child, it is good to see you again. Your father tells me you have come a very long way in search of the Machulu Buddha."

"The Rimpoche recognized me from the wedding," Howard explained. In other words, Nagasena remembered her father from one brief meeting seven years ago. She wasn't surprised—very little slipped past him.

"Yes, Nagasena Rimpoche," she said. "This is my good friend, Dr. Kathleen Carlisle."

He shook Kathleen's hand and complimented her on her books, two of which he'd read, then returned to the subject of the statue. "It was allegedly taken from the ruins of a village nearly two thousand years old, but there is no proof of its age other than its stylistic similarity to certain other works of the period. We believe that it depicts an early incarnation of the Buddha, and since there is a snake coiled around one arm, that the artist perhaps belonged to an early snake-worshiping cult."

"It's a unique work of art," Kathleen said. "As a historian, I would like to see it studied."

"It is a holy object," Nagasena replied, "and as such belongs in a holy place. One must revere it, not poke it."

She smiled. "I suspected you might take that position. May I see it?"

"Perhaps." He gestured toward the door. "First, however, I would be pleased to show such a distinguished visitor our *gompa*."

They saw some glorious *tankas* and wall paintings that morning, but not the golden statue; it was evidently in one of the rooms Nagasena had skipped. Sabrina thought her father would burst from frustration when the lama excused himself to attend to the monastery's business. "Ten to one the statue's in his private chapel. It must be somewhere near his room—"

"Don't even consider it," Kathleen said. "I got you this far, and if you violate his hospitality... My professional reputation is at stake."

He pecked her on the cheek. "Forgive me, sweetheart—I got carried away. I thought I'd go into town. Do you want to come?"

She gaped at him. "But you said the king would throw you out of the country if he caught you. Wasn't that the whole reason for doctoring the papers?"

"Don't worry—I won't be recognized. I'll wear my Pahan tribesman robes."

Sabrina was as appalled as Kathleen. "But Dad—"

"On second thought, I'll go alone. I'll be back in a couple of hours." He ignored their stunned protests and strode out of the room.

Sabrina would have followed him, but Brad stopped her. "Don't waste your time. If he's really determined to go, nobody's going to talk him out of it."

"But he's up to something," she mumbled.

Kathleen's jaw tightened. "So help me, if he so much as looks covetously at that statue—"

"Let's go for a walk, ladies. We need to talk." Brad led them outside, heading for the trail that circled the *gompa*.

He'd done some hard thinking the night before and reached the conclusion that it was time to tell Kathleen the

truth. Howard had kept her in the dark because ignoran[ce]
was a form of protection, but she was in this up to her ne[ck]
and deserved a chance to back out. He didn't so much a[sk]
for Sabrina's permission as inform her of his decision. S[he]
nodded uneasily but didn't object.

Kathleen looked enormously relieved afterward. "Th[at]
must be why Howard went into town—to make arrang[e]-
ments with Ali Sayyid. Of course you've got to get Maya o[ut]
of the country. She's only a child—it's outrageous that [an]
educated man like the king could countenance such [a]
thing."

"Dad called Sayyid from Delhi, Kathleen. He was a[l]-
ready in Khapalu by then." Sabrina sighed. "They di[s]-
cussed everything they needed to discuss. There was [no]
reason to risk another meeting."

"Unless it doesn't concern Maya," Brad said. "I'll ha[ve]
a talk with him when he gets back. He's not walking out [of]
here with that statue even if I have to strip-search him b[e]-
fore we leave."

Howard, however, insisted the idea had never occurred [to]
him. While admitting he'd gone to see Sayyid, he claimed [it]
was only to double-check their arrangements. Sayyid was [a]
smuggler, after all, hardly the most reliable fellow in tow[n,]
so one couldn't be too careful. As for the statue, he pr[o]-
fessed to be shocked that Brad believed him capable [of]
stealing it. He loved Kathleen far too much to do anythi[ng]
that might cause him to lose her.

Brad was skeptical, especially in view of how feveris[hly]
Howard's eyes glittered when Nagasena agreed to sho[w]
them the statue. It was late afternoon by then, and the lam[a]
had fetched them in from outside. "I admire your work to[o]
greatly to deny you in this matter," he told Kathleen. "A[f]-
ter all, this is still the year of the snake. Your friends a[re]
welcome to join you if they wish."

They made their way to the *gompa* in silence. As How[-]
ard had guessed, the statue was kept in the Rimpoche's pr[i]-
vate chapel, inside a jewel-encrusted box covered by a *tank[a.]*

Sabrina had expected something large and awe-inspiring, but the figure was quite small, about ten inches high. One hand was at its waist; the other arm was circled by a snake and outstretched in reassurance. Though dressed in a monk's robes, it lacked the grace and serenity of a classic Buddha. Instead, it was robust and very much of this world, like an early Hindu *yaksha*. Still, there was something magnetic and transcendent about it. Though slightly pitted, it shone with the patina of great age, and an unmistakable aura of holiness surrounded it.

Kathleen studied it for several minutes, then smiled. "Thank you for letting me see it. It reminds me of the ancient Buddha in the museum at Sarnath, but it's even more remarkable—not so much because it's made of gold, but because it seems to radiate goodness."

"Indeed." Nagasena touched it reverently, then carefully put it away. "Shall I be besieged with visits from your colleagues now that I've shown it to you?"

"Not if you don't wish them to come."

"Anyone may come. It is the reason we exist."

"But you don't promise to show them the statue."

"Precisely."

"Then I'm doubly honored, Nagasena Rimpoche."

"Quite so," he said with a chuckle. Sabrina had always adored his sense of humor. A man so wise and virtuous should have been horribly intimidating, but Nagasena wasn't.

They had dinner with the monks that evening. Howard was in a jovial mood, discussing philosophy, theorizing about the statue's provenance and entertaining everyone with anecdotes from his travels. Sabrina, on the other hand, was too tense to eat; she didn't understand how a man who was about to risk his freedom or even his life could be so relaxed and cheerful. It was unnatural, she thought, even neurotic.

She would have given almost anything to be able to guard him, but women weren't permitted in the monastery after eight o'clock. Brad walked her back to the nunnery after dinner, but rather than leaving her at the door, he led her down to the parking area where they'd left the Jeep.

He followed her inside, then took her in his arms. The sun hadn't set yet, but it had dipped behind the mountains and the air was quite crisp. She shivered and clung to him, feeling as if she'd never warm up. "I'm frightened," she said. "That statue—it's extraordinary...mesmerizing. My father will never be able to resist it."

"I'll make sure he has no choice."

"If he offers you something to eat or drink, don't take it." He smiled, and she gripped his jacket and gave him a little shake. "I'm serious. I don't put anything past him."

"Neither do I." He cupped her chin. "Nothing will go wrong, sweetheart. I promise." His lips brushed her mouth. "I love you. I hate having to leave you."

"It's only for one more night."

"That's one too many." He kissed her again, deeply and possessively. She responded with quick hot passion, wanting to crawl inside him, to surround herself with the comfort of his embrace. For a few brief moments nothing existed except his mouth and her own desire.

Finally he eased her away and repeated that he loved her. she buried her face against his neck and held him tightly. "Is it so hard to say?" he asked gently. "Four little words? 'I love you, Brad?'"

She wanted to but couldn't. "I need you," she said instead.

"You love me," he corrected, "but I'd rather kiss you than argue about it." Then he found her mouth again, and the fear went away for a little while longer.

Chapter Nineteen

The guest room Sabrina shared with Kathleen was on the second floor of the nunnery, its lone window looking out over the pathway between the road and the monastery. She didn't bother going to bed once they'd gone upstairs, but pulled over a chair and sat down. Without a word, Kathleen joined her. After the first few minutes their eyes grew accustomed to the dark and they were able to make out shapes in the moonlight. There was nothing to see except the mountainside rising behind the trail and the branches of willow trees waving in the breeze.

"I'm worried about him," Kathleen finally murmured.

She meant Howard. He was supposed to pick up Sayyid in the Jeep, then drive to the road above the palace. Sayyid would position a ladder against Maya's second-story window, climb up and wake her. She knew him well; he'd been one of her favorites during his years as an aide-de-camp. He would have her write an hysterical note saying she couldn't go through with the marriage and had left, then bring her down and take her to the Jeep.

Howard was the driver and cover man; if Sayyid was challenged and couldn't talk his way out—if anyone started shooting—Howard would shoot back. The Pathans would be waiting about thirty miles to the west on the other side of the Indus River, the border between Jammapur and Pakistan. Maya would be ferried across, and Sayyid and Howard would return to Machulu.

They were hoping that Maya's absence wouldn't be noted right away, and if it was, that her letter would buy them enough time to get out of Jammapur safely. They planned to leave at dawn, hours before anyone in the palace normally stirred. Since Maya didn't know how to drive, the logical assumption would be that she was with friends in Khapalu or hiding in a nearby *gompa*. If they were lucky, the king would check the obvious places before ordering the borders closed.

"I am, too," Sabrina said, "but I keep telling myself that Sayyid is taking the worst risk. Of course, he's being paid a fortune for it."

"And that's the only reason he's helping?"

"He was fond of Maya. I think he enjoys the danger, too. Some men do."

"Howard, for example."

"Probably."

They lapsed into silence. The minutes dragged by. Then Sabrina saw a light on the pathway and squinted. They were watching for her father to go down to the Jeep, but somebody was walking in the opposite direction. He was holding a flashlight and pointing it to his right, as if he was looking for something at the side of the path. Finally he stopped and bent down. A moment later he focused the light on a piece of paper and studied it. Moonlight played over his head and shoulders, revealing a peaked hat—a soldier's hat.

Sabrina abruptly stood up. "I'm going outside. I think that's Ali Sayyid. My father must have left him some sort of message. I'm going to follow him and see what he does."

She reached for her jacket and Kathleen did the same. Neither of them put their shoes on—they would have made too much noise. They couldn't go out the door—it was kept locked at night and a key was needed to open it from either side—so they slipped out a window instead. By the time they reached the path, Sayyid was nowhere in sight.

They hurried after him, entering the courtyard as he unlocked the front door. Sabrina's anger and disgust didn't prevent her from realizing how clever her father had been. He'd known Brad would watch him every moment—that he wouldn't be able to take the statue himself or unlock the door for someone else—so he'd stolen a key from one of the monks and taken it to Sayyid that morning. The message he'd left must have contained directions to the statue's location.

Unlike the nunnery, the *gompa* had no first-story windows; the prayer room they entered was totally dark. The monks' rooms were on the third floor, too far away for their warnings to be heard, so they groped their way along the wall to the staircase. Sabrina started calling to Brad and Nagasena when they reached the second-story landing.

Only seconds later, a handful of lights clicked on. As Sabrina and Kathleen hurried to the third floor, Brad, Howard and half a dozen monks ran out of their rooms and dashed toward the head lama's quarters at the end of the hall. Sabrina distractedly realized that her father was carrying his rifle. She and Kathleen followed the men, hanging back a little, aware that their presence here was proscribed.

There were two doors off Nagasena's private sitting room, one leading to his sleeping quarters, the other to his private chapel. By the time the women entered the sitting room, Nagasena was standing by the first door and Howard and Sayyid were directly across from him, poised by the second. Sayyid was clutching the statue, Howard was pointing his rifle menacingly, and Nagasena was holding out his hand serenely and requesting that the statue be returned.

Howard stabbed the air with his rifle. "Forgive me, Rimpoche, but that won't be possible. I have a sizable investment in this statue. Please tell the monks to move aside. I don't want to hurt anyone."

He and Sayyid started forward, and two of the monks began to whisper frantically in Jammapuri. Sabrina recognized the one nearer to her; he was the *loban*, the head lama's chief assistant. Suddenly he darted sideways, grabbed Kathleen by the arm and said to Howard, "If you wish to see Dr. Carlisle again, you must return the statue. Do you understand?"

Howard hesitated, but surely not out of concern for Kathleen. He was knowledgeable enough about Buddhism to know that the monks wouldn't have hurt a fly, much less a human being. They were devoted to charity and goodwill, and the preservation of life was considered a duty leading to joy and serenity.

Kathleen looked angry and very shaken, but with Howard, not the monks. "You're despicable—blinded by greed and inconceivably selfish. You've profaned a holy object and you've broken your daughter's heart, and for what? *Money?* I hope it keeps you warm at night, because *I* certainly won't!"

Nagasena took a step forward. "All of us take the wrong path at times. It may be difficult to turn back, but it is never impossible. One has only to seek help." He looked at the *loban* and said in Jammapuri, "Dr. Carlisle is our guest. I am sure she knows you will do her no harm, but to be physically restrained is unpleasant." The monks released her at once, visibly abashed.

Howard turned to her. "This statue is worth a fortune. We could be set for life."

"We already were," she said scathingly. "I'm a wealthy woman, and I was prepared to marry you and share everything I have with you. You know it isn't the money."

"Maybe not." He paused. "Damn it, Kathleen, I've been searching for this for years. I can't just give it up—"

"Oh? Do you plan to keep it?"

"I have a buyer, but that isn't the point."

She nodded. "Of course not. It's the glorious satisfaction of having stolen it in the first place."

He grimaced, shifted his weight from one foot to the other, looked at the statue. Finally he sighed and shrugged. "If my choice is between you and the Buddha—"

"It's not. You're not the sort of man I want to spend my life with."

He took the statue from Sayyid and held it out to Nagasena, flashing a grin at her. "The Rimpoche says there's hope for me if I seek help. Compassion is a cardinal virtue, sweetheart. Think about it."

She looked away in disgust as Nagasena reclaimed the statue. "You and your friend will leave Jammapur at once," he said to Howard. "We shall escort you to the border so that you do not lose your way."

"I'm afraid that won't be possible," Howard answered. "We still have business to conduct here."

"I see." He smiled. "What else do you plan to steal?"

"Nothing. It's humanitarian in nature."

"Forgive me for not trusting you, but you will do as I ask or I shall summon the authorities. I am a patient man, Mr. Lang, but you have committed an intolerable offense. You must leave at once."

The Rimpoche was a gentle man, but Sabrina knew that he could also be totally implacable. Still, she couldn't let him throw her father out of the country without an argument. "Please, Nagasena Rimpoche, let him stay until dawn—for me. Nothing else will be taken from the *gompa*. I promise."

"So this business of his was to be conducted tonight."

She reddened. "Yes."

He switched to Jammapuri. "Is it a coincidence, my child, that your beloved *gyalmo chhunun* is to be married in two days, much against her wishes?"

Lying to him would have been as profane an act as stealing the statue. "No."

"And you felt it necessary to save her." He didn't wait for a reply, but continued, "Remember, Sabrina, there is no objective reality to our existence, so the circumstances of Maya's life will only *appear* to change. Married or not, she can still follow the Noble Eightfold Path to tranquillity, peace, and ultimately nirvana."

"Forgive me, Nagasena Rimpoche, but I'm a Christian and I don't see it that way. The girl is fifteen years old, and she's being forced into this marriage so that an old man can use her body to breed his sons and so that the king can do a favor for his brother-in-law's business partner."

Nagasena shook his head sadly. "Ah, Sabrina, the pain our attachments bring us!"

"Please...don't lecture me about cravings being the source of all suffering. Maya is like a daughter to me, and I won't have her in torment for the rest of her life because you say it's not real. What benevolence is there in that?"

"You always were a difficult pupil, my child—so stubborn, so impassioned." He put his hand on her shoulder. "I cannot fault you for doing as the Buddha counseled—endeavoring to protect someone in your family—but your father must leave. His disrespect and blasphemy leave me no choice. Beyond that, we shall see."

Sabrina knew his decision was final; it they resisted, he would summon the police. Sayyid and Howard would be charged with robbery, and *she* could wind up in jail for traveling with false papers. She explained the situation to her father as concisely as she could, clinging to the hope that Nagasena would still decide to help her.

Howard handed her his rifle afterward. "You may need this, honey. I'm sorry about the way things worked out. I thought I could have it all—the statue, Kathleen, Maya..."

"Ethics have never mattered to you. You don't care who you hurt or whose trust you abuse."

"I care," he said. "Maybe just not enough."

In the end, Kathleen went as well, both because Brad wanted her safely out of Jammapur and because she felt an obligation to make sure Howard didn't slip away and try to steal the statue again. She, Howard and Sayyid left in his Jeep, two monks following them in another vehicle, while Brad and Sabrina remained behind in the monastery for a private meeting with the Rimpoche.

He listened intently as Sabrina described their rescue plan, then remarked, "Your father is a daring man, but perhaps too optimistic. The king has increased security about the palace, a precaution against citizens who are as unhappy about little Maya's marriage as she herself."

"Sayyid told us that, but he said the soldiers spend the nights inside."

"I visited her last week. I saw six guards, four inside and two patrolling the grounds . . . less than enthusiastically, to be sure, because they are Buddhists, but that will not prevent them from doing their duty as Jammapuri soldiers."

"But the marriage troubles them, just as it troubles some of their fellow citizens."

"Perhaps."

Nagasena was probably the most virtuous man Sabrina knew; dishonesty was alien to his nature. Seeing the flicker of unhappiness in his eyes, she asked pointedly, "And you, Nagasena Rimpoche? Does it trouble you as well?"

"You are not only stubborn, Sabrina, but observant— you have seen my ambivalence. As you know, the Buddha taught us that *metta*, a feeling of compassion and goodwill toward others, is not enough. One must act on one's feelings as well." He sighed. "The girl has tried to resign herself, but she is anguished. She has a good mind and a deep faith, but what will become of them? I interceded with the king, but to no avail. He is determined that the marriage will take place. He puts politics above *metta*, I fear."

Her hopes rose. "If you help us, we can save her. Please, Nagasena Rimpoche, lend us a ladder and Jeep."

"It would be sheer folly. The guards will surely see you and try to stop you. Killing may occur. I cannot countenance that."

She looked at Brad, silently pleading for his help. He hadn't said a word since Howard had left and she was beginning to fear the worst—that he had no intention of taking part in a rescue. If Nagasena didn't stop her, he would.

She wasn't far wrong—Brad would have given anything to drag her away—but the situation wasn't that simple. He couldn't disregard his repeated promises to help her simply because the worst had happened; he had to make good on them. It didn't even matter that he was terrified she might get hurt. He'd given his word, their relationship wouldn't be worth a damn if he backed out, and if they didn't at least try to get Maya out of Jammapur she would agonize about it for the rest of her life.

"It seems to me that you have a unique position in this country," he remarked to Nagasena. "The people revere you as the wisest, holiest man in Jammapur."

There was no false modesty in the Rimpoche. "Indeed. I must confess to great curiosity about where your charming flattery is leading, however. The king, as we have seen, is decidedly less reverent than his subjects, so appealing to him again would be pointless."

"But if you were to come with us...if you were to distract the guards who patrol outside the palace by engaging them in conversation..."

"They would be honored to be in my presence and put their duties aside temporarily. You are correct."

"And afterward, even if the king suspected you were involved in the rescue, he wouldn't be able to prove it—not if you insisted it was mere coincidence. He wouldn't be able to act against you, either, because the Buddhists in this country would be outraged."

The Rimpoche smiled. "You are correct again."

Brad was keenly aware that Nagasena still hadn't agreed to help them. "It's always been a wish of mine to meet the Dalai Lama," he remarked. "Not only is he a holy man; I admire him tremendously for the way he's led the Tibetan resistance against the Chinese occupation."

The smile turned into a chuckle. "If political action in the name of freedom is good enough for the Dalai Lama, it is good enough for a humble monk from Machulu, eh? But we are talking about one young girl, not a whole country, and lies and deception are proscribed according to the Eight-fold Path, the third step of which is right speech. What do you say to that, Mr. Fraser?"

"That I'm not in your league as a philosopher, Rim-poche. All the same, I suspect you could justify helping us if you put your mind to it."

"That is quite true," he said sternly, "but I am not in the habit of playing sophist games. I must do what is right."

Brad felt like a little kid who'd been called to the princi-pal's office. "I'm sorry, Rimpoche. I didn't mean to be flippant."

"Nor I to be moralistic. Please excuse me." He walked into his private chapel and closed the door.

Brad and Sabrina had no choice but to sit and wait. They couldn't even talk because the Rimpoche was evidently meditating and the slightest noise might disturb him. Nei-ther of them had a watch on, so they had no idea how much time passed. It felt like forever.

The Rimpoche emerged looking utterly at peace. "Maya's marriage will benefit neither the child herself nor Jamma-pur. I would not have the fragile balance of opposing forces in my country upset, nor see it go the way of Tibet, swal-lowed up by a more powerful neighbor. I will help you."

Sabrina wanted to throw her arms around him and thank him, but that would have been too familiar. Instead, she took Brad's hand and drew him forward. This had been an exhausting evening, full of trauma and tension, but at least one good thing had come out of it. She didn't have to put up

barriers against her deepest feelings anymore. She didn't
have to be afraid of trusting and loving. Brad had not only
kept his promise to help her; he'd appealed to the Rimpoche to become involved when she herself had run out of
arguments. It was more than she'd had any right to expect.

She held his hand tightly and said to Nagasena, "We love
each other very much and plan to spend our lives together.
Will you bless us before we leave?"

He did so, then patted her cheek affectionately. Since they
wouldn't have time to come back here, she returned to the
nunnery to pack, then met the two men outside. Brad was
carrying a ladder as well as his duffel bag, her father's rifle
poking out through the top. She wondered if he knew how
to use it even half as well as she did. Howard had taught her
young.

He shut off the Jeep's headlights before they reached
Khapalu, took a roundabout route to the palace, and
dropped Nagasena off at the end of the road that twisted up
to the entrance. The road behind the palace was little more
than a track, more suitable for trekkers than vehicles, but
Brad parked well short of the palace behind a stand of trees
so they couldn't be spotted. He was adamant about Sabrina remaining behind in the Jeep; if anything went wrong,
he wanted her to leave immediately.

He handed her the rifle and unloaded the ladder. Even
without the trees, she would have had trouble seeing what
was going on; the palace was too far away. Not daring to
speak, she hugged him fiercely and watched him walk away.
Her heart was pounding frantically, she was sweating despite the cold and she wanted to run after him and tell him
to forget the whole thing. She didn't, though. Maya—once
the joy of her life, still singularly precious to her—would
suffer forever if she did.

Brad was far from a coward, but he was easily as scared
as Sabrina. The only thing that kept this rescue attempt
from being totally suicidal was the presence of Nagasena. If

the worst happened and they were noticed, the guards wouldn't shoot them. The Rimpoche wouldn't permit it.

He waited a few minutes, then crept to the back of the palace. According to the Rimpoche, Maya's room was where it had always been—on the second floor in the far corner. He planted the ladder and started climbing, turning on his flashlight when he reached the top. He was supposed to cut the glass and unlock the window, then go inside and wake Maya up. He only hoped she didn't start screaming bloody murder before he got a chance to show her what he was carrying: a note from Sabrina and a picture of her and Maya taken in Delhi that she carried in her wallet.

Wanting to make sure he had the right room, he shone the light through the window and searched around inside. Then he almost jumped out of his skin, because Maya was sitting up in bed, staring straight at him. Either she'd been too troubled to sleep or the light had woken her up. He pulled the picture out of his pocket and focused the light on it. She squinted, leaned forward and nodded. For a teenager, the girl was extraordinarily self-possessed.

She made her way to the window and unlocked it. Without a word, Brad slipped inside and handed her the flashlight and letter. She read it, then crept to her desk and pulled out a sheet of stationery. Sabrina had told her exactly what to write. "I won't marry him. I'd rather die of hunger first. I'll kill myself if you find me."

She left the letter on her desk, then pulled some clothes on over her pajamas. Brad wasn't especially relieved by how well things had gone; none of this seemed real. His mind couldn't comprehend the danger they were in—it was like a dream or a movie. Ordinary guys from Boston didn't get involved in rescue attempts in obscure Himalayan kingdoms.

Maya pulled on a pair of boots and grabbed her coat; the hanger jumped off the rod and clattered to the floor. She was so startled that she cried out in alarm. Unnerved to have made such a loud sound, she ran to the window, her boots thumping on the floor. As she climbed outside, a door opened somewhere not too far away. Somebody had evidently heard them. There were footsteps in the hallway, a hurried slapping of bare feet against the wood, coming closer and closer. It didn't feel like a dream or a movie anymore, but like real life—and completely terrifying.

Brad followed her outside and slammed down the window. A moment later the room filled with light. Somebody was inside. Maya frantically descended the ladder, Brad right behind her. He heard the window being yanked open and then a man's voice . . . yelling Maya's name, screaming furiously in Jammapuri. The moment she reached the ground, Brad jumped the rest of the way down, grabbed her by the hand and started running.

He heard an engine running and looked at the top of the hill. Sabrina had turned the Jeep around and parked it directly above them. He and Maya scrambled up the hillside and hurled themselves into the back; Sabrina switched on the headlights, gunned the accelerator and sped away. Windows were lighting up all over the palace.

Brad stared through the darkness as they skidded down the track and rounded the side of the palace, trying to see what was happening. Guards were milling around by the front entrance, Nagasena among them. Two Jeeps were approaching to pick them up, but suspiciously slowly considering the emergency at hand. He smiled grimly. The soldiers were doing their duty all right, but as sluggishly as they could. Someday, if they got out of this in one piece, he was going to ask Nagasena exactly what he'd said to them and whether the Buddha would have approved.

A short man in civilian clothing waved his arms excitedly and ran toward the lead Jeep, then opened the door and shoved the driver aside. The track they were on paralleled the palace driveway at this point, but they had a lead of perhaps a hundred yards. "We're about to be followed," Brad said.

Sabrina nodded. She was better at shooting than driving. "Climb over the seat and take the wheel. I'll keep my foot on the accelerator while I slide over."

They lost some ground making the switch, but the track crossed the main road farther west than the driveway, and west was the way they were headed. Brad swung around the corner and floored the accelerator. Sabrina looked out the back window at the Jeep behind them and saw a rifle pointing their way. She hugged Maya desperately and told her to get down. Several shots rang out, but the soldier seemed to be aiming high.

"He's deliberately missing us," she said, grabbing her father's rifle. "There's a second Jeep, too, but he's losing ground fast. The only one who's really trying is the man driving the Jeep right behind us."

"He was short, dressed in civilian clothing. His room must have been very near Maya's. We didn't make that much noise, but apparently it woke him up."

"Ved Pradham," Maya said hoarsely. She sounded very frightened. "I recognized his voice."

The two Jeeps barreled down the deserted roadway, their tires and brakes squealing as they tore around one curve after another. Pradham wasn't as good a driver as Brad, but his Jeep was newer and faster than the monastery's utilitarian vehicle and he gained ground on them every time the road straightened out.

The Shyok River was on their left, the peaks of the Karakoram mountains on their right. Their destination was thirty miles away, just past the point where the Indus River met the Shyok and Pakistan was across the border rather than India. At the rate they were going, they would never make it; Pradham would overtake them and force them to stop.

"I could try to shoot out his tires," Sabrina said.

"He could lose control of his Jeep. The soldier with him might be killed."

Brad was right. They couldn't risk an innocent soldier's life—a soldier who was doing his damnedest not to hit them—unless there was no other choice. She kept the rifle on her lap, her fingers convulsively gripping the handle.

Brad's skill as a driver kept them in front for the next twelve miles or so, but then they hit a long, flat straightaway and Pradham gained on them more quickly. There was no sign of the second Jeep; it had either turned back or deliberately dropped behind. The next section of the road was straight and rising, the worst possible combination. Sabrina prayed silently, not for divine intervention but for courage. She was more frightened than she'd ever been in her life, but she had to stay calm and concentrate on helping however she could.

Brad tried to go faster, but it was impossible. Pradham was so close that his headlights were illuminating the inside of their Jeep. Sabrina yelled for Maya to keep down and twisted around. Pradham was struggling with the soldier for control of the wheel. She wasn't sure what happened next, only that the soldier stopped fighting and slumped in his seat.

A moment later Pradham slammed into the back of their Jeep, making it lurch wildly. It careened into the opposite lane and collided with a large boulder at the side of the road. The sickening sound of metal scraping against rock filled the air as the Jeep crunched past the first boulder and several others before bouncing free.

Brad had barely managed to get the Jeep under control when Pradham hit it again. Suddenly everything seemed to slow down, turning the situation into a nightmare at quarter speed. The Jeep caromed off the mountainside on their right, Pradham hit it again, and it rocked like a ship in a stormy sea. Finally, in apparent slow motion, it rolled the other way, throwing Sabrina violently against her door. As the door flew open, she was thrown outside onto her hip. Pradham smashed into the Jeep a final, brutal time, the engine died, and the Jeep came to a stop.

Badly dazed, she rolled over and looked up. The Jeep had righted itself and her door had snapped shut, but she couldn't see Brad or Maya. A shot exploded in the still night air and Pradham yelled in Jammapuri for Maya to come out. There was no response; Maya neither moved nor answered.

Pradham got out of his Jeep and strode forward. Sabrina could see his legs but nothing else; their own Jeep was blocking her view. She shook her head, desperately trying to clear it, and realized she was still clutching the rifle. She heard a rattling sound—Pradham was trying to open the Jeep's doors—followed by an angry, frustrated curse.

There was a loud, vicious crash—the sound of a rifle butt smashing into Brad's window. Sabrina bolted to her feet, terrified but suddenly clearheaded, and looked into the car. Maya was huddled on the floor, Brad was slumped against the steering wheel and Pradham was turning his rifle around. He was so intent on watching Brad that he never noticed Sabrina directly across from him, standing on the other side of the Jeep.

Inside the car, Brad steeled himself not to move. He'd been out for a few moments but had regained consciousness as Pradham tried to open Maya's door and then his own. Neither would budge; the collision with the boulder had apparently jammed them. He couldn't fling open the driver's door and knock Pradham out of the way, and he would be an easy target for Pradham's rifle if he attempted to escape out the passenger door. Aware that he was trapped, he played dead and looked for a way out.

As Pradham smashed his window, Brad realized he had only one option. Adrenaline coursed through his system as he waited for exactly the right moment to act. When Pradham pointed his rifle through the window, he would grab the barrel, force it aside and wrest the gun away.

His body tensed in anticipation. Pradham turned the rifle around. Then, out of the corner of his eye, Brad saw Sabrina outside the Jeep, her chest only inches beyond the window on the passenger side. His relief that she was all right gave way to horror. When he grabbed the gun—when

Pradham pulled the trigger—the bullets would crash straight through the window into Sabrina's body. He had to come up with a different plan of action.

Sabrina saw Pradham aim his rifle at Brad and knew she had to divert his attention. He wasn't going to shoot the man she loved or take away her little girl without killing her first. She raised her own rifle and spoke to him in Jammapuri, softly but fiercely. "Lying pig. Filthy butcher. Put down the rifle or I'll kill you."

His head snapped up. She saw the shock in his eyes. He yanked up the gun. Suddenly, out of nowhere, Brad yelled at her to get down. But before she could move, in a horrifying fraction of a second, Pradham's body jerked violently, he cursed loudly and a deafening explosion roared in her ears. On some level she realized the shot had gone wild—somehow she was still alive—but the thought that grabbed and held her was more primitive. *Protect what you love. Kill or be killed.* When he pointed his gun at her again, she did as her father had taught her—squeezed the trigger gently but quickly, hitting her target exactly where she intended... squarely between the eyes.

There was a dull thud as Pradham's body hit the ground. She slumped against the Jeep, reeling with dizziness and nausea as her mind conjured up the obscene details of death that her eyes had luckily missed. Then, sobbing Brad's name, she opened the door and flung herself inside.

Brad pulled Sabrina into his arms. He was horrified by how close he'd come to losing her just when he'd finally won her. "That was so damn dangerous... why in the hell didn't you get down?"

"Maya..."

"I'm all right," she answered.

Sabrina was shaking violently now. "Brad, I thought you were unconscious. I thought he was going to shoot you."

"I was, but only for a second. I came to when he was trying to open the door. When I realized it was jammed, I decided to pretend I was still unconscious and grab the rifle before he could fire it, but then I saw you stand up and I couldn't take the chance." His arms tightened around her back, as if he were still afraid of losing her. "He might have gotten a shot off and hit you through the window. I punched him in the gut and reached for his rifle a moment before he fired, but I couldn't do more than push it aside. Thank God you killed him when you did."

"I've never shot anything before—not even an animal. Dad used to tease me about being squeamish when I wouldn't go hunting. It was so awful—"

"You had no choice. Pradham would have come after you and tried again. He wouldn't have stopped until both of us were dead and he had Maya."

Maya. Sabrina twisted around and held out her arms to the girl. Pradham had destroyed six of her babies, but at least he hadn't gotten Maya. As awful as this had been, she couldn't regret the fact that he was dead. "Darling... Thank God you're all right."

They embraced, kissed, clung to each other. Then they heard footsteps and broke apart. The soldier from Pradham's Jeep was staggering toward them. Brad managed to kick open the door. In the other Jeep's headlights, she could see that the soldier's shirt was soaked with blood.

"Is the princess all right?" he asked in Jammapuri.

"She's fine," Sabrina replied. "And you?"

"The bastard knifed me, but it's not as bad as it looks. Take my Jeep and go. We'll have to make at least a pretense of pursuing you."

"But we can't leave you here alone...."

He pointed down the road at a set of headlights. "They're a few miles back. The keys are in the ignition—leave now, and we'll take our time chasing you."

They thanked him and walked to his Jeep. They would have to leave Jammapur with Maya now; they couldn't return to India the way they'd come because the borders would be closed as soon as the proper orders were issued and received. Communications in this part of the world were erratic, so the process could take anywhere from minutes to hours.

Compared to the terrifying twists and turns of the first fifteen miles, the rest of the trip was almost tranquil. The tensest moment was at the junction of the Indus and Shyok Rivers, when they passed within fifty yards of the twin border checkpoints into India and Pakistan. The guards inside probably hadn't received instructions to watch for them yet, but even if they had, they were traveling in a Jammapuri army Jeep—the best camouflage there could be.

Sabrina knew the exact spot they were headed for—it was a few miles past the checkpoints, marked by a Buddha carved into the hillside on their right. The trail leading to the river was a short distance beyond.

They drove the Jeep to the edge of the river and got out. Brad waved a flashlight at the opposite shore and somebody waved back. Sabrina put her arms around Maya and wept with a mixture of relief and joy. They were finally going home.

Epilogue

It was the middle of April and slushy snow from an early spring storm was piled up along Boston's streets, but the weather was sunny and balmy—a perfect day for a wedding. Sabrina, the matron of honor, was about to walk down the aisle of a local church. Her own wedding the previous September had been a quieter affair than this one—only the immediate families had been present—but her in-laws had thrown her and Brad a lavish reception at Christmastime. She'd been both impressed and grateful; Royce and Emily Fraser hadn't batted an eyelash at introducing their new daughter-in-law to their friends and relatives, even though she'd been almost seven months pregnant at Christmastime.

She smiled at Kathleen, the bride, and Royce, who'd be escorting her down the aisle. Her opinion of her father-in-law had risen immeasurably since the days when she'd been a princess and he'd been an ambassador. Brad had phoned him as soon as they'd arrived in Nepal, explained the situation in detail and asked for his help. Within eight hours they'd been on their way home; within twenty-four a spokesman for King Ashoka had announced that Princess Maya's wedding was being postponed indefinitely so she could attend school in America. As far as the public was concerned, the rescue had never taken place and Ved Pradham had been killed after discovering two terrorists in the palace and trying to capture them as they fled. Sabrina had always known that the official version of an event could be markedly different from what had actually happened, but she'd never seen such a graphic example of it.

As she started down the aisle, she spotted her brother and Grace Fitzsimmons and winked. They'd just flown in from New York, where Grace worked in an art gallery and studied painting and Josh went to school and ran a take-out sandwich business that Brad had helped finance. Although they enjoyed each other enormously, they wanted to establish themselves in careers and explore everything the city had to offer before they thought about settling down.

Two pews in front of them, Maya was sitting with Sabrina's mother and stepfather, dabbing her eyes with a handkerchief. Seeing her here—having her present at a family occasion—was such a joy that Sabrina needed a handkerchief herself. After an initial period of homesickness, Maya had adapted beautifully to life in America. She was a high school junior now, a little less emotional than the average teenager but just as talkative, involved in school activities and popular with her classmates.

Hassan Muhmar, Maya's former fiancé, had married the daughter of a Pakistani diplomat three months after she'd left Jammapur. Ashoka had realized by then that he'd given her too much freedom to expect her to adapt to life as a traditional Jammapuri wife. She'd since told him that she had a lot to offer her country and wanted to return there after college, but would only do so if she could live her own life and choose her own husband. Ashoka wasn't happy with the idea, but Sabrina suspected he would eventually come around. Royce had seen to it that he knew the truth about Pradham's activities, and he was guilty enough about the way he'd treated Sabrina to want to make amends. Indulging Maya was a way to do that, and besides, he'd admitted to Ranjeeta Singh that he missed her more and more.

Sabrina had almost reached the front of the church now. When she saw Kathleen's mother she smiled and fought back tears at the same time. Diana was holding a very small boy—one month old today—with a very big name, Bradley Royce Fraser V. Sabrina wasn't sure she approved of saddling him with such an intimidating name, and the nickname Brad had come up with—Bear—wasn't much better. To live up to names like that, the poor little thing would have to become either a foundation president or a college football coach.

Sabrina had planned to leave him with a baby-sitter that day, but Diana wouldn't hear of it. It amazed Sabrina that a woman who'd never been the slightest bit maternal would adore her little boy so much, but Diana did. Of course, he had the good sense to coo and smile whenever she held him and had never been so ill-mannered as to cry or spit up.

She took her place at the front of the church and looked at her father, who was standing with his younger brother, the best man. Howard was surprisingly nervous for a man who'd been married so many times before, but then, Kathleen was to be his wife forever. Having seen his wives come and go, Sabrina was sure of that. Howard had worked his tail off to persuade her to forgive him and accept his proposal, but she wouldn't have done either if he hadn't changed in the past seven months. He was more thoughtful and less selfish, more trustworthy and less restless.

For the first time in his life, he was not only compromising, but putting somebody else first. Kathleen wanted a child immediately, and he'd agreed. She expected him to be an attentive husband and father, so he was in the process of changing careers. Over the next year or two he would scale down the number of tours he led until only his summers were booked, building up a full-time consulting business in the meantime. He already had two clients—companies that had hired him to use his expertise and contacts to help them design interesting, marketable tours.

Kathleen was walking down the aisle on Royce's arm now, and Howard couldn't take his eyes off her. Neither could anyone else—she was a lovely bride—but Sabrina's gaze strayed to Brad, who was sitting with the rest of the Frasers in one of the front pews. Sometimes she couldn't believe how lucky she was. She had a beautiful healthy son, and if the Shey oracle was any guide, would eventually have three daughters as well. Maya was safe, happy, and here in Boston. Next fall, there would be two students in the family—Sabrina was going back to school part-time to earn her teaching credential in elementary education. Somebody had once remarked that teaching kindergartners or first graders wasn't much of a dream for a woman who'd once been married to a crown prince, but it was Sabrina's dream and she was thrilled about fulfilling it.

Most of all, she had Brad, who treated her more like a princess than Ashoka ever had. He was everything she'd ever wanted in a man—best friend, empathetic partner, exquisite lover and devoted father—and it gave her a profound sense of pleasure to make him happy. She'd looked at love all right, but the illusions and disappointments were a thing of the past. Brad had taught her everything she hadn't known.

*   *   *   *   *

Silhouette Special Edition

COMING NEXT MONTH

#487 A CRIME OF THE HEART—Cheryl Reavis
"Outsider" Quinn Tyler returned to Lancaster County, hoping the old scandal about her and Amishman Adam Sauder was forgotten. But to Adam and his people, one crime could never be forgiven....

#488 SMOKY'S BANDIT—Barbara Catlin
Holed up in a remote Texas cabin, Jerri aimed to kick two nasty addictions: cigarettes and Tyler Reynolds. Yet when the irresistible cowboy appeared, good intentions went up in smoke!

#489 THE LIEUTENANT'S WOMAN—Janice Kaiser
Anne-Marie was no longer a naive German girl in love with a dashing American lieutenant. But decades later, a savvy Californian, she found she still hadn't outgrown Royce Buchanan.

#490 GHOST OF A CHANCE—Andrea Edwards
Holly Carpenter reluctantly moved into a rickety old house, only to encounter a pesty poltergeist...and a dangerously tempting tenant. Could Zach Phillips mend Holly's broken heart?

#491 THE RIGHT MISTAKE—Janet Franklin
When a wilderness walk proved perilous, Jessica needed a hero...and Seth Cameron did just fine. Back on solid city pavement, however, she feared loving Seth was a mistake.

#492 THUNDER HIGH—Linda Shaw
Hired to buy off a senator's mistress, Brad Zacharias hadn't expected compassionate, spirited Catherine Holmes. He soon cursed his political ties, which threatened Cat's good works...and their thunderous attraction.

AVAILABLE NOW:

TALES OF THE RISING MOON
A Desire trilogy by Joyce Thies

MOON OF THE RAVEN—June (#432)
Conlan Fox was part American Indian and as tough as the Montana land he rode, but it took fragile yet strong-willed Kerry Armstrong to make his dreams come true.

REACH FOR THE MOON—August (#444)
It would take a heart of stone for Steven Armstrong to evict the woman and children living on his land. But when Steven saw Samantha, eviction was the last thing on his mind!

GYPSY MOON—October (#456)
Robert Armstrong met Serena when he returned to his ancestral estate in Connecticut. Their fiery temperaments clashed from the start, but despite himself, Rob was falling under the Gypsy's spell.
